Tangled Encounters: A Sapphic Circus Romance

Cirque Callisto Series Book One

Madison Nicole

MN Books LLC

PREFACE

Tangled Encounters is the first book in the Cirque
Callisto Series, a four-book series of interconnected
standalones. Each book can be read on its own but is best
read in numerical order. Enjoy!

This book is a work of fiction. All of the characters, organizations, companies and events in this novel are either products of the author's imagination oar are used fictitiously.

Editing & Proofreading: Rose Santoriello

Cover Art: Amanda Hawkins, Eternal Geekery

This book is for 18+

 Created with Vellum

To those who wanted to run off with the circus when they were younger...
I promise you still can.
And my mom. You've always encouraged my dreams and my unhinged antics. Thank you for being my number one fan.

Before you read...

This book contains adult themes such as sex work, explicit sex scenes, misogyny, homophobia, kink, slut shaming, and more. This book is intended for mature audiences and reader discretion is advised. If you have any concerns about the content of this book feel free to email the author, Madison Nicole at info@madisonnicolebooks.com, your mental health matters.

PROLOGUE: OZZIE

There are moments in time that etch themselves on your skin and send you spiraling towards another path. Today was one of those days. Last night had been a fucking disaster. Sean was an absolute asshole. The decision to break up with him at that moment was one of the easiest ones I had ever made. Especially after he tried to thrust some woman on me in an attempt to get us all to sleep together and then proceeded to get mad when I said no thanks.

I didn't really know why he thought he could handle two women at once, when the reality was, he could barely handle one. Not to mention we had never talked about adding someone else into our very new relationship, if you could even call it that. I felt like we were still in the beginning stages of defining what we were. Our relationship label was like a slightly upgraded form of a situationship, honestly.

Being queer was also not synonymous with doing whatever sexual bidding your partner wanted without actually talking to your partner about it. It was an easy split for me. I liked Sean well enough, but not *that* much. It had just sort of happened since we worked and trained circus together. We were both looking to slide our bodies together in more ways than one, and that was sort of that.

We weren't that serious, but I did feel comfortable with him and he ruined that when he tried to claim I wasn't queer. He thought because I didn't want a threesome; I didn't want women at all. Women were lovely, but I didn't appreciate being blindsided by him last night.

I was too old to be dealing with this fucking shit. But I had hoped that we could still work together in peace. After all, we had met in our current circus group and we were professionals. It felt like a very obvious thing to act like adults at our jobs. But alas, that was not the case.

Instead, the shitstorm continued as I walked into our training facility, and all eyes whipped to me. Attempting to stand tall, I painted on a grin and set my stuff down, trying to gauge the weird tension in the room. My skin felt itchy and like I wanted to crawl into a hole to avoid everyone's harsh gaze.

It couldn't have been all from the break up last night? How had news traveled so fast? I knew for a fucking fact that I was nicer and more enjoyable to be around than Sean. Plus, I was a more talented and dedicated performer. No one could juggle like me and I certainly held my own in the other disciplines. There was no reason all of that would mean nothing to them after a fight between two romantic partners, right? Swallowing, I tried to ignore the slight nausea rolling through me.

Christ, I don't even know why I engaged in our stupid relationship, anyway. The sex was good, but not *that* good. It had obviously been a judgment error, and yet here I was anyway, trying to just do my job while the whole room seemed to be waiting for me to fall on my face. This would all blow over soon enough. Someone else would have other gossip to share and soon our breakup would be in the past where it firmly belonged.

"Ozzie." Brittany, one of the other professional members of the company, strutted over to me with her hands in fists like she was ready to brawl.

Oh god, oh god, oh god. It was probably nothing. She sounded like she was looking for a fight, but it couldn't have anything to do with the blow up from last night. Why would anyone else need to be involved?

"Brittany, how's it going?" She wasn't my favorite person, but again I did my best to mind my own business and do my job as opposed to getting wrapped up in the bullshit that was the gossipy cliques of the space.

It was truly the antithesis of circus. It should have been about community, creating art, being inclusive and instead, this place was like a country club. Where money and connections were more important than your skill, talent and artistry. Unfortunately, it was my best option right now with where I lived. They had the best access to training facilities, coaches and paid opportunities. So it felt like my only option despite it being like high school all over again. My anxiety was already high in the space sometimes but today it felt dialed up to an almost full body discomfort.

"Not good, Ozzie," Brittany said, scowling at me. The annoying gremlin in my head wanted to mess up her perfect blonde high ponytail just for the fun of it. It would undoubtedly bring me a small semblance of joy.

"Oh...Um... Well, okay," I said. My throat felt scratchy, and I fought the urge to clear my throat. What if I just didn't ask? Then maybe it would go away? Today I wanted to train like usual, not see Sean's stupid face and then leave and go home. The end. I let the silence drag on and begged whatever god existed out there that she would simply leave. Apparently, no one was answering prayers today.

"You're not even going to ask me why it's not good, *Ozzie?*" She practically spat my name out. Her venomous words made me flinch, and I desperately looked around for something to get me out of this awkward conversation.

"Uh, I—I feel like you're going to tell me whether I ask or not, so why don't you just say it, Brittany," I said, trying to match her snarky tone. It came out high and squeaky instead. Damnit. I wasn't ready for this today. My emotional walls were crumbling from last night and all my bad bitch energy had been used up telling Sean to go fuck himself. The only thing left was a growing pit in my stomach from her menacing gaze.

"Sean told us all about your blatant disrespect last night," she hissed at me. There were more people inching closer to our little confrontation. I felt like a feral cat in a cage. Suddenly, the space felt too small. There wasn't enough oxygen in the room as they loomed closer, throwing accusatory stares my way. I clamped my mouth shut and inhaled deeply through my nose, praying that enough air was getting to my brain. My stomach rolled as I tried to figure out what to do.

"What's going on? We just aren't seeing each other anymore. He was kind of a dick to me and said some hurtful things about my identity," I said. The words tumbled out in a rush. "He's the one you should be mad at, not me!" The words felt childish even as they came out. In reality, none of them should be involved in any of this, anyway. It was our private business. Couldn't they just leave it alone?

Brittany's mouth dropped open. "How dare you try to manipulate the situation and take no accountability, Ozzie." She looked like she was going to lunge at me, and then suddenly Sean was there, pulling her back into his arms.

What's actually happening right now? I took a step back and nearly tripped over my bag. The surrounding circle kept getting smaller and smaller and frantically I looked for a way out.

"Ozzie, please stop trying to play the innocent party here. You went off the rails last night. You need to apologize to me." His tone was so patronizing that my mouth dropped open. Did we experience the same thing last night? Because in what world would I need to say sorry to him?!

"Sean, you can't be serious. Why are you lying like this?" Tears pricked the backs of my eyes and I tried to calm my racing heart. None of this was going as planned. My skin felt hot, and I blinked a few times, trying to regain focus. I could calmly explain our fight last night, right? Then everyone could go on about their day and forget it ever happened, just a lover's spat. I tried to convince myself it was possible despite the disapproving looks around me.

"I told them about your other thing too," he scoffed at me, keeping an arm around a scowling Brittany. Nearly every single person in the gym was bearing witness to this now. My vision started to go fuzzy as tears gathered in my eyes.

"About what, exactly?" My voice came out in a whisper, and I dug my fingernails into my palms.

"I told them about the whore you are and how you make money."

It was like a dagger to the heart and a punch to the gut all at once. I lost my footing and stumbled over my bag, crashing to the floor. Scrambling up, I wiped at my eyes.

I should have never told Sean I had an OnlyFans. The facade this man had put on to act like a safe and genuine person when we were alone was truly Oscar worthy. Instead, he was a manipulative asshole who traded information about people whenever it was convenient for them and made villains out of people who didn't deserve it.

Don't cry in front of these assholes, Ozzie. Just get out.

"Why are you doing this?" I asked, my voice cracked. This was going downhill really fast.

"You sell naked photos of yourself, people deserve to know the truth," Brittany said, pointing her finger at me and everyone in the crowd seemed to gasp collectively.

"I'm allowed to do what I want with my own body. And these are not your secrets to tell," I whispered, looking down at the floor. I didn't expect people to understand why nudity was empowering to me, but they sure as shit didn't have to shame me for it.

"You work with children!" Sean threw it at me like holy water on a sinner's face.

"And you're the one who is going around telling people!" I said tears were flowing freely now. The pain in my chest radiated through my body, and my tears turned to snotty whimpers. This was absolutely horrible.

"Well, we all voted and you're fired. I already talked to Leslie about it." Sean smirked, and it was like another emotional bomb went off inside me. My composure was fractured into a million little pieces and there was no way I could recover from it.

Leslie was Sean's aunt and barely here so she let Sean and his other little minion's run the place. Today, apparently, they had decided that instead of treating me like a human being they wanted to slice me to pieces and leave me flayed open, to gawk and jeer at.

Again, why did I get this involved? So many mistakes led to this moment, and I wanted to tell them all to fuck themselves, but the betrayal I felt was crushing. There was no room for bad bitch Ozzie right now, only a shell of who I was crumbling under the anguish of trusting someone I shouldn't have.

"You voted on it?" I gasped, finally finding the words. "But I'm one of the most booked performers and one of the hardest working professionals. You're firing me because of personal things I told you while we were in a romantic relationship?" Even as the words left my mouth, I knew they wouldn't make a difference. My fate was sealed the minute I had trusted Sean.

I looked around at the faces surrounding me, no one—not a single person seemed to empathize with me. They all saw me as this weird, slutty villain that Sean painted me out to be, even though he was more than happy to date me until twelve hours ago.

"You're unfit to be a coach and a performer and we don't want to associate with the things you associate yourself with," Brittany echoed, and any fight left in me was gone. I took one more moment to plead with my eyes to those around me. People I thought who had my back, who were maybe not my friends but at least co-workers who cared.

Some people looked away or down to the ground but a lot of them just shook their heads at me and seemed to think the only way for this to fix itself would be for me to be kicked out.

"You better not show your face around here. You're banned, Ozzie. You're never allowed to set foot in this studio ever again. No recommendations or associations will ever be made from this company for you, Ozzie," Sean said seriously.

"Great. I wouldn't want to be associated with the likes of you anyway. I quit!" Grabbing my things as quickly as possible, I practically fled to the door, fighting back the tsunami of sadness that threatened to topple me to the ground.

As soon as I made it to my car and sat down, the tears erupted and my heart broke entirely. What the hell was I going to do now? I needed a new plan, and I needed one fast. So I drove home trying to think of a new future while the one I had imagined crumbled behind me.

———

"Trevor! We have to move. We have to move right now." Tears were still streaming down my cheeks as I slammed the door shut in our apartment.

"Oz? What's going on?" Trevor rushed in from his bedroom and he scanned my face. His dark hair was sticking out in every single direction humanly possible. If I wasn't so upset I would have laughed, instead I felt like two seconds away from collapsing. "Is this about the breakup? I thought you didn't even like him that much?"

Sniffling, I dropped my shit on the floor and let Trevor usher me to the couch. "No, it's not about that dumb boy. I was fired. Well, I quit. Okay... technically, I was kicked out of the company."

Trevor's eyes widened, and his jaw dropped. "What? Because why?"

"Because Sean spun this horrible story about me being this whore of a villain. When in reality his ego is hurt because I dumped him and now he says I'm unfit to work with kids or be a part of the company because I have an OnlyFans."

"It's 2024. What the hell is wrong with him? Also, you never told anyone except him, so why is he sharing information that is not his to share?" Trevor asked.

"That's what I said. But they voted on it and I don't want to be somewhere that doesn't accept me for who I am. And I'm like the only queer person there and it's not fun. This isn't what I want." I buried my head in my hands.

"I know, Oz." He wrapped his arms around me and let me cry until I had nothing left in my system to give. "Well, our lease is up in the next few months. You know I have connections all over. I've been over this place for a while now. You know I get itchy to go somewhere shiny and new. Let's start another adventure together. Pick a place and a few new circus companies to browse, and let's write a new story." Trevor's voice went wistful, as if this new imaginary place we would go together was magical and wonderful and exactly what we needed.

He was always better at diving headfirst into the unknown while the idea sent a slight panic through my body. But what other options were there? There certainly weren't any good ones here anymore.

"Really? Do you want to do that?" Sniffling, I tried to imagine what a new start would look and feel like. Maybe it would be exhilarating as opposed to vomit inducing.

"You and I both know that as performers, we can get booked everywhere. We've got the talent and the drive. We just need the opportunity. We're both kick ass instructors and damn good at what we do. Let's get out of here and go somewhere that feels better for both of us. We've outgrown this place. You know the dating pool is nonexistent. So let's go fuck some shit up somewhere else," he said confidently. I was jealous of how easy it was for him to decide his next move while I felt frozen in place.

"I love you, Trevor," I said, wiping at my face. If he believed we could do it then I could at least pretend to believe it too.

"I'll tell the leasing office that we aren't renewing and then you get to researching some places you might like to try. Let's narrow it down to a few places and see what opportunities are available."

"Okay, let's do it." Laughing nervously, I tried to bolster my own attitude. I could do this. I could do hard and brave shit.

That night I got to researching right away. Over the next few weeks Trevor and I had decided on a place that seemed to have ample opportunity for both of us. Emails had been sent, connections had been established, Instagram accounts had been followed, and we both worked on performance resumes and video content.

Not once did I hear from anyone after that day I got fired. Instead, I found random gym and outdoor spaces to practice my juggling and keep my strength up for my other skills. I refused to step foot in that horrible place again, so I just made do with what I had.

My other side hustles and my OnlyFans kept me financially steady even though I missed performing and creating movement art. It was just a short-lived break. Only a few months to get moved and settled somewhere else. Everything would work out the way it was supposed to. Plus, I was really excited about some of the places I found, specifically Cirque Callisto.

The director, Logan, was a fantastic trapeze artist who started her own company. It seemed like they were booked and busy with lots of performers. All of them seemed incredibly talented. But you know what they were missing? A juggler. Desperately I hoped I was what they were looking for. After we moved, I needed to try to get to one of their shows for some face-to-face time.

Trevor had several places he was looking to teach and perform at. But he was a classically trained dancer, and I was a circus artist, so we each needed different things.

The final days at our apartment were filled with giddy excitement as we loaded up our shit in a U-Haul and got our plans together. We had already found a place to rent for a while and then we would see how it went.

I was ready for a new chapter. One filled with people who actually gave a fuck about me outside of what I could simply provide for their business. What was that even like? It had been a long time since I felt like I had a community of people. Which is probably why I ended up creating a thing with Sean. It felt better than being alone at the time, but in reality, my time with him just made me lonelier.

No longer would I settle for mediocrity in my life. This

was the start of something new where all parts of me would be celebrated and encouraged.

"It looks like that's the last of it. Are you ready to do this thing?" Trevor asked. Nodding my head, I grabbed his hand.

"Yeah, you're the bestest best friend ever."

He blew me a kiss. "I know. How lucky are you?"

"So lucky. Let's get out of there."

We turned in our apartment keys and hopped in the car. At least we had one another. Trevor and I had been best friends for years and roommates for a while. We were each other's family, so it was only fitting that we start something like this together.

"Alright Ozzie, let's go!" Trevor plugged in his phone for our road trip playlist and we were on our way.

Things felt lighter with every mile that we traveled. This was the right direction. Things were looking up and no one from my old company would be bringing me down again.

ONE

OZZIE

"How did you hear about this show again?" Trevor asked. At this point, I had dragged him to attend several performances, all with varying levels of skill and professionalism. Some were extraordinary, while others were... not so much. But this one? This one felt different.

"It's another one of the circus companies I reached out to. I'm thinking about auditioning for them depending on how this goes, and it's their spring show." I flipped through the pamphlet in my hand and scanned the acts. It was an aerial cabaret show, and my skin was already buzzing. The auditorium was U shaped, so the audience hugged the stage. Soft red lights wrapped around us, and the backdrop dazzled and sparkled across the audience in the dimly lit room.

The seats slowly started to fill up, and I tried not to keep checking my watch for the official start time. This was always my favorite part of a show: the blossoming energy of the room, the frisson of anticipation that skittered across my skin and left me smiling in its wake. Cracking my neck from left to right, I tried to file away every small detail that brought this experience to life.

"Well, it's giving Christina Aguilera *Burlesque* vibes, and I'm here for it. Want me to go grab another round before the show starts?"

I looked over to where our empty drinks sat. I sure as hell wasn't going to get up; the pre-show atmosphere fueled me and warmed my chest. My brain was fully rooted in waiting mode and incapable of doing anything else but sit my jittery ass down.

"Sure, I'll take whatever their specialty cocktail is."

Trevor nodded and made his way through the red velvet seats and over the legs of everyone in our row with only ten minutes until showtime. My knee bounced erratically as I tried to read more of what the pamphlet said. My eyes scanned the page, hungry for more information about Cirque Callisto, the company putting on the show tonight. There was a slight blurb about inquiring artists and my heart sang. I had already reached out to them, but I couldn't wait to see their work firsthand.

Trevor and I had just settled into a rental house, and I wanted a circus space to call home. My skin tingled with excitement at the thought of training and performing again; it hadn't even been that long since I left my last company, but my body ached to create movement art. Even a little time away made me anxious.

It was hard not to listen to a song these days and immediately put together an act. The creativity inside me was fucking desperate for a release, despite the hellish ordeal my last company had put me through.

Glancing at the pamphlet nearly crumpled in my hands, the words on the pages blurred together, so I tried to focus on the pictures instead. They had pronouns included with the artists' bios, which was a great indicator that they would be queer friendly, and the roles in the production seemed to give the middle finger to gendered stereotypes. My smile grew bigger and my shoulders relaxed at the thought of having a community that would be safe and supportive of who I was. Coming out every time you met someone new as an adult got old, especially when you didn't know what their reaction would be. My job wasn't to manage anybody's emotions about my identity. They could fuck the fuck right off if it bothered them, but alas, sometimes it could not be avoided.

"Okay, it's some sort of dressed up Cosmo. It's good, but I couldn't tell you the name of it." Trevor's eyes danced as he handed me the bright pink liquid. He looked gorgeous in his black sequined tuxedo jacket and floral print button-down. He wore perfectly tailored slacks that hit just above his ankles, and the whole look was tied together with a pair of sparkling loafers. He fit right in with the sultry vibe of the evening.

All around us, people were dressed up to various degrees. The show had encouraged audience participation in their sexy aerial cabaret, so there was everything from full-on latex kink gear to suburban khakis and sweaters. It was a glorious mix, a beautiful reminder of how art could bring otherwise contrasting people together into a melting pot of appreciation and respect.

The lights dimmed, and my stomach did a flip. A hush fell over the audience, and I tried not to hold my breath as I death-gripped the arms of my chair. My eyes bounced around the room, waiting to see what would happen and how the spectators would react.

The emcee came out dripping in leather and chains. She was a beautiful Black woman who introduced us to the show with a megawatt smile and the crack of a small crop against her palm. The audience roared as she began to sing and dance in her dominatrix style outfit. She high-kicked and shimmied across the stage, belting out notes only Broadway stars hit, and finished in a jump split to the ground.

What a fucking star.

The crowd yelled and hollered while she blew kisses, and then, with a bow and a wide sweep of her arms, she welcomed the next act. Fog started to pour out, and the music changed from an upbeat jazz interlude to a deep sexy pulse. My heart seemed to thump in time to the bass, and I scooted closer to the edge of my seat.

I watched in awe as a white woman strutted on stage in a two-piece set that was made entirely of rhinestones and left little to the imagination. Her dark brown hair cascaded down her back and showed off the cords of muscles in her shoulders and arms. I swallowed as my eyes took in her athletic form.

There was a fluttering deep in my belly as I watched her command the stage. The stage lights turned to deep purples and blues, and the ensuing reflections from the rhinestones covering her body danced across the audience's faces. Her limbs flowed effortlessly on the ground until a hoop was lowered down, and she grabbed it with both hands. Floating up, she hooked a leg and blew a kiss to the audience.

People whistled and cried out all around me as she began her dance on the hoop as it was lifted, higher and higher. She moved like she was making love to it, and I tried to still my queer little heart.

Circus and aerial weren't inherently sexual. It was an athletic feat like any other professional sport mixed with performance art that could be a beautiful narrative of all kinds of stories.

But tonight, the things that woman was doing with her body felt practically carnal. My stupid imagination was running off in a million different directions, and I scolded myself for not keeping my weirdly horny ass in check.

Focus, Ozzie.

Her eyes were bright as she committed to her confident character and art in the air. It felt like she was looking into my soul each time her eyes swept across the crowd. Splits and spins were thrown out one after the other; audible gasps rang out from the crowd as she dropped from the top to the bottom of the hoop. Emotion that I couldn't place swelled inside me and had me breathing hard while heat crept up on my cheeks.

I wondered idly if I had ever made anyone feel like this when I performed. How was it possible to inspire such a visceral reaction in someone? Swallowing, I tried my best not to objectify her like some dumb man—I was literally no better than a horny fourteen-year-old boy by the way my body was reacting—and to focus instead on her creativity and talent. Performance artists worked hard to have their skill and strength recognized. Circus could be sexy and strong; I knew that firsthand.

My body was just reacting to a beautiful person, that was all. It was normal and natural. Nothing to be ashamed of, just something I needed to monitor. Probably just needed to get laid, honestly. Mentally, I put it on my to do list.

The audience continued to be enthralled by her as she wrapped and weaved her final moments in the air. She finished her act by spinning so fast she was practically a blur and then stopping on a dime, so that her hair fanned down and her chest heaved dramatically. She winked at the audience as she was lowered down slowly and gave us all a little wave as she exited the stage.

Who was she? My mouth was nearly dry as I sucked down the rest of my cocktail.

How could I create a mesmerizing experience like that, one where the audience was eating out of the palm of my hand? Every drop and spin had been met with gasps, claps, and whistles. I had never seen someone move like that on the hoop; it was practically mouthwatering. A spell had been cast over every single person here, and I wondered how she seemed to bewitch all of us so easily.

Trevor lightly coughed, and I whipped my head around to him.

"What?" I hissed.

"You just drooled all over that performance." He took a sip of his drink and lifted his dark brows.

"It was a beautiful display of athleticism." I narrowed my eyes as he rolled his.

"*Right*, had nothing to do with the performer?" he teased.

"Everyone was enraptured by her. She was extraordinary!" My voice was getting higher as I shifted uncomfortably in my seat, trying to ease some of the weird tension that had built in my belly.

"Yeah, but the hunger coming off of you is palpable, Ozzie." Trevor cackled, and I scowled. The lights were shifting, and our gorgeous emcee was back. I waved him off and took a deep breath.

Turning my attention back to the show, I exhaled loudly. The show flowed beautifully from silk performers, contortionists, dancers, singers, and acrobatics; all of which had the crowd singing and cheering. However, nothing had captured me quite like the first aerialist in the hoop. Maybe Trevor was right. I did have a little crush on the performer, but it was harmless. Nothing to be concerned about. I had lots of crushes on lots of different performers, and it literally meant nothing.

My mind wandered to the way her bright red lips cracked open, a smile that looked like she was holding on to a secret. Her eyes seemed to be glued to everyone in the crowd, like she could see the most intimate parts of my soul.

Before I knew it, the show was over, and I had half my mind on the first performer and had only been half watching the rest of the show.

Goddamnit, Ozzie.

"That was fantastic. I can see why you would be interested in joining them. Also, a very diverse cast. I think you'd fit right in," Trevor commented. Slowly we oozed out of the auditorium, where a happy buzz infiltrated every corner of the building. The performers were out in the lobby by the bar, greeting the spectators and taking photos with anyone who wanted them.

I scanned the lobby for the hoop artist and came up short. Why was I looking for her? I didn't even know her and how weird would it be for me to go up to her and be like, "Hey I was obsessed with your act and you're really fucking hot. Are you into women and are you single?" That would be a guarantee that I would never work with this company and that they would call me a weirdo.

"Ozzie Nelson?" someone said from behind me, and I turned around to see the director of the show in a pink feather boa and a hot pink lingerie set.

"Hi, Logan Beaumont?"

"Yes! I'm so glad you could make it tonight. What did you think of the show?" she asked happily. Logan's long, light pink hair was piled high on the crown of her head, and she grinned, showing off straight white teeth. Tattoos snaked along most of her body and she practically glowed from all the glitter on her skin. Logan had been walking around the aisles, teasing people with her feathers and flirting with the guests during the show.

"Thank you so much for the tickets! It was amazing. The first hoop artist was magnificent. Truly one of the best lyra acts I've ever seen." I blushed slightly, thinking of her hard muscles and the way her body moved around the apparatus.

"Jess is truly a star. You should come take her class sometime. I'll send you the schedule. You should come hang out this next week and see what you're interested in. Obviously, I'm biased, but we have amazing coaches and contacts here.

And we're always looking for people to help diversify our acts." She beamed at me.

I had already sent her my videos on lyra, as well as juggling, and I knew I was good. I had been training in a circus for several years now, but I wasn't captivating like Jess was. She moved in ways that felt impossible and magical all at the same time. Not that it was a competition, but it was hard for my mind not to wander there, to feel like an imposter in my art sometimes.

"I would love that." Tension prickled across my shoulders. I had been in my hometown for so long, but I needed a city with more connections and more action. This seemed like the perfect place to go, despite my own anxious energy.

"Oh, there she is! Jess!" Logan waved her boa frantically, and Jess seemed to pop out of nowhere. She still wore her dazzling rhinestone two-piece, but she donned a pair of black circular glasses. Oddly, she was even more endearing with the dark frames surrounding her light blue eyes. She was more petite than I realized, but all the muscles in her body seemed to ripple as she moved. Jess's dark brown hair looked even shinier up close. She had chunky teal pieces framing her face that I hadn't noticed while she was on stage. I had the urge to reach out and run my fingers through the silky strands.

Ugh, I needed to get it together.

"Jess, this is Ozzie. Ozzie, Jess! She just moved here and is looking for somewhere to train. I'll have to show you her videos. The juggling you do is truly phenomenal. We don't have anyone who object manipulates right now, and she's also a lyra artist!"

My cheeks grew hot again. Juggling was my main trick, and I was really fucking good at it when I actually gave myself due credit. I loved to blend it with dance, clowning and other apparatus work. It was like a puzzle to solve every time. People didn't often brag about me, though.

Jess's eyes crinkled as she beamed broadly, and a dipping sensation happened in my stomach. It was like her whole face lit up. She reached out a hand, and I stared at it a second too long before grabbing it and folding my sweaty palm against hers.

"Nice to meet you, Ozzie. Can't wait to see you in the studio sometime."

"You too! Your piece was enthralling, truly could not stop thinking about it the whole show. I would love to take a class from you sometime." I realized I still had a hold of her hand and let it go quickly, wiping my hand on my leather leggings.

Jesus, why were my hands so fucking wet?

Jess gave me a funny look, and I realized she probably thought I was wiping her touch off. My eyes widened, and a knot formed in my belly, but before I could explain myself, someone interrupted us and took the two performers away. Logan gave an apologetic grin, and Jess grimaced.

"Fuck."

"What happened? It looked like it was going well!" Trevor sidled up next to me with a new drink in hand from where he had been eavesdropping.

"I wiped my sweaty ass hand on my thigh, and I think Jess, the girl who performed on the hoop, thought I was wiping her touch off. Christ, I'm just stressed because I have an insta-crush on her. Pretty women are my weakness. My little queer heart can't help it." I bit my lip and sighed.

"Well, I'm sure it wasn't that bad. You'll just have to be extra nice when you see her next. You're visiting their studio this next week, right?"

I nodded. Butterflies erupted in my belly. I wanted to dazzle Logan, and I really wanted to impress Jess. She was breathtaking up close, and I had royally screwed it up.

"Come on, let's go drink some of your embarrassment away." Trevor dragged me to the bar with a knowing smirk. He was all too familiar with my embarrassing ways. Hopefully she would forget that I had been a total asshat and did that. Maybe she hadn't even noticed at all.

TWO
JESS

"Are you sure about Ozzie? She wiped her hand off after shaking mine." I frowned, trying to figure out why she would be so against my palm touching hers. Maybe I was thinking about it too much, but it felt really dramatic and exaggerated when she did it. Sitting down, I removed my glasses to start the egregious task of taking off all this stage makeup.

"Maybe she just has a weird thing about physical touch?" Logan suggested and shrugged, removing the pins from her hair, and peeling off her bajillion layers of tights to get ready to go home. Most of the other performers were gone, it was just a few of us left. We usually stayed later as we liked to debrief before we got home. Some of us needed some time to decompress after our performance high, and let our nervous system level out.

Even though it was annoying to take off all the makeup, hair accessories and costumes, it was methodical and a way to wind down after the intensity of the show. A little bit of catnip for my brain after the delicious chaos of performing.

"Who's Ozzie?" Aven asked before gulping down her

water. Her dark brown skin was already scrubbed free of makeup and glitter. She looked dewy and relaxed; her adorable freckles stood out on her nose and cheekbones now that all the makeup was gone. And here I was, looking like a disco ball gremlin. How the hell had she gotten all the glitter off so fast? Mine seemed to stay permanently adhered to my skin for what felt like weeks.

"Ozzie just moved here and is first and foremost a juggler. She's also an incredibly talented lyra artist. Not like Jess, but pretty fucking good. She sent me some videos last week, and I invited her to train with us and see if she wants to audition," Logan said. She rubbed her scalp and sighed when the last pin came out of her hair.

She hadn't performed on stage tonight and instead kept an eye on how the show looked from the audience's perspective. She could have easily hopped up on stage with us, but she loved directing and seeing her vision come to life.

"And she thinks Jess has cooties?" Myla teased. She was already undressed and bare faced. How was everyone done so fast? I swiped at my eyes and moved to rid myself of the red lipstick that seemed to be permanently stained on my lips. Ugh, I just wanted to go home.

"I thought you had left. Isn't Jake supposed to take you home with him?" I asked, squinting at her.

"He, uh, couldn't make it tonight, so I was wondering if one of you could give me a ride?" She casted her mahogany eyes down and ran her fingers through the strands of her hair, fiddling with the deep purple tresses.

"What?" Logan narrowed her amber eyes and looked ready to tear him limb from limb. My heart dipped. Jake was being super fucking flaky with Myla lately. My blood boiled at the thought of him leaving her high and dry.

"It's not a big deal. He has some work stuff going on. He'll catch the next one. Just drop it, okay?" Myla swiped at her eyes and Aven wrapped her in a hug. I wanted to punch Jake in his dumb face.

"I'll take you home, lovely. No worries." Aven popped a kiss on her pale cheek and Myla's lips turned up in a wobbly smile. Her eyes watered and she hugged her arms around herself. Jake had been withdrawing himself more and more over the past few months. Myla didn't like to talk about it, even though it was clearly hurting her heart.

"Anyway, Ozzie seemed great if not grossed out slightly by Jess's callused hands. But you'll meet her this next week and we'll take a vote on whether she's a good fit. If she auditions with us and it goes well, I'm interested in asking her to join us," Logan announced gently, drawing the attention away from Myla back to my own conundrum. I sighed, wiping off the last little bit of foundation and wrapping my hair up in a messy bun before putting my glasses back on.

We moved on to the topic of the show tomorrow since it was a two-month long residency performance and then chatted through some slight costume alterations. My mental to-do list was getting longer and longer by the second. I couldn't forget that I also needed to get some more chalk and finish up my lesson plans for this week's classes and double check enrollment.

Myla and Aven left first. Logan and I finished cleaning up and shutting down.

"Do you think Myla is okay?" I asked, shutting off the lights.

"No, but she isn't ready to talk until she's ready, you know? She's an avoidant person. All we can do is be here for her when she's ready." Logan sighed as we walked to our cars.

"Yeah, I know."

"Don't think too much about the Ozzie thing, okay? It probably has nothing to do with you. Plus, she's a kick ass performer, so unless she's a bigot or a narcissist, she'll probably be offered a spot here." Logan raised her eyebrows at me, and I laughed.

"Okay, I'll play nice." I would do my very best to befriend her, even if our first interaction was off.

After we said our goodbyes, I drove back home in silence. My eyes were really bothering me tonight, but I tried not to get too distracted about it. They often were like this after I had a treatment done. A little raw, sore and blurry until a few days later. Sometimes they were worse than others and today was just a hard day, thankfully they weren't so blurry that I couldn't drive tonight. Thank god one of the other performers had time to do my makeup tonight, otherwise I would have been absolutely fucked since I could barely see up close right now. Everything close to my face was foggy.

I could do lyra blindfolded, in fact I had, but I couldn't do my hair or my makeup very well. Idly, I wondered what about me had turned Ozzie off. She had such a strange reaction to me when I had walked over there. Even though she seemed totally chill when it was just Logan and her.

Ugh, I didn't know why it was bothering me so much.

I pushed those thoughts away to what I needed to focus on, which was prepping my costume and show bag for tomorrow. Unloading my car, I headed inside and immediately threw some things in the laundry and ran a hot bath trying to give my aching muscles a break when my phone buzzed.

"Who wants something from me right now?" Grumbling, I snatched it aggressively.

Genevieve: You looked great tonight.

Groaning dramatically, I closed my eyes. I didn't see her when I went to chat with everyone after the show. Surprisingly, she hadn't come up to me afterwards. Why the fuck was she there?

We had broken up months ago, and it was getting weird how she would randomly pop up. The breakup had been fine. Not like a huge blowout, but maybe she still had lingering feelings for me.

Me: Thanks. I'm surprised you came.

I sunk into the steaming hot water and exhaled. Oh, this felt amazing on my bruised and battered body tonight.

Genevieve: I still want to support you. You're a very talented artist and performer.

I tried not to roll my eyes at that. I didn't want to do this with her tonight. So, I just liked the message and moved on. Instead, I checked out Ozzie's Instagram. It wasn't difficult to find with a name like Ozzie. She had already followed Logan, who had a ton of followers.

Ozzie's blonde pixie cut popped up almost immediately, and I checked out her videos. She had loads of reels of her juggling all sorts of things. Balls. Rings. Clubs. Knives. Cigar Boxes. She was fucking good. We hadn't had anyone with this skill set come to our studio in probably ever. She even could manipulate light sabers and swords. It was impressive. Her body moved fluidly like she was made to do this kind of art. Her thick waist and strong thighs were only a *little* distracting as I scrolled.

Some videos she was also doing acrobatics and other random circus things. There were only a few on the hoop. She moved well, albeit a little less fluid than she did on the ground. She needed some coaching, but Ozzie had a solid foundation and good strength. There were photos of her laughing and smiling with large groups of people. She looked way more friendly in these images than she did when we had met. I wondered what her deal was.

It wasn't my intention to look at every single video of Ozzie, but there were a few that were different from the rest. She was sexy and sultry. Much different from the clowning and it felt like someone had reached into my stomach and lit a fire low in my belly.

Her navy eyes tracked the camera as she writhed around a chair dancing, her body on full display. It was like I was hypnotized. A siren song that I couldn't look away from as she moved and beckoned me in. Swallowing, I scanned her profile some more and found only a few of the other side of Ozzie. Something about the way her demeanor changed in these moments had my core tensing and the urge to reach for my vibrator was strong, I didn't realize my hand was already going for it until I was interrupted once again.

Genevieve: We should catch up sometime
and talk about your show.

Goddamnit. I didn't want to do this. I had plenty of friends and I didn't really need an ex to be another one. These casual check ins were annoying and uncalled for. Ignoring her message, I sank deeper into my steam filled tub. Sooner or later, I would need to tell Genevieve off, but today was not that day. I set my phone on _do not disturb_ and went back to Instagram.

I told myself I would watch only one more video of sexy Ozzie and then I would be done. It meant nothing. It certainly was in no way correlated to me deciding at this exact moment in time I needed to get off to loosen up. It was simply my overall irritation with Genevieve contributing to my overall sexually frustrated body and Ozzie just happened to be what I was looking at when all this occurred. No connection *whatsoever.*

Satisfied that I worked that out in my brain, I grabbed my toy and slid it to my clit and turned up the intensity. I sighed as the pressure started to build and I rolled my hips along the vibe until I moaned and felt a rush of pleasure and release. I was most definitely not thinking about Ozzie's body in any way, shape, or form. In fact, when I was done I was hardly thinking about anything at all besides how much I needed a fucking break.

Three

Ozzie

"Oh, hell yes. Are you a trapeze bitch because you know trapeze is the best?" Logan taunted me as I walked into her class the following week.

The studio was fully decked out. There were tons of aerial equipment, mats and ground space as well as a dance studio, warm up space and a few other rooms I hadn't yet seen. It was a circus performer's dream, and it was filled with so many happy looking people.

Logan came over and gave me a big bear hug for such a petite person.

"It's not my main apparatus, but I can keep up a decent amount. I figured I would come check things out and see what all the hype is." Winking, I looked around. "I'm excited to take class."

So many other athletes were training right now, and it was glorious. It looked like there was another silks class going on and then a few people training their own thing. One of them happened to be Jess. I tried not to stare as she spun aggressively on the hoop. My crush had obviously not gotten the notification that I should chill the fuck out.

"She's obsessed with spinning." Logan smirked beside me. "She's fucking great at it, too."

"Yeah, she is," I said a bit breathlessly as I watched the muscles in Jess's back flex as she moved. I tried not to think about the sweat that was sliding down her smooth skin. Coughing awkwardly, I tried not to choke on my drool.

"Well, here's the trapeze class!" Logan introduced me to several other company members, and I grinned, nodding at each of them. There was a wide array of people here. All shapes, sizes, ages, skin tones, and genders. It was beautiful. My shoulders relaxed slightly, and I took a deep breath.

Logan was the director of the circus and the head trapeze coach. She guided us through a warmup on the ground and then we moved into the air. I kept sneaking glances around the warehouse, my eyes seemingly magnetized on Jess. At one point, she took off her tank, and the moment crystallized in my brain. The way her arms flexed as she tore off the fabric like it was inconvenient to her, and her abs showed with every inhale and exhale. I hoped to god no one had noticed me watching her.

She seemed to be trying to perfect something. Jess would set up her phone to record the same move over and over again, then go back to watch the video and scowl. From my point of view, every time she did it, it looked great, but clearly she was dissatisfied with her performance. The more I watched her, the greater the weird tingling sensation in between my thighs diverted me from the class I was supposed to be fully partici-pating in. I nearly screamed at my genitals to calm the fuck down.

"Ozzie, you're up." Logan's voice drew me back to what we were doing on the bar. I nodded and hopped up to the high bar where we practiced different beats and swings. It was a little clunky at first, since this wasn't my main thing, but I got the hang of it quickly. Everyone rallied behind me and nodded encouragingly as I tackled each thing. There was a sense of belonging here, like I could see myself laughing and training alongside these people.

Soon, the class was practically over and we were all instructed through a cool down and moving away from the bars.

"Ozzie, will you show us a demonstration?" Logan asked as class started to wrap up. I stopped dead in my tracks, excitement skittering down my spine. I loved showing off my skills. But it was mixed with a sinking feeling in my gut, too. This was my time to shine, and I didn't want to fuck it up.

"Like a juggling demonstration?" I asked innocently, my muscles already tensing up at the thought of an impromptu performance.

"Yes ma'am. I want to see some balls fly, if you know what I mean." She winked at me, and I snickered. Logan was quickly becoming one of my favorite people. I hoped we could be good friends.

"Do you have any juggling balls here?"

Her face fell, and she frowned. "No, actually we don't. I guess we should change that." She tapped a manicured fingernail against her lip like she was calculating how quickly she could get some juggling materials here.

"That's okay. I always have some with me. Let me go get them from my car." I turned to head out of the complex, colliding head on with Jess.

"Jesus Christ," she said as our sweaty bodies smacked together in a rather unpleasant sound. Scrambling, we both grabbed onto the other in an effort not to fall over. Our hands were slick against one another's skin, and we clung to each other for a moment before we toppled to the ground.

My breath came out of me in a whoosh as I practically body slammed on top of her. My thigh was in between hers and my hands were on either side of her head. Our mouths were inches apart, and I glanced quickly at her lips. So much of my body was touching hers and I was rendered speechless. Heat went straight to my lower belly and suddenly I was dizzy.

"Oh my god, I'm so sorry." My face heated as I hovered above her, looking deeply into her ice-blue eyes.

"It's okay, no harm, no foul." Jess grimaced, and I jumped up and off her aggressively and nearly fell as I took a few steps back. The warmth of her body suddenly taken away from mine was a bit jarring. I realized I was just staring at her sprawled on the floor and tripped, rushing forward to offer her a hand to get her up.

Why was I so awkward with her?

She looked at me quizzically and grabbed my palm. In one fluid motion, I pulled her hard to her feet. She stumbled forward and my hand lingered with her fingertips against mine before dropping her palm quickly, like I had touched a hot stove. Flexing my hands at my sides, I wiped them on my pants. Jesus, my hands seemed to sweat aggressively every time she was around.

Jess gazed at me with an annoyed look, and I realized I had done the same goddamn thing I had done the first time we had met, which was act like her touch was battery acid. In reality, I felt like my body responded in weird ways to her and I didn't even know her. I had no right to have lewd thoughts after touching her skin only twice.

"Right, well, I'm going to go get my balls."

I got another funny look from her. Ducking my head, I hustled out to my car and tried to breathe. It was fine. Surely, she had met more uncomfortable and awkward people than what I had just displayed, right?

Right.

I grabbed my juggling bag, which was full of balls, rings,

clubs, and a few other random objects, and walked back into everyone sitting down. Expectant expressions lined everyone's faces in the warehouse. My nerves were fucking fried now, but I needed to put on a show.

Butterflies erupted in my belly, and I tried to calm my pounding heart. This was my job. I was good at this. My training prepared me for situations exactly like this. So why was I so goddamn terrified to juggle some balls in front of these people?

Not people, just Jess. She tilted her head to the side and watched me closely, like she couldn't figure out what the hell to do with me. With the way I had acted towards her, I totally got it. I was acting like someone who did not live on Earth and was learning to be a human in my skin suit for the first time.

"Ozzie is going to juggle for us!" Logan clapped enthusiastically and everyone cheered except Jess, who seemed to glare even harder at me. Logan gave me a thumbs up encouragingly and then I got into it.

Three deep inhales and exhales to start, and then I threw. I started with three balls and worked my way up to five, then alternated between rings and balls and finally finished with clubs. I added fun flourishes and swishes of my hips and contact juggling where I would roll things across my body. My natural rhythm and cadence came easily as I let instinct and trained discipline take over.

I added some spins and cartwheels to everyone's delight as I clowned around and moved fluidly. At one point, music played, and I moved to the beat. The songs seemed to go faster and faster until I was about to pass out from exertion. The small crowd cheered as I took a final bow. My smile was genuine and broad as I looked at the small community around me.

"You're so cool!" Logan rushed up to me and gave me a tight squeeze. Jess hung back. Not that I noticed.

"That was seriously amazing," someone else said next to me. "I'm Myla." She reached her hand out, and I shook it. I immediately recognized her from the other night. Her hooded brown eyes were warm and kind as she introduced herself.

"Yes! You're the silks artist that performed the other night. Your piece was beautiful. The drops were seriously show stopping. Also not to be weird, but I've also totally seen your parents perform before. Their acrobat duo changed my life." I sounded like an obsessed fan. But it was hard not to be when her parents were like one of the coolest and most famous circus couples known to man. Two young circus artists from two very different worlds. Back in the height of their careers, they made a whole show about their love story and how, even though her dad was Russian and her mother was Korean, their home was with one another wherever the world took them. The entire show had made me sob uncontrollably.

"Thank you! They are pretty spectacular. They will be delighted to know people still talk about them," Myla said. She didn't seem fazed at all that I knew of her parents. Thank god I didn't screw up this introduction. "I'm also the head silks coach," she added.

Okay, so far so good.

"Juggling is lowkey so goddamn hard and you made it seem as easy as breathing." Another girl came up to me, her high ponytail bouncing with a massive tumble of black curls as she walked over.

"Thank you. It was a disaster when it started. I couldn't catch a damn thing. But then I got addicted to the small bits of progress and I just never stopped." I shrugged, trying not to ramble too much. Juggling was hard. Everyone knew when you messed up. If you dropped one ball out of a hundred juggles, it looked like you failed. Even though in other performances people wouldn't always be able to recognize a fuck up. Juggling practically held a neon sign to your mistakes.

"I'm Aven. Nice to meet you," she said, and I shook her hand, too.

"You did the ground piece, right?" I had been mesmerized by her control over the wheel. It was epic.

"Yes! I'm in charge of the acrobatics program here." Aven gave my shoulder a squeeze.

"And you know, Jess. In charge of lyra," Logan said. She looked over at Jess, who continued to scowl at me, and I shifted uncomfortably in front of her.

"Right well, should I show you what I can do on lyra? Now that I've impressed you with my juggling skills, you can see if you'd like me to also hop on the hoop?" I teased, since Logan already knew that lyra was my secondary thing.

They all agreed to watch as the rest of the company and students shuffled out. This felt more serious, like this is where I would prove myself to the coaches and the company and...Jess.

"Jess and I used to be lyra partners. But the company needs more of my attention these days, so I need a few less things on my plate to maintain my sanity. Which means Jess is looking for a lyra partner. You know, just throwing it out there in case you're interested," Logan said. She squeezed Jess's shoulders, and she smiled a little sadly at a frowning Jess.

"Well, I don't want to presume that you'd want to work with me," I said. My body felt like a weird ball of nerves as I quickly added, "but I would be honored to be your student and partner if you'd have me...." I shifted from side-to-side itching to know her answer. Our interactions were now zero-to-two, so I hoped this could make up for some of it.

"Sure Ozzie. Let's see how this goes first." Jess gestured to the hoop, and I cued up a song. Within a few beats, I mounted the hoop and began a solo I had worked hard to perfect at my previous company. It was more like a dance than it was an aerial act, but I knew it was captivating by the way they all seemed to stare. Breathing hard, I finished the act with much less spinning than Jess and gently hopped off and took a small bow.

"Hold please." Logan held up a tattooed hand. Aven, Myla and Jess huddled around her as they dove into conversation together, whispering harshly with laughter bursting out randomly.

I looked around absently and twisted my hands together, not sure what I should be doing at this very moment while they deliberated. Maybe I should leave? Slowly, I started to edge my way out of the space.

"You're in if you want it." It was Jess who delivered the news. I froze and then beamed at her.

"I would really like that."

"Great! I'll send you some details about rehearsals, upcoming shows, and all the boring administrative stuff. We're so excited to add you to the professional team, Ozzie!" A group hug engulfed me, and it felt nice. I hadn't had a community that celebrated who I was in a while. The last company I was with didn't exactly love all the details about me.

"Thank you," I said as Jess looked at me with those intense eyes again, and I tried to shake off the sensation that she loathed me.

"First gig is this next week if you want it. I'll send you all the details about the schedule." Logan did a little happy dance like this was the most exciting news ever.

"Welcome to Cirque Callisto," Jess said curtly. She walked out of the space and the others lingered, asking me questions about juggling and shows I had been a part of. Usually I was better with people. But something about Jess made me feel like my body and my brain were disconnected. The things that came out of my mouth when we talked were so cringy I just wanted the floor to swallow me whole. I had been around many talented and beautiful people, so what exactly was my deal with her? Ugh.

Clearly, we would have some work to do, and I was going to do my fucking best to get Jess to like me.

Four

Jess

With the five of us in here, the dressing room was crowded. Everyone was frantically trying to get ready except Ozzie, who had shown up in full hair and makeup, ready to go. Clearly, she was exceptionally prepared. For some reason, that annoyed me.

Logan grumbled as she worked on her own face while Myla and Aven debated on what they wanted to do with their hair. I opened my bag onto the counter and makeup spilled out everywhere. Helplessly, I squinted at my face in the mirror and was met with a blurry and wobbly image. There was no way I was going to be able to do this by myself today.

"Hey, Lo."

"What?" she said in the middle of caking on foundation.

"Um."

Logan looked at me in the mirror with her eyebrow raised. She knew what I was going to ask.

"Ozzie, any chance you can help Jess with her makeup? Her eyeballs aren't working so well today." Logan didn't miss a beat, and I tried to keep my face neutral. Logically, it made the most sense. Ozzie was ready and Logan still had to do her whole routine. But Ozzie and I were on weird terms even if she didn't realize it yet. My body and mind just couldn't figure her out. It put me on edge and it didn't help that she seemed to be exceptionally nice and hot in a muscle mommy kind of way.

Ozzie's eyes looked up from her phone. "Sure, I can't promise it'll be great, but I'd be happy to help."

I scowled at Logan. But I needed help, and this was my best option. Why did Ozzie have to be so prepared? Ugh.

"I have an eye condition that messes with my vision." That was all I offered for an explanation. The corner of Ozzie's mouth ticked up, and she simply nodded, not asking any questions.

"Tell me how you like to do your makeup," she said softly, like she didn't want to scare me. She looked at my things and a small smile played on her lips. I straightened my spine and tried to relax my rigid shoulders. Ozzie was helping me. This was nice; there wasn't any reason I needed to be snappy about it.

"Uh, usually I start with this primer and this brush."

I handed her the makeup brush, and our fingertips touched. I half expected her to shake off the sensation like she seemed keen to do anyway, but she simply grabbed it and got to work. Her hand was steady and sure.

Huh, maybe she was just exceptionally anxious the first time we met? Maybe I needed to give her a fucking break. Or maybe I just needed to forget about it entirely and calm my tits before I bit someone's head off.

"Close your eyes, please," she whispered. Her voice seemed to slide against my skin in a warm caress. I tried to refrain from shivering, even though I was practically burning up.

Gently, I closed my lids, and the soft presence of her body pressed into me. Her heat brushed against my cheek. Tingles went down my spine as she gently coated my eyelids. This felt oddly intimate, and I had no idea why. Logan had done my makeup a million times, and it was never like this.

Was I attracted to Ozzie?

"Is it okay to use this brush for eyeshadow?" she asked, her dark purple lips splitting into a soft smile. It took me a moment of blinking and breathing heavily to understand what she had just said to me. Her makeup looked flawless in my blurry haze as I squinted at her. Dramatic lines and dark smoky accents with glitter across her skin. I got distracted by her dark purple lips again and had to refrain from licking my own.

"Jess?" she asked again, her dark blue eyes dancing with amusement. Her cropped, bright blonde hair framed her face in a sleek and sophisticated way. I wanted to reach out and touch it.

What is happening to me right now?

"Yes." I swallowed, barely recognizing my voice. "That's great."

She continued to ask for permission as her fingertips would sometimes dust across my cheekbones and her breath would flutter against my lashes in minty cool freshness. I tried to shake off this weird attraction that was budding rapidly in my belly. Minutes ago, I was annoyed and put off by her. What the hell had happened in the moments in between then and now? Was I so sex deprived that the touch of a new woman was sending my horny ass into a frantic state?

Damnit, I needed to get it together. I tried to focus on my breathing and ignore the quivering that seemed to travel lower and lower in my abdominals.

"Okay, well, I think I'm done. Does it look okay?" She looked at me sheepishly. I narrowed my eyes in the mirror as the other girls gathered around us. The outlines of it looked great, but I couldn't see the exactness of it, so I looked at the others for some help with validation.

"It looks lovely! Ozzie's a natural." Aven stood behind me and I looked at her in the mirror as she patted my shoulder.

"Ten out of ten," Myla added.

"She's beauty and she's grace," Logan teased, and I rolled my eyes.

So, it looked good. My chest seemed to grow exceptionally warm, and I fought the urge to rub at my sternum. I wondered why it was oddly attractive that Ozzie was good at makeup and specifically good at doing my makeup? Probably something to unpack later on my own time.

"Thank you, Ozzie. I really appreciate it."

"Anytime." She gently put all the brushes and compacts in exactly the same way she found them. I watched silently as she zipped up my makeup bag. Her hands were strong and confident as she finished cleaning up. I wondered idly if they were like that from all the aerial and juggling. I reminded myself that these same strong hands seemed intent on wiping off my touch.

I snapped my head up, realizing I had been staring at her palms as she stood up, avoiding my eyes and cracking her neck from side to side.

Grabbing her hand, I felt a zap of electricity go through my arms. It was on an impulse that I needed to know what her touch would feel like in this exact moment, as my body seemed to shift in how I felt about Ozzie. We both looked down at where our skins touched, and I let go quickly.

Fuck. Here I was, irritated at her for doing the same thing. Could it be that she felt this weird vibe between us? My body seemed to be responding on its own. Is that why she had let go of me so aggressively and wiped her hands off?

Unlikely. Clearly, we were both a little socially awkward and anxious. That was the most logical explanation. I scowled at myself for having such a funny thought. Ozzie was still looking at me expectantly since I had snatched her arm.

"Uh, good luck out there," I said, forcing myself to look pleasant. Ozzie gave me a quizzical look.

"You too." She left the room to go grab some water.

"Good luck?" Logan raised a brow at me.

"What?"

"Jesus, Jess." She snorted, and I grimaced again. Logan was so fucking tuned in to everyone around her; it was unnerving. Aven walked over and patted my hand lovingly.

"Do you need help with your hair, or are you good?" She gently combed the ends with her fingertips.

"Will you work your magic?" I batted my very long false eyelashes at her, ignoring Logan's pointed stare.

"I would love to, darling," she drew out her words and got to work making an elaborate braid with my long brown hair.

"I don't know what the heck was happening there, but it was hot." Myla winked at me, and my mouth dropped open.

"Nothing is happening here." I hissed as Aven continued to move hair pieces around.

"*Okay*," Logan said airily.

What *was* happening here?

My body and my brain were clearly confused. Obviously, I was just a little horny, and it was nice to be touched by someone. But there was nothing going on here. No vibes were happening. This was a *no vibe zone*. It was just a fluke moment of intimacy.

Everything was exactly as it had been.

Ozzie eventually came back and settled into warming up for the gig and changing into her costume. I tried not to look when she stripped off her sweats and tank for the skin-tight, mirrored ensemble. Powerful muscles lined her legs and forearms, contrasting the softness of her hips and belly. There were a few tattoos scattered across her body and I wondered what they meant to her, and what they were.

Pushing that silly thought away, I pulled my focus back to

my own costume. I didn't know anything about Ozzie except that she popped out of nowhere and seemed to be everywhere all at once. Eventually, the party began, and we all filed out in our elaborate costumes and moved to be ambient performers like decor on the wall.

The partygoers shined and glittered around us as we weaved in and out of them . The theme was neon glam western for a high-profile client in the city. It wasn't that abnormal for us to be hired to enhance a party experience by being walking performers. For the most part, it was enjoyable. Usually, it just involved lots of sinewy movement and saucy smiles. We weaved around the dazzling elite and flirted our way through the throngs of alcohol, money, and laughter.

I spotted Ozzie off to the side, juggling rings and rolling them across her toned body. The full body suit with mirrored paneling bounced lights off in so many directions, making her look absolutely brilliant. Like a shining star amongst everyone else.

"Why are you glaring again?" Logan brushed by, looking like a widow who just killed her husband with her long mesh robe lined with a fuzzy collar and matching wristlets.

"I'm not." I plastered on a smile as Logan and I hung on one another for a moment before we strutted back to our green room.

"You like Ozzie," Logan stated like it was a fact. Fuck, she was practically a mind reader.

"I don't know anything about her." I gulped down water and gnashed into a granola bar. Aven waltzed in laughing and then immediately slid her normal face on. Each of us had masks to protect us as we performed in these spaces. On stage, we were mostly free, but at these parties we played a part.

"Good god, I'm tired of these men trying to grab at me." She patted at her damp armpits and slick forehead.

"Who was grabbing at you? You know I have a zero tolerance, no harassment policy at gigs. I will light their goddamn ass on fire." Logan's eyes seemed to fill with flames.

"I can handle it, Lo. I told them to fuck off unless they wanted me to sue their ass, and that seemed to get them out of my space pretty fucking fast." The corners of Aven's mouth tipped up and Logan looked dissatisfied with that answer.

She was technically the one in charge and she would fight people for our safety. People sometimes felt entitled to touch us at these types of events, and that was absolutely not the case.

"It's hot as hell out there." Myla slipped into the room as well.

"Is Ozzie the only one out there right now?" Logan's eyes widened as she looked around, fanning her face.

"It's fine. She's killing the crowd with her light up rings. They're eating her shit up." Aven waved it off like it wasn't a big deal.

"Okay, we have to get back out there." Logan flipped her light pink hair and plastered on a sugary smile.

"If you smile any harder, you will break your cheekbones," I said, poking at her exaggerated expression.

"Fuck you." She flipped me off playfully and exited the room, with Aven and Myla in tow.

I took a moment to breathe and sit down, needing to collect my thoughts. Genevieve had texted me again, and I was trying to find a polite way to say fuck off without her making it into some huge thing. Confrontation wasn't usually my thing, and I was avoiding a blowout at all costs.

She couldn't seem to let us go, even though she was the one who had been doing questionable things with other people. I was a monogamous kind of girl and Genevieve often did some things that weren't exactly cheating, but I felt betrayed, nonetheless. I didn't know if that was a *me* issue or a *her* issue, but eventually it got too big in my head and I decided it came down to a breakdown of my trust. After that, I was done. Considering it was months ago, I had no idea why she was trying to keep up this weird attachment to one another.

I liked a clean break. There was no reason for her to keep contacting me.

Thoughts of Ozzie's fingertips brushing against my skin kept popping up, and I tried to shake it off. It created an odd warmth in my chest that bloomed across my collarbones and down to my belly. Realistically, she was not as bad as I had made her out to be in the beginning, but that didn't mean I liked her. It meant that I was neutral towards her. No vibes were happening. *None.*

Sighing, I decided to not think about it too much and instead went back out to the crowd to do my damn job.

FIVE

OZZIE

I showed up at Jess's class the next week and tried to keep my cool. Our faces had been so close the other night and I was sure she could feel my hands shake as I tried to apply her liquid eyeliner. I hoped my breath didn't smell weird or she couldn't hear me practically panting in front of her.

The gig was straightforward and enjoyable. The crowd was super into my juggling tricks and a few people had asked about booking me for their events, which was a lovely compliment. I had guided them to chat with Logan, who oversaw all our experiences. She was fiercely protective of us as performers and had an ironclad contract that ensured we were safe, happy, and financially compensated appropriately.

Aven and Myla were an absolute delight to work with. I really hoped we would all become close friends. Nobody told you how fucking hard it was to find your people as an adult. Desperately, I wanted to find a family here. Jess and I seemed to have a funny moment in the dressing room. I swear I was getting a vibe off her, but maybe I was just reading into it because of my attraction to her. There were so many reasons why that was a terrible idea.

Rolling my neck side to side, I tried to work out the constant tightness in my shoulders and not think about the train wreck that was my last relationship.

In my previous training company, getting involved with another performer ended in a ball of flames. In reality, I should have known better, but in my stupid, naïve head, I thought it would be fine. We were consenting adults and professionals, after all. The ripple effect our falling out had on the surrounding company was nauseating. The asshat had started a witch hunt, and people ate that shit up. He started the fire, and I was simply consumed in the aftermath. He had tainted the space with his exaggerated tales of what the hell had happened. That motherfucker was on my shit list and if I never saw his face again, it would be too soon.

Even though I was a better and more professional performer, I was the crazy one. It seemed like women always were. Fuck him.

Cracking my knuckles, I decided that those thoughts were not helpful or productive anymore. This place was different. I was different. The situation with Jess and me was practically nonexistent, so there was nothing to get overly invested in.

Breathing deeply, I tried to center myself and calm my mind to take Jess's class. A distracted head was a great way to fuck your own shit up on any apparatus, and I did not want to do that today with my already injury-prone shoulders and hips.

My body was already grumpy with me for not cooling down properly from the gig. My joints had screamed at me this morning and for the first few hours of the day I had hobbled around trying to get my body back in working order. Thank god for Advil, ice, and heat packs. The beauty of my hypermobile body was that it was upset when I didn't move it consistently, but then would get pissed if I did too much. A delicate, ever moving target of what actually felt good.

The surrounding chatter died down as Jess clapped her hands, beaming at her students, who were eager to take class. She stood confidently in front of us and instructed us on how to begin the warmup and conditioning exercises. There were about eight of us with varying degrees of skill. I was by far the closest in caliber to Jess from what I could tell, but still nowhere near to her grace and control on the apparatus.

She had a special bit of sorcery that came from love and passion that could only be spell cast by herself. Her mastery of the lyra was apparent in every interaction she made; it inspired something deep within my soul every time she demonstrated a trick.

Every once in a while, she would come over and assist or show me something and I would try not to get distracted by the way her body moved. It was intoxicating to watch her elegantly maneuver through the air. A few times she physically spotted me and laid gentle fingertips against my skin, and I had to fight the urge to shiver. My reaction to her touch needed to be reined in.

Breathe, Ozzie. You can do this.

The class went by swiftly as we all took turns playing a sequencing game and pulling moves out of a hat before then linking them together with a chosen song. Each person had their own personality, and it was lovely to see the individualization that made each performer shine. Everyone celebrated one another over and over again.

My heart warmed at the collaboration and community that was practically tangible in the space. The way a circus should be.

We all started to pack up and Jess called out to me, "Ozzie."

I looked at her eagerly and tried to slow my rapid heartbeat. "What's up?"

"Uh, not to be weird, but Logan mentioned where you

lived, and I was wondering if you could give me a ride to the next gig we have together. I get a bit nervous to drive sometimes, with my eyes how they are, and I would really appreciate it." She wound her hands together tightly and looked at me openly.

This was clearly a vulnerability for her. I wanted to say something encouraging, but I wasn't sure of the right words, and we still barely knew one another. I wanted it to come off as support, not pity. We all needed accommodations for things —it made us human. I certainly understood, my autoimmune disease and hypermobile ass were practically a full-time job sometimes.

"Absolutely. What's your number?" I asked, grabbing my phone.

She prattled off her answer, and I sent her a text.

"Just send me your address and I'll come grab you before we have to be there."

"Great, I'll uh see you then," she said softly. I stood there for another moment, unsure of whether I should go.

"You're incredible, you know," I blurted.

Jess looked at me in surprise. I wanted to bridge this chasm between us, but maybe this was the wrong approach. Was that just the dumbest fucking thing to come out of my mouth? I groaned internally and my miserable self continued to run with it.

"On lyra. You're the best I've ever seen. And a great teacher," I said, fumbling through the words and tried to make it sound less disastrous as it tumbled from my lips.

"Oh, thank you. That's... very sweet of you to say."

We stood silently until I bowed my head in an odd manner and hustled out of there before I said something else strange. Driving home, I tried not to think of what Jess thought about me. With everyone else, I could act like a total normal human being, but I always clammed up around her. I needed to get this weird attraction under control.

Attractive people were around me every day. So why exactly did my human function die whenever I was around her?

Ugh.

Walking into my house, I unceremoniously dropped all my shit on the floor and turned to face Trevor, who was lounging at the dining room table.

"Why do you look like you just ran over something?" he asked, eyeing me suspiciously.

"I'm like an extraterrestrial being in a meat suit with this girl at the circus," I grumbled, plopping down next to him.

"The hoop artist?" Trevor raised a brow.

"God damnit yes."

"You've got a crush and you just don't know what to do with yourself," he said with a laugh, seeming to enjoy my discomfort.

"Exactly, I don't want to make it uncomfy because I just got here, and I have no idea if she's into women or whatever and we're working together and we know how that worked out last time. I just feel like every time I'm around her I can't stop staring at her or saying a cluster fuck of things."

An image of her flashed in my mind of moving around in that tiny rhinestone two piece, doing impossible physical feats on the hoop and it sent a weird searing heat right in between my thighs.

"First of all, what happened at your last studio was because Sean was an absolute asshole who used his manipulative charm to paint you as the nasty girl." Trevor sat up straighter and leaned forward. "We all should have clocked his ass as an ignorant man a lot sooner, but mistakes were made, and we got you the fuck out of there."

"I know." I ran my fingers through my short hair.

"I still can't believe he outed you like that and then made you seem like a predator. Who the fucks asks for a threesome and then when you politely decline, says that your sexuality is a lie and your OnlyFans work is deplorable? What a fucking tool." Trevor narrowed his gaze.

"The audacity of men truly has no bounds." I remembered the night he found out quite vividly. We were out with everyone from the training company and dancing the night away. We had only been exclusive for a few weeks with one another, and I had disclosed to Sean that I had an OnlyFans. Nudity was an art form that paid well. Sex work was fucking work, and the circus hadn't always provided. Plus, the human body wasn't dirty or uncomfortable.

It was powerful. It made me feel alive and free.

At the time, Sean had taken it well. I wouldn't have continued to see him unless he had. But then I added the layer of telling him I was bi and suddenly, he took that as an opportunity for me to be his slutty little fantasy with little regard to what I wanted. Sean had drunkenly just hurled the threesome at me by cornering me at the club and saying that this girl wanted to fuck us both. She seemed excited and eager and that was great, but I wasn't into it.

I was still figuring out if I wanted to put a serious label on Sean and me, emotionally I wasn't ready to have another intimate partner involved. I said I didn't want to do it and he made a huge scene saying I lied about my sexuality and that I was a whore, which made no fucking sense.

Then he left with the girl.

In my head, that was the end of our relationship, and I was fine with it. We weren't that serious yet and the next day everything blew up. Sean spun his web of lies so fast that no one was interested in my side of the story.

There were times I thought about trying to tell my own truth, but what was the point? Sean had gotten to everyone first and, in reality, those people weren't my friends. We just happened to be occupying the same training space. They wanted me out. If their loyalty was so fragile that it could break our team's trust in one another by the inflated tale of someone else, then I didn't want any part of it.

"This place isn't like your last studio. They were a glorified version of mean girls from high school. You were like their one token queer bitch. It doesn't seem like that's the case here," Trevor said.

I nodded. The atmosphere already felt different. There were many more openly queer folks loving other queer people here. It felt better, but the wounds from my past still made me cautious.

"Why don't you just take a breath and try not to overthink it. You aren't going to screw anything up, and I will fuck some bitches up if they try to mess with you." Trevor wasn't kidding, either. He really would.

I laughed at that. "I appreciate your willingness to get violent."

"And it's okay to have a crush." Trevor winked.

"I also did her makeup the other day," I blurted, thinking about how close we were and the heat that had coursed through my body at being a breath away from her skin.

"And?"

"It was weirdly personal. I thought my heart would pound out of my chest as I was touching her face."

I had wanted to run my entire hand across her cheek, and I wondered what her lips felt like against mine when we were so close together. My mind had taken a huge detour into horny land when I just needed to complete the task at hand.

"I mean, what would be so bad if something did happen? This is genuinely different from what happened before," Trevor said gently.

"I don't know. I would get kicked out or be forced to quit

again?" Nerves tingled along my spine. I didn't think that it would get to that point. Things were not the same here. They were, in fact, on the opposite end of the spectrum. Plus, Sean was a dick hole, and I just didn't want to admit it to myself at the time. The sex was kind of fun, so I just coasted by all the glaringly obvious red flags.

"No, you won't. You're too talented and they need you," he said, like it wasn't a big deal or that the trauma of my past wasn't knocking at my door. Even if logically I knew what he was saying made sense, my nervous system disagreed whole-heartedly.

"Right, well, either way, I'm nervous as fuck."

"I know, feel those feelings. They're valid and recognize the reality in front of you." Trevor patted my hand, and I rolled my eyes.

With that, I headed to my room and took a shower, trying to shake off the heaviness that seemed to hang over my head about Jess and me. I was making an enormous deal out of nothing.

How complicated could things get? It couldn't be any worse than before, right?

I had to believe that to be the truth.

Six

Jess

A ding sounded on my phone, and I figured that must be Ozzie saying she was coming to get me. I squinted at the phone and held it as far away as I could. The fuzzy letters seemed similar to *on my way*, so I figured it was time to go. Quickly, I ran around trying to gather all my things. My eyes should be fine in just a few more days. This treatment had just really taken a doozy on my near-sighted vision this time. Probably because I was stressed and really fucking busy.

I grabbed my bag and double checked that everything I needed was in there. Snatching a granola bar, I filled up my water and headed towards the door. Another ding sounded from my phone, and I figured that meant Ozzie was here, so I walked out of my house to see her in my driveway.

She waved. Her makeup and hair already seemed done. She knew that's why we got to things so early, right? So, we could prep there? Maybe she just liked to be extra ready. Either way, I was impressed by her punctuality.

I opened the car door, and she grinned at me.

"You can put your bag in the backseat if you want."

"Okay, thanks." I shoved my large duffel back there and settled into her car.

"Thanks for doing this. I should be fine to drive in just a few days."

"I'm happy to help, Jess," Ozzie said, her eyes dancing over me from head to toe and it made my heart ache for some reason.

"Do you, uh, think that you could help me with my makeup again?" I twisted my fingers in my lap. Was I being awkward because it was Ozzie or because I was just awkward. I had no problem asking anyone else for help, but they all knew my story and my situation, so it felt less vulnerable in a way. Or maybe it was the fizzy feeling in my stomach that seemed to pop up whenever Ozzie's face was close to mine.

"Totally. I would love to help." Ozzie seemed unfazed by my discomfort.

"So do you do anything else besides circus work, or is this like your main thing?" I tried to broach what felt like a safe topic. In reality, even though things were warming up between Ozzie and me, I barely knew her. There were still a lot of things that neither of us really understood about the other. Part of that was my fault, so here I was trying to thaw my icy walls.

"Mainly this. I have some people that I mentor via zoom for juggling and I used to have some in person students. I also sell some things on Etsy, like queer merch and do some brand collabs on social media and other random things," she said casually, and not just like she listed five different jobs. That sounded extremely exhausting.

"That's cool. I would love to see your queer merchandise sometime." Now that I thought of it, I remembered seeing some queer stuff on her Instagram, but I wasn't sure where she landed on her sexuality. Plenty of people wore queer stuff and weren't actually queer but were just vocal allies. Women especially were hard to decipher, even though the circus was practically a queer playground most of the time.

"Are you queer?" Ozzie had a teasing look on her face, her bright red lips smirked.

"Jesus, you just went for it, didn't you?" I laughed. People didn't just flat out ask the fucking question, but here Ozzie was just whipping it out there. No guessing games for us then. I was starting to gather that things just came out of Ozzie's mouth with little thinking or inhibition. The transparency was honestly nice, a little jarring and surprising sometimes, but better than the alternative.

"Yeah, I mean, if you're comfortable sharing. I'm just very loud and queer after being quiet for what felt like a long time. So, I'm not as polished about it, you know?"

"Sure, yeah. Yes. Well, I'm into women." I tried to make it sound airy and light. It wasn't like I was admitting I was attracted to Ozzie. I just said I liked women. That meant literally nothing in the context of our relationship.

"So, I'm a lesbian." I added. "Not that you probably needed clarification. You know what a lesbian is." Wincing, I wanted to smack myself in the face. "You know what? You should probably say something now, so I'll stop talking." I placed my face in my hands and sighed. Now I was being weird again. Ugh.

Ozzie snorted loudly. "Okay, I'm also queer, but I'm into people, not genders. Sometimes I identify as bi or pan or queer. It just sort of depends on who I'm talking to, and the understanding of what sexuality can mean. Most of the time I say I'm bi."

Labels could be comforting or confining. I understood that.

Well, at least it was out in the open that we both were a part of the community. Not that it meant anything, since we were literally just talking like anybody else. Nothing had happened. This conversation was just that. A conversation, nothing but words ping-ponging through my head on repeat.

"Well, either way, I would still love to see what you've got in your online shop." It was my attempt to get this conversation back on track away from my own budding attraction that had nothing to do with Ozzie personally and all to do with the fact that I was going through a dry spell. Absolutely unrelated to the way Ozzie's eyes crinkled when she was happy or the way she lit up a room with her energy. It was simply the desert that was my sex life.

"I'll send you the link and you can browse sometime." Ozzie's easy confidence settled my nerves as we rolled into the gig.

"Do you do anything else besides this?" she asked, turning to me.

"Yeah, I'm a fitness instructor on the side, but mostly this. Occasionally I'll get roped into some other stuff, especially with kids. It's more like a steady way to keep money coming and going through slow seasons. But we've been busy lately, so I've been able to ditch some hours of the things that I don't like." I liked the stability of my other things, plus it was only like ten to fifteen hours of my week. Mostly, I was able to do what I loved, which was to perform and teach. I was grateful for that.

"Kids are definitely not my number one thing, but those jobs are way easier to get than adults sometimes," Ozzie commented as we hopped out of the car.

"Agreed and unfortunately, they sometimes pay better." We walked into the venue, which was a giant high-rise apartment building. Today was ambient aerial performing on the hoop and tonight we would be next to their rooftop pool.

We would each take turns on the hoop for a couple of songs and then hop off when we needed a break. Logan found us quickly and ushered us into our green room, where we could get ready and warm up before we began.

"Is this always the dream team?" Ozzie asked as Myla and Aven shuffled in.

"Yeah, we're the full-time professionals here and some of our other company members pop in when they can, but since this is our full-time gig, we get priority of jobs. Our cabaret show has a ton of guest artists from all around, so it just depends on who is available. We happen to all be available most of the time. Logan is the head bitch in charge because she started the company and the three of us are the most seasoned," Aven responded.

"Got it. That's good to know." Ozzie set her things down and leaned against one of the vanities.

"Is that how your old circus company worked?" Logan asked innocently, but something glittered in her eyes. I could practically smell drama from the way Logan's long lashes fluttered innocently.

"Uh, not exactly." Ozzie bit her lip. The air in the room suddenly felt charged. Ozzie's hands clamped into a fist beside her and a line formed between her brows.

"I'll level with you. I knew some shit about your previous place. Shit, that I didn't love." Logan was as straightforward as they came. She didn't fuck around. The whole room seemed to hold their breath. Myla's eyes widened and Aven frowned as we all looked at one another.

"So why did you take me?" Ozzie stiffened like she was afraid of the answer.

"You're an amazing performer." Logan put her hands on her hips like a power stance.

"Thank you."

"But I had a feeling that the same shit I didn't like was what drove you away?" Logan asked it like a question that she already knew the answer to.

"I take it you asked around?" Ozzie cracked a smile as her hands visibly relaxed.

"I did." Logan's face softened.

"So, you probably know some shit went down with me?"

Aven, Myla and I didn't even pretend to not be listening. We fully watched the verbal volley that was happening around us. There was so much that wasn't being said and clear secrets surrounded Ozzie's old circus.

"I do," Logan said softly, the tension dissipating in the room. Clearly, whatever had happened had probably fucked Ozzie over too. I wondered if Logan would tell me about it later or if she would make me wait for Ozzie to bring it up.

"I can promise we won't outcast you. Sean is a grade A asshole, and you deserved better. And I'm glad you found it." Logan gestured to us sitting in the room.

"Fuck yeah, you got better!" Aven pumped her fist in the air.

"I don't know who Sean is, but he sounds like an idiot," Myla hummed.

Ozzie cackled. "He was. I should have never let it spiral out of control. But it was too late before I realized everything had fallen apart, you know?"

"I know," Logan said as she walked over and hugged Ozzie fiercely.

Whatever had gone down at her previous place had obviously changed her. My heart ached for her. Our little circus was family, and I couldn't imagine being shunned by them.

"Thank you for letting me be a part of this. I'm excited to be here," Ozzie said quietly. She took a deep breath in and looked around at each of us.

"God, if we weren't about to hop on a hoop, I would say let's all take a shot or something together right now!" Aven smacked her lips and dabbed at her eyes.

"Let's plan a night sometime next week?" It was the first thing I had said in the whole conversation.

"I'd really like that." Ozzie turned her big navy eyes to me, and it felt like everyone else in the room had disappeared for a split second. I could see hurt and anguish in her irises. The urge to punch this Sean guy came in fierce and fast. I didn't even know who this guy was, and I wanted to slap him.

"I love you all and think you're the best fucking people. If anyone tries to fuck with you, you know who to call?" Logan stared at each of us, and we laughed loudly.

"Got it, now let's get this show on the road, people! We're up in twenty minutes!" Myla said as she put the finishing touches on her makeup and hair.

Shit. I hadn't even gotten started.

"Don't worry, we'll get it done." Ozzie sat right in front of me and got to work. I nodded, choking back tears. I don't know why I was so emotional about this. Ozzie handled my brushes with care as her light touch swept across my skin. At one point, I was holding my breath as her fingertips and minty exhales skittered across my cheeks. With her so close, I tried to look anywhere but directly at her face.

My eyes lingered on the tattoos scattered across her skin. One on her wrist and another on her collarbone. My hand itched to trace them with my fingertips, but I tried my best to be as still as a statue. Ozzie's gentle voice commanded me to close my eyes. My fingertips tapped against my thigh and I realized I was holding my breath. Sighing, I tried to relax.

Okay, I think we're done," Ozzie whispered, and it caressed my ear, and I fought the urge to lick my lips. It happened too fast. Her touch here one minute and then gone the next. Fuck, why was I craving the lightness of her hands on my face?

"Thank you, Ozzie." I opened my eyes and blinked at her. She was only a few inches away from me and even though her features were a little wobbly, her closeness made me feel funny things.

"Sure thing."

"I don't know what happened at your old place, but I'm glad you're here," I said quickly, wanting to hold this moment in my hands, but it slipped away like sand.

Ozzie sat back, and she came into better focus in front of me. "Thanks Jess. That means a lot coming from you." We held each other's gaze for a few more moments before Aven hustled over to help with my hair and Ozzie moved out of the way.

We all quickly finished and slipped into our costumes, getting ready to head out to the performance. It was a beautiful evening with throngs of people walking about, sipping on drinks, and giggling with their friends.

A live string quartet was our background music, and they began to play covers of songs that were familiar. I stepped up to the hoop first and began a gentle movement journey around the apparatus. I got claps for spins and splits until I was ready to come down and Logan took my place.

She winked at me and mounted the hoop. It wasn't her favorite apparatus, but she was strong and elegant, as she was on most things. Our fearless leader conquered everything in her way and it was beautiful to see.

"Jess!" someone yelled, and I stilled, looking through the crowd of people who had said my name. It couldn't be her, right?

"Jess!" they yelled again. My eyes went wide as Genevieve appeared in front of me. I caught the slip of Logan's smile as she performed. Why was she even here?

"Oh, my god I didn't realize you all would be here. It's so good to see you!" Genevieve grabbed me and hugged me as my arms hung limply at my side.

"Hi," I said curtly. Myla and Aven crossed their arms and

glared at her. Ozzie looked confused as she tried to put two and two together.

"Have you been avoiding me or something?" she asked playfully. I was for sure avoiding her, but I sure as shit wasn't going to admit that to her. Her energy was bubbling around me like mosquitos I wanted to squish and bat away. Genevieve grated on a special part of my brain that made me feel itchy and skittish.

"Why are you here?" I tried to keep my tone light, but I felt like I wasn't doing a good job. My tongue was heavy in my mouth.

"I'm here with some friends from this apartment complex."

I attempted to keep my face blank. Genevieve had lots of friends who she seemed to have questionable boundaries with. It was one of the many reasons our relationship had inevitably ended, but it seemed like she was eager to keep all her options open despite me giving off major *I don't want to fuck with you* vibes.

"Hey Jess." Ozzie sidled up next to me, looking a bit concerned.

"Hi, I'm Genevieve! Jess and I used to date." She winked at me, and I wanted to scream in her face. Why did she have to just throw that information around? I know some people were super comfy with their exes, but I wasn't one of them. Especially because this ex would not leave me alone.

"I'm Ozzie." She grinned politely, but there was a bite in her voice.

"You're a part of the circus as well?" Genevieve asked, oblivious to the tension in Ozzie's shoulders.

"Yes, I—" Ozzie started, and I interrupted to do something so incredibly stupid. So dumb and yet so fucking brilliant that I wish I could give myself a gold star sticker.

"And my girlfriend." I wrapped my arm around her waist

and pulled her close. To Ozzie's credit, she didn't look fazed in the least bit as she settled her arm around me. She was just a smidge taller than me, but not by much. Our bodies folded into one another perfectly, like the girlfriends we were pretending to be.

"Oh." Genevieve's face fell slightly, and she seemed to lose some of her enthusiasm. "That was fast. I've never seen you before." She narrowed her eyes at Ozzie like she was seeing her for the first time.

This was a bad idea, right? A very, *very* bad idea.

But fast, my ass. Plenty of time had gone by and I knew she had already been seeing plenty of people since our breakup.

"Well, I joined a few weeks ago, and it was practically love at first sight," Ozzie said, tone dripping with honey. I swallowed and tried to smile with all my teeth and not have it look like a snarl. That's right, we could sell this. *I* could sell this.

"Sorry I've been unavailable; we're just enjoying our time together you know? That honeymoon phase is just the best," I said, looking back at Ozzie with wide eyes. What was even coming out of my mouth right now? Lies, lies and more lies, but I couldn't stop. We had started this shit show, and I was committed to see it to the end.

"Well, we should all hang out sometime. I'm surprised it isn't a messy, dynamic being in the same company and all." Genevieve pursed her pink lips at us.

"You can't stop true love, can you?" Logan had appeared by my side. They had never liked each other and that should have been my first red flag, but the sex with Genevieve had been good, and we had had fun until we, well, didn't.

"Hello Logan," she said in a clipped tone.

"Hi," Logan responded saucily. "Ozzie, it's your turn after Aven. If you don't mind, Genevieve, we have a very challenging job to do. Enjoy your drinks."

Genevieve looked taken aback as Logan thoroughly dismissed her. She stomped off looking like she just ate a lemon.

"Well, that was fun." Logan looked the two of us over. "So, dating, huh? Good luck getting out of that." Logan cackled as she walked away.

"Don't say a goddamn word." I looked at Ozzie, whose sneer was practically screaming mischief.

I had just made things so much more complicated than necessary.

SEVEN

OZZIE

"Cheers to a busy season that kicked our ass and thickened our bank accounts!" Logan made a toast, and we all whooped and hollered excitedly. "Also, Dani should be joining us tonight. I'm going to add their straps and flute act to our upcoming shows because they're moving here for a while."

"Who's Dani?" I asked. There were so many guest artists who floated in and out all the time and, as the new kid, I didn't know all of them very well. I was a full-time performer and resident with Cirque Callisto now, but I knew others came and went as they took shows all around. Time had been a blur lately. Everything happened so fast since I got here. It seemed like yesterday when Trevor and I had agreed to stay at least for a year as we both needed this fresh start and now it had been months.

"Dani is an amazing musician and performer. Truly. Hardly anyone else can play the flute in a suspended middle split like they can," Myla said in a dreamy tone, practically petting her purple hair, her eyes gazing off into some distant sunset. It was honestly adorable.

"Myla is a fangirl," Aven teased.

"Oh, please." Myla blushed.

"Speaking of fans, where's Jake tonight? You invited him, right?" Jess's voice rang out, laced with an edge. She tossed her brown hair over her shoulder, but one of the teal pieces slipped from behind her ear. I had the urge to tuck it back, but sat on my hands instead. Her icy eyes narrowed like she already knew what the answer was to her question, and Myla pointedly avoided her hard gaze.

"Uh, he's taking a night in." Myla bit her lip and sighed.

"When are you going to cut him loose, M?" Logan sighed and wrapped her arm around Myla's shoulders.

"I don't... I just...." Tears slipped down Myla's flushed red cheeks and Jess reached to squeeze her palms.

"Myla, are you alright?" Someone I didn't recognize stepped up to our table. Their strawberry blonde hair was long and wavy on one side and shaved on the other. Their dark green eyes seemed to hold all the care and sympathy in the world for Myla. I racked my brain for who this could be, until Logan solved it for me.

"Dani, you came!" Logan beamed lovingly at them.

"Sorry, just stupid relationship drama. I'm fine," Myla said. "I mean, it will be fine. If you'll excuse me." She sniffled and got up to hurry to the bathroom. Her arms hugged around her body as she practically fled from our group.

"I'll go check on her in a few minutes." Aven took a swig of her drink and Dani settled beside me.

"I'm Ozzie. I'm new! I uh, juggle," I awkwardly explained. Nice.

"Yes! Aven was telling me about how you and Jess are apparently dating, right?" They said it so calmly and casually I nearly spit out my drink. News traveled fast, apparently.

"Yes, we're dating." Jess cuddled up next to me and put her hand on my own and intertwined our fingers.

There was a zap of electricity through our palms, and I looked at her with a heated stare. Jess looked ravishing tonight in a black minidress and high-top sneakers. The long mesh sleeves of her dress showed off the taut muscles on her arms. Her lips were a bright red, and I had the urge to take a bite out of her, even though that was absolutely out of the question.

Totally inappropriate thoughts about my incredibly hot pretend girlfriend.

"Wow, I love it! You all are so cute together." Dani beamed at us, and Logan smirked from across the table. Aven had trailed after Myla, and I was shocked at how far Jess was willing to play pretend.

"You know, I'm going to get a drink. Jess, want to come with me?" I tugged her up without waiting for a reply and dragged her through the brewery, where plants and ferns popped up all around, creating an indoor jungle oasis. People joked and chatted as we weaved through the tables and chairs until I was positive we were out of earshot.

"What the hell are you doing?" I asked, amused. I wasn't upset at being Jess' pretend girlfriend, but I did want to know why.

"What do you mean?" she asked innocently, batting her incredibly long eyelashes.

"I mean, what is up with this charade?" We hadn't gotten a chance to talk since our gig the other night. Jess had high-tailed it out of there with Logan and had avoided me the rest of the evening.

"I don't know. Genevieve is on my last fucking nerve with all her texts and just popping up wherever I'm performing, and I needed her to back off. She knows I would never be with Myla, Aven or Logan, so you were my best option." Jess shrugged her shoulders like it wasn't a big deal.

"Okay, but what about Dani? It sounds like you all are friends. I figured this pretend dating thing would be for one night only." Crossing my arms, I tried not to let my gaze snag on her full red lips.

Focus, Ozzie.

"What if we just did it for a few weeks? I need Genevieve to get the hint and stop popping up places. When she's around, I need it to look like we're together and she's a snooper. So, if we could just keep it up on the regular until she's off my back, then we can say it didn't work out and go back to just being friends," Jess said it like it was that easy.

"Yeah, but don't you think the training company will be weird about this?" I had flashbacks to what it meant when Sean and I broke up. My face fell at the thought of that happening again. Was I just doomed to repeat my past mistakes over and over again?

"Hey." She stepped into my space, and I breathed in her lavender and vanilla scent.

"I just can't do this again. This is how my last company went to shit." I took a step back, and she reached out, grabbing my hands. Her calloused palms felt heavy and warm in mine.

"Logan knows what's going on and she would never put up with that fuckery."

It was easy for Jess to say that, because she probably didn't know the whole story. Not only had Sean blamed the breakup on me, but he also freaked out about my side hustle. And then the whole company lost it. I was practically told I was unsafe to work around children and then I got blackballed from teaching and performing in my hometown because of it. I didn't necessarily hide what I did anymore, but I certainly didn't shout it from the rooftops. It was my information to tell.

This was a bad fucking idea. A powder keg waiting to explode and here I was, setting fire to it myself. But I wanted to help Jess. Ugh, why was I so weak in my own resolve around her?

"Only a couple of weeks?" I looked into her pleading eyes, and I saw the desperation. I should really say no. There was so much that could go wrong with this and lying to the people around you was never a good idea, but I had no idea what was up with this Genevieve girl. It sounded like she was determined to be on Jess's ass.

I pursed my lips and closed my eyes.

"Fuck, I'm going to regret this, but okay. We can pretend for a few weeks. But I swear to god if this blows up in our faces you have to take the fall for it. Okay?" I looked at her seriously.

"Don't worry Ozzie. I will take care of you." Jess winked at me, and it did weird things to my lower belly. The crush I had on her would just need to be put on hold while we played pretend. I couldn't add that to the mess of this situation. This was bound to end in disaster any way.

"I actually need a shot now, and you're buying it." I shook an accusatory finger at her, and she giggled; the sound warmed my chest. She pulled me along and we snuggled right up to the bar, where she waved the bartender down for two shots.

"Ozzie, is that you?" a voice said behind me, and my blood went cold.

Shit. Why was the past determined to keep its claws in me?

"Hey Brittany." My voice sounded unlike my own. It was tight and pitched high.

"What's up! I'm just in town visiting. What are the odds that we would meet?" Her eyes narrowed, and she looked practically feral, like I was her prey and she was the predator. There was absolutely no way she was happy to see me unless it was to dump my body in a dark alley trash can.

I imagined punching her right in the teeth and enjoying the blood on my knuckles. She was one of the worst offenders at my old company, the true leader of harsh whispers and scathing stares. Why was she was acting like we were best fucking friends?

"Fucking great," I mumbled underneath my breath.

She flipped her platinum blonde hair and narrowed her gaze as Jess turned and handed me a shot.

"What are you doing here?" her voice dripped sweetness bull dozing past my obvious discomfort.

"Ozzie is a full-time performer for Cirque Callisto now." Jess slinked her arm around my waist like she was trying to hold me together. My hands trembled from my barely controlled rage.

"Are you two together?" Brittany looked Jess up and down, then looked at me with a smirk. "You really moved on quickly, didn't you?"

It had been fucking months. How dare she act like my behavior was anything but normal.

"Sean was a mistake that I kept making for far too long." My tone was cold and detached.

"I think the only mistake was Sean ever being interested in someone like you in the first place," she shot back, fire burning in her eyes.

Why, oh why, was this happening right now?

"You know, men tend to disappoint women most of the time. But you seem like someone who would be fine with mediocrity." Jess threw back her shot aggressively and shot daggers at Brittany.

"W-well." Brittany stuttered through clenched teeth, her eyes wide as she seemed to search for a retort, as Jess's words hung in the air. "At least I'm not a whore!" She practically spat at me.

My mouth hung open. What was this fucking middle school? This could not actually be happening. *No, no, no, no.* Please, someone kill me now. Jess' arm tightened around me, her steady warm touch grounding me through this madness.

"You have five seconds to get the hell away from us before that drink in your hand ends up all over that pretty little dress of yours," Jess said with a smile. She took a looming step forward, her fingers flexing as if to say *don't test me*. Christ, I needed more alcohol for this. Grabbing the shot, I poured it back, letting the heat settle in my veins.

"I would listen to my girlfriend. She really likes whores, but has a particular disdain for hateful homophobic cunts." I raised an eyebrow at her, daring her to say something else.

She looked between the two of us and must have decided that two against one was not in her favor. Her eyes went wide and her voice shook slightly. "Wait until everyone else hears about this, including Sean. What was the name of the company you're with? Sounds like I should send an email to them, too." She backed up slowly, her steps a little wobbly as her gaze darted back and forth around the room.

Logan suddenly appeared. I hadn't even noticed her walking over. Was she clairvoyant? I swear she always showed up when we needed her most.

"I own the company and I can assure you I know everything I need to know about Ozzie. Now it's three against one, Brittany. Did you need an escort out, or can you figure it out on your own?" Logan said with an icy tone, tilting her head to the side.

"Fuck all of you," Brittany said and stormed off and I breathed a sigh of relief.

"Are you okay?" Jess asked, looking at me. She said it softly, like I may break apart at any moment. Swallowing, I nodded.

"I'm fine. Just wasn't expecting to see her ever, actually."

"Fuck that bitch. Let's do another round." Logan flipped off the direction in which Brittany stomped away, and we took another round. The tequila seared my throat and made my stomach warm.

"Does that mean this whole made up relationship thing is advantageous for you, too?" Jess teased me.

"Maybe." I rubbed at my neck and the knot in my stomach loosened a bit.

"Oh, this should be good." Logan had gotten another drink, and her eyes sparkled.

"Let's rejoin the party." Desperate to forget the last twenty minutes ever happened.

Aven, Myla and Dani were already dancing in the mass of people with drinks in their hands, screaming Dua Lipa lyrics at the top of their lungs.

Jess gently pulled me into the group and I quickly was hypnotized by the way Jess's hips moved and the way the lights danced off her skin. She was stunning. I felt weightless when I was in her orbit and Brittany seemed like a far off memory from years ago as opposed to mere minutes.

Being in an invented relationship with Jess felt like it was the most natural thing in the world. The way we had easily stepped up to be on one another's team was as simple as breathing, and just maybe it would help keep the Brittanys of the world off my ass and out of my life for good.

I only hoped that things wouldn't get messier than they already were.

EIGHT

JESS

"Are you sure this is a good idea?" I looked over to where Logan was, the events of the other night flashing through my mind. The moment I clung to Ozzie in front of Genevieve. Ozzie's surprise when I stood up for her in front of that Brittany bitch. Telling Dani that we were dating, even though we weren't. This was turning out to be quite the elaborate lie, and I was the one who had insisted on it.

Ugh.

And if I was being totally honest, my feelings towards Ozzie weren't cut and dry. She made my blood boil in the weirdest ways. One day she was pissing me off and the next I was thinking about the way her skin felt against mine. Now Logan was adding fuel to the fucking fire. She was meddlesome and nosy, which was one of the many things I loved about her. But dammit, being on the receiving end of her scheming wasn't ideal.

"I mean, since you're lovers now, I think it would be beautiful to have you do a big duo piece together," Logan said, batting her impossibly long eyelashes at me, and I had the sudden urge to shove my best friend, hard. She would be fine. There were mats all around. Her ego would be the only thing really bruised.

"Oh, fuck off," I jeered loudly and sat down on the mat underneath our hoop.

"She's the best hoop artist we have except for our core team. And you know I love you to the moon and freaking back, but I need something off my plate. The business side of this is getting out of control. Which is great because it means we're making good money but also, it's demanding more of my time, and you know my love is really the trapeze." She looked at it longingly, like it really was her soulmate. We had been partners for a long time, but she was right. The business needed her elsewhere and sadly, it meant that I lost my best friend as my duo partner.

"I know you only ever did the hoop stuff for me. Which I appreciate. A lot."

"I think it'll be good. We already have someone who wants to book an event for a duo lyra act." Logan's smile turned sour.

"Why does your face look like that now?"

"Hi friends!" Ozzie walked in with her duffel bag.

Her hair was a little ruffled, but the cropped tank and sweatpants she wore did a really great job of showing off her body. The way she somehow had muscular lines and soft hips. It hit me like a gut punch, but I would never admit that to her face. I had to practically fight myself not to take a slow perusal of her body.

Bad, Jess.

This was exactly the type of thinking that would make this farce of a dating thing even worse. No hot thoughts about Ozzie. None.

She smirked crookedly at us, and I swear to god my heart fluttered. That shit needed to stop. Who had time for proper feelings when a fantasy relationship was what we had agreed upon?

"Hi! I was just talking about how we had a gig for a duo lyra piece." Logan got up and grabbed a swig of water.

"Yeah, and you looked like you had just eaten a lemon after you said it." I scowled at her while chalking up my hands and doing some shoulder shrugs on the bar. Logan's avoidance of answering my question was not helping the situation. She purposefully avoided my gaze, so I stalked over to her.

"Logan!" I grabbed her shoulders and shook her hard.

"Fine, fine," she said, swatting at me. Ozzie snorted as Logan sighed.

"Why oh why do I feel like this is already a bad idea," I grumbled. Ozzie's eyes danced between the two of us and I took a deep breath.

"Well, it was from Genevieve." Logan tried to sound unbiased about it, but you could hear the annoyance in her voice. My jaw dropped open.

"You've got to be fucking kidding me," I growled.

Part of the reason it was so hard to avoid Genevieve at these events is because she worked for a huge event company in the city, and she was always at the latest and greatest things. The last thing I wanted to do was fucking work for her.

"It's a huge gala too, with a super large price tag," Logan added.

"Why can't someone else do it? It feels gross that it's from her." I crossed my arms and stuck my tongue out.

"She does seem to be particularly invested in you, Jess, like all the time," Ozzie said, sounding annoyed. Was that a little jealousy I detected in her tone? Impossible.

"Well, she specifically asked for you and said she would pay more. And she expressed that they were looking for a *real couple* who are in love and said, I quote, 'Jess and her new partner could be the star performers.'" Logan air quoted that, and Ozzie's face went blank.

There was a special place in hell for the way Genevieve seemed to want to pull me around like a puppet, months after our breakup, mind you, to do her weird bidding.

"That's some of the most manipulative bullshit," Ozzie grumbled.

"It really is. You can say no to the job, but I thought you might want to look at how much it pays before you do. Genevieve is for sure trying to get under your skin and she is throwing her company's money around to do it."

Ozzie and I huddled around Logan to look at her phone, where the initial email for the gig was pulled up. The number was incredibly inflated, tens of thousands of dollars, and I nearly vomited right then and there. There was no way this job was worth that much. Which meant Genevieve really was just trying to keep her hands in my business at all times.

"Are you fucking kidding me?" Ozzie gasped.

"No. I mean obviously it's not perfectly split evenly as there might be other performers for ambient shit and we would take some for the company overhead to set up and take down and all that shit but we haven't had a budget like this for a private event in well, ever."

Damn Genevieve and her stupid high budget event.

"It's up to you, Jess. I won't do it unless you're okay with it," Ozzie said seriously.

"You would really give up that kind of money because I said so?" I looked at her incredulously.

"Yes." She didn't even hesitate, and warmth filled my belly. What a nice thing for my not-real-girlfriend to do.

"Okay."

Logan raised an eyebrow at me as I paced around the studio for a minute.

"I'm taking the fucking job and it needs to be the most

sexual lovey dovey shit she has ever seen. I want her to seethe with jealousy for doing this bullshit power play," I said through gritted teeth.

"That's my girl!" Logan clapped her hands and then stood up. "Well, I have to go answer a trillion emails like this one. You too get started on your sexy set up." She winked and sashayed away.

"Thank you for taking the job. That money could really make my life a lot easier." Ozzie looked openly at me. "I have a lot of body things that I have to keep up with and between that and paying for health insurance. It could really put my mind at ease."

Ozzie clearly had her own ailments to deal with and oddly, that made me feel better about doing this with her. We could both do this for ourselves. Nobody else.

"Yeah, I mean, it's an enormous amount for one performance." It would be, and I would enjoy the look on Genevieve's face when she realized she had made a mistake asking for us as a couple. I wanted her to melt from second-hand embarrassment.

"And thanks again for standing up for me the other night with Brittany," Ozzie quietly added as she began to warm up on the bar.

"Sure." There was an awkward pause, and I wondered if I should push the boundary further. "What exactly happened at your last company?" That girl had been throwing a lethal attitude at Ozzie. It was hard for me to imagine why she would be so hateful.

Ozzie sighed and chalked up her hands. "Well, on top of Sean, my old sort-of-fling-sort-of-relationship trying to push me into a threesome because I'm bi. He also said I'm a prostitute. He threw it in my face and so did everyone else in a disgustingly degrading way." Ozzie's shoulders sagged and the urge to wrap her up in a hug nearly sent me careening towards her. But it didn't feel like the right move, so I kept my hands to myself.

In fact, I didn't say anything. I looked at her intently and waited for her to go on.

"And I am a sex worker. I've had an OnlyFans for a long time. Nudity is beautiful and artistic, and it pays. I mean, you know we don't always or ever get gigs that pay like what Genevieve's offering. Most people think performance art is something that everyone can do and it's highly undervalued. So, I did what I needed to do along with some other things, and I ended up really liking it. It's empowering in a different way than circus arts. I like it and I'm a fucking adult who can do what she wants with her body."

"Ozzie..." I began, but she kept going.

"I wasn't ashamed of it. Sex work is work. I did what I needed to do and nudity, it feels beautiful and freeing. It's art, just like what we do here. But the rest of my company didn't see it like that. They kicked me out of everything and said terrible things." Her eyes welled up with tears. As she hugged her arms around her torso, leaving chalky handprints on her clothes and skin.

"They said I was unfit to work with kids. It wasn't a secret, but I didn't advertise it like they were doing. I understood the need for discretion when working with minors and teens. And fuck, I don't even like working with kids that much, but it fucking stung."

My heart ached for her, and how unfairly they had treated her.

"So, I had no choice but to leave. They weren't supportive, in fact, they were destructive. Turns out none of them were friends, just people who happened to be working in the same circus space that I was..." Ozzie trailed off like the words still stung. I couldn't hold back anymore, so I gently walked over to her. My arms wrapped around her and squeezed as tightly as I could. She sniffled into my arm and I wished so badly I could tell every single one of her old colleagues exactly what I thought about their hostility towards Ozzie.

"Fuck them," I said as she shook against my shoulder.

"Logan and I have done several nude shoots for things on our own terms. You get to decide how you use your body and fuck anyone else for thinking they have any right to judge or ridicule you for that." I pulled away as she wiped her hands across her face.

"Thank you for saying that. I knew Logan did a lot of boudoir and assumed that she would be safer for me. I had reached out to her on Instagram first and she immediately quelled my fears and that's when I came here." She shrugged like it wasn't a big deal, but I knew what it meant to feel accepted, seen, and heard. Not everyone was like Cirque Callisto. Some places only focused on aesthetics and a certain look, talent and training be damned. Others only cared about who you knew and how much money you had. And some were just elitist clubs that prided themselves on being exclusive for no other reason other than they could.

We were founded on community, love, artistry, safety and support. We were all on the same team, no matter what.

"I'm glad you're here." I squeezed her hands, and it was like this moment hung in the air. Like time had suspended, leaving only me and Ozzie. We both breathed in and out loudly and then a flute started playing somewhere and the fragile moment of time broke into a million little pieces that seemed to fall around us in a blink of an eye.

"That must be Dani." I cleared my throat.

"Right. Should we get started?" Ozzie asked, and I nodded.

For the next several hours, we tried to iron out who would do what on the hoop. Our coordination and timing were awful. Absolutely tragic. We both kept bumping into one another and awkwardly apologizing as one of our faces would plummet into the other's stomach or boobs.

The amount of times sorry was mumbled between the two of us was getting out of control as our sweaty skin slipped against one another and our limbs tangled. We bumped around for a few hours, where things really only seemed to get worse. There was a terrifying moment where we both nearly clocked each other in the face with a hand or foot, almost giving each other black eyes.

At one point, we both fell face first into one another's crotches and I nearly died of giggles.

"Ya'll look like an absolute fucking mess." Aven stood in the corner howling with laughter.

"That was really bad," Ozzie agreed.

My cheeks hurt from how much fun I was having.

"Honestly, the first time Logan and I worked together, I threw her off the bar. She accidentally kicked me in the head, rendering me unconscious, so as long as none of that happens, I think we will be fine!" I joked, thinking about what a disaster we were when we began. It was one of the reasons doing it with someone you loved and cared about and worked well with was essential. Things would get real personal in duo.

"It's true. It can only get better." Logan appeared again. "Let's try to not kick anyone into unconsciousness, though. That feels like a one time mistake that no one else needs to make."

Aven and Ozzie fought back giggles.

"Part of it is, we're still getting to know each other, and duo is really intimate." I said, walking over to where my snacks were stashed.

"Good thing you're *fake dating*, then." Myla said as she walked in and winked at us.

"Okay, but everyone needs to play along because no one else knows except us in this room!" I was practically begging, but I didn't care. I needed this. Especially now that Genevieve had hired us for this stupidly well paying event. We needed to sell this shit so she could die of secondhand embarrassment.

"Your secrets are safe with us." Aven tucked a wayward curl behind her ear.

"Ozzie, um, speaking of what are you doing tomorrow night?" I asked sheepishly. Hopefully, this would probably be the last time I needed to ask for this favor, at least for a while.

"Uh, probably nothing except a date with my couch and some pizza, maybe."

"Can you come over to my place and do my makeup one more time?" I asked, batting my eyelashes at her.

"Anything for my girlfriend," Ozzie whispered against my ear, and her breath tickled my cheek. I felt my face get hot and something else as she stepped away and winked. "Text me the time and I'll be there."

I nodded, squishing my thighs together to release some of the pressure that was building there. *No, no, no.* This weird muscle mommy spell she had on me was getting out of hand.

Get it together, Jess.

"Of course," I said breathlessly, hoping she didn't notice the redness that was surely on my cheeks. "Well, I'm going to go practice juggling then. Thanks for the disastrous rehearsal, Jess." Ozzie sauntered off, and I watched her walk away with awe.

"You're in trouble," Logan hummed, popping up out of nowhere, so she was right behind me.

"Fuck."

I really was. What had I gotten myself into?

"You've got no one to blame but yourself," Logan whispered and then cackled maniacally like this was all a part of some evil plan.

"This should be interesting," Myla added, looping her arm around Logan.

"Should I get some popcorn or something?" Aven teased, joining Logan on the other side.

"All of you, shut up right now!" I hissed.

But they were right. I couldn't stop the stupid smile on my face from growing even wider, despite feeling like this was an absolute shit show that I had created.

NINE
OZZIE

J ess' little house was nestled close to the other homes on her street. I pulled up and knocked on the door, where she took two heartbeats to answer. She swung open the door in an adorable pajama onesie that looked like it had bunny ears while nursing a cup of tea.

"This is cute," I teased as she let me in.

"It's comfy okay. I'm a proud 36-year-old woman in a pajama onesie." She topped off her tea before she went on stomping about. It was sort of like a small child throwing a tantrum, and it was hard to control my smile.

"And I respect your choice," I giggled. "I didn't know you were thirty-six..." I felt like I was in that weird time in my life where I wasn't sure how old anyone was. Age was just a number, and we were all bumbling around trying to figure our shit out. I just assumed everyone was sort of close to my age, even though that made no sense.

"How old are you?" she asked, leaning against the counter. Her usually long hair was pulled back in a tight ballerina bun and her face was a blank slate waiting for my magical makeup touch.

"Twenty-six," I boasted.

"Ah, to be young," Jess teased.

"Please, these bags of bones feel like they're ancient. All the pops and cracks sound positively medieval." I rolled my eyes, and she grabbed another mug for me, filling it up and handing it over to me while I scanned the tea choices she had set out.

"Take your pick," she said.

We had settled into a more comfortable coexistence since yesterday when we had been all up in each other's, well, everything, while trying to do our duo act together.

"Thanks. Want to get started?" I added a little bit of honey and took a long sip.

Jess nodded, and we headed over to her kitchen table. Her house was cozy and quaint, with warm colors and wood finishes all around us. It smelled like her, too. The urge to take a big lungful of her scent was tempting, but I didn't want to make it weird. So I tried to remember how to breathe normally.

"I want all the drama tonight." She sat crossed legged on a barstool as I started to go in on her eyes. It was silent except for our breaths as I powdered her eyelids and dusted glitter and bold splashes of liquid black liner. There was a heavy layer of tension in the air as I finished up one eye and then the other.

Surely this feeling was just me. There was no way Jess reciprocated this crush. I simply needed to pull myself together and be a good fake girlfriend and real-life friend like we had agreed upon.

I swallowed and felt like it echoed throughout the whole damn place. Jess's lush lips were parted as I worked, and I had the urge to run my tongue along the seam of them and see what she tasted like.

Fuck, my overactive imagination was getting out of control.

"How's it looking?" Jess asked, eyes still closed, and it snapped me out of my trance.

"Good. Your eyes are mostly done. Let's add some lashes?"

She nodded, and I went to work gluing her falsies on and blowing on them to dry. Everything in this process felt oddly special. I tried to cherish every moment that I touched her face and not think about the fact that I was dying to do more. We were friends and fake girlfriends. Friends. *Not. Real. Girlfriends.* I chanted that shit at least five more times so my brain and body would get the picture.

I had no business lusting after my phony partner despite how soft her skin looked.

Swallowing loudly again, I grabbed some highlighter and blush, making her glow and glitter like the beautiful performer she was.

Ugh.

"What's the gig tonight?" I asked, doing the finishing touches on her cheeks, my voice low and breathy. This would be a needed distraction from my own thoughts.

"It's some wealthy guy's birthday party where he wanted ambient performers. It should be easy and hopefully he gives us a big tip." Jess smiled, and it made my heart flutter. I sat back away from her face and observed my work.

"I think this looks good," I said, proud of what I did. Honestly, I was getting better at it since I had now done it a few times for her. I wanted her to be impressed with me. This crush was getting out of control and I needed to rein it in before I did something I would regret.

"Okay, let me go try to look at it." Jess hopped up and her hooded onesie flopped around behind her as she went to the bathroom and did her best to examine it.

"What do you think?" I asked.

"I think it looks good, from what I can tell." She blushed as she sat down.

"Great! Want to do lips now?"

"Let me eat something really quick and then we can do it." She pulled out some ingredients and started to whip together something with rice and chicken in what felt like 10 minutes flat. "Are you allergic to anything?"

"Uhhh, I don't do gluten or dairy." I cleared my throat. I wasn't embarrassed to say it, but I also usually didn't let other people cook for me.

"Got it. Logan doesn't do those either, so I've got lots of practice at it." Jess winked at me, and it made me feel less anxious to eat her food, which in turn made me feel even more attracted to her.

I really needed to get it together.

"Great," I whispered as she hurried around the kitchen. What I really needed to do was get out of here and away from her before my mouth said something stupid.

"The least I can do is feed you." She slid a plate in front of me and it made my heart melt a little. No one had really done a lot of cooking for me. Including myself. I was bad at domestic things. Always forgetting to go to the store and having to order takeout at the last minute because I didn't have anything left to eat.

"This is sweet. Thank you." I took a bite of the rice and groaned. "Oh my god this is so good."

"I'm so glad you are making love to my chicken," she teased, and we both snickered. It felt easy and light and fun. I couldn't remember the last time I had really felt like I could just exist with someone like this.

"Ozzie, can I tell you something?" Jess said in between bites.

"Of course." I didn't know what she was going to say, but it felt important.

"I have an eye condition called central serous chorioretinopathy. Without treatments, I could lose my vision and I could still lose it, anyway with some of the complications I have. It gets worse when I'm stressed and basically means my eyeballs are just not that great at this whole seeing thing. So, thank you for helping me. It sometimes gets hard to ask for help and I appreciate it," she said quietly and I grabbed her hand.

"Thanks for sharing. Just tell me what you need and I'm there." It was as simple as that. I paused before thinking about sharing my own shit. "I've got several autoimmune disorders, and it has some implications about the food I eat, the way I train and how my brain works and socializes."

"Just two weirdos trying to figure life out with funny bits and pieces of ourselves that work in ways society doesn't understand," Jess said, giving me a crooked smile and my own mouth tipped up. I liked that definition.

We finished the rest of our food and cleaned up in amicable silence, and then we sat down again to put the finishing touches on her look so we could get her sent off to the gig. One of the other performers was picking her up.

"You want to do red or dark purple?" I asked, since she was looking for the drama.

"Let's do red." Jess' voice dipped low as I got in closer and started to paint her lips. I could feel my heart race with each stroke of lipstick. I got a little out of bounds on her cupid's bow and gently tried to swipe it away with my thumb. Our eyes locked, and it was like electricity where our skin touched.

It felt like we were magnetized to one another, gently moving forward until there was only a millimeter of space between our lips.

Was this really happening? Jess was actually leaning in close to me?

Without thinking or planning, I cupped her jaw, pulling

her into a kiss. It was slow at her first, her lips barely moving against mine. I started to think maybe I had read everything wrong about this moment.

Fuck.

But then she was kissing me back, her pillowy lips pulling and tugging me in. Our tongues danced together, and I lost myself in the taste of her on my tongue.

I groaned as she slid her hands down my arms, warmth spreading in between my thighs as Jess straddled me. We both grabbed at one another's bodies, trying to make contact wherever we could as our mouths explored, like two people starved.

A quick knock at the door sent us flying apart. Jess's lipstick was absolutely wrecked, but the rest of her was relatively intact.

"Just a minute!" she called.

It was her ride. Without any words, I grabbed a makeup wipe and cleaned her up in silence and then reapplied her lipstick in sixty seconds flat. Breathing heavily, we looked at one another, her eyes wide as I chewed on my lip, the taste of her still fresh on my tongue. I took a makeup wipe to my mouth and then grabbed my bag, heading to the door.

"Good luck, Jess." I opened the door to one of the student members, Emily.

"Hey, Ozzie!" she said cheerily, and I grimaced as I hustled out, leaving them both behind.

I got into my car, slammed the door, and took a few gulping breaths. Quickly, I flipped down my mirror and noticed there were still smudges of lipstick on my face.

What the fuck had just happened? Why did I run out of there like someone who was on fire? I groaned, wondering what Jess might think and how this would affect everything that we had in motion. The only thing that could fuck up this opportunity even more was us liking each other and then legitimately dating because what if we broke up and real feelings were involved?

My mind went to the worst-case scenario, which would be a repeat of what happened to me before.

It was one thing to pretend to date and go back to being how we always were and then it was another thing to actually date and do all that shit together and then if it didn't work out, it would be miserable. I would probably have to leave again and damnit, I had promised Trevor we would be here at least one fucking year.

Gripping the steering wheel tight, I tried to figure out what to do next. I didn't know what the right answer was, so I just drove home and hoped I didn't just make things horrible for myself and for Jess.

TEN

JESS

"I have a secret," I confessed to Logan. She lifted one sculpted brow at me. Her long pink hair was up in a claw clip, and she had an espresso martini in one hand and her phone in the other.

"Oh, do tell." She scrolled on her phone like I wasn't about to drop a bomb on her.

"Ozzie and I kissed." In my head, fireworks popped off and an air horn blew. The kiss had knocked me on my ass, and I couldn't stop thinking about it.

Logan gave no reaction, and an awkward pause filled the room.

"Well, aren't you going to say something about it?" I nervously nibbled on some popcorn. Why was she not freaking out about this? This was huge. I was freaking out about it.

"You're dating, so I assume some intimacy would be normal," she mused.

"We're not actually dating. It's not real."

"Semantics." She finally set her phone down and waved her hands. Her grin turned absolutely villainous.

"This could make things super weird and awkward." My voice pitched high, and I hardly recognized it. Her lack of reaction made my anxiety skyrocket.

"Why are you so worried about it? What would be the worst thing if you actually dated?"

I said nothing as I ran my fingers through my hair, tugging at the teal pieces in front.

"You're adults. You're hot. And you both clearly like one another. Just let it happen." She folded her long, tattooed legs underneath her and I could practically hear the eye roll happening.

"It's not that simple," I tried to argue.

"No, babes. It really is. You're the one who is making it complicated. In fact, why don't you ask her out? Make it official that you like her."

Logan made it sound so effortless. Her blasé attitude was annoying the shit out of me and I knew that was her exact goal. She knew me too well.

"Fine, maybe I will," I threw back. Logan fucking played me like a fiddle and I couldn't even be that mad about it.

"Stop being a baby and do the damn thing!" Logan flung a pillow at my face and I swatted it away.

"What the fuck?!" Laughter bubbled up out of me.

"You just need to loosen up a bit. Genevieve really got your panties in a twist, and I think Ozzie would be perfect at unraveling them." She winked at me, and it was my turn to roll my eyes.

"Okay, yes, I get it. Fine. I'll think about asking her out. You weird sorceress of human behavior, you," I said, returning to my popcorn.

"It's not sorcery, it's me knowing my best friend even better than she knows herself. Plus, I want you to be happy and Ozzie does that for you," Logan said, her voice going soft.

Her phone chimed, interrupting the movement, and she looked at it and scowled.

"What's up?"

"One of our performers for our future residency show dropped out, so I need to find a new one like yesterday." She tapped her fingers on the chair she was snuggled into.

"Which performer?"

"Lacey."

"Ah, so we need a singer. Fuck."

"You want to volunteer?" Logan's eyes twinkled with mischief.

"Hell no. No one wants to hear me holler on stage. It would literally send everyone home." That was not one of my gifts, and that was fine. The only time I sang was in the shower.

Logan cackled loudly. "I know. Our little company can do so much, but singing just isn't one of them."

"Actually wait, I know a hand balancer who also sings. He's pretty good. You probably remember him from the performance we went to in Arizona."

"Bex, if I remember correctly." Logan searched through her phone, looking him up.

"Yeah. I mean, the odds of him being available ASAP are slim, but hey you could at least ask? Plus, we have no one else, so better than nothing, you know." I could see the wheels turning in her head as she scrolled through his page.

"I sent him an IG message, looks like he's English but travels internationally and is currently in the states. We'll see if he responds. It says he's mutuals with Aven. I wonder if she knows him better than we do. Might be a good way to convince him to come instead of me sliding into his DMs." Logan squinted at her phone.

"Is this you claiming a kinship to him because you were

born and raised in Paris for the first few years of your life, Miss Beaumont?"

"Oui." She winked and the corners of my mouth tipped up. In reality, she had only been there for a little bit as a small child before her mom moved her back to the states because she and Logan's dad didn't work out. It wasn't long after that we became friends.

"I'll try to think of some other people we could hire." But in reality, Bex would be our best bet.

Logan sighed loudly, like the world was inconveniencing her.

"Speaking of dating," I said, waggling my eyebrows at her.

"No."

"You got to be up in my business about Ozzie now it's my turn. This is what friends do. We talk. We share! Laugh, cry and drink." I grabbed another handful of popcorn and grinned broadly at her.

"There's no dating happening for me. I'm running a business while also being a performer." Logan gave me a *no duh* look.

"Right, and you could still get some if you wanted." I nudged her with my foot and she kicked it away.

"That's the problem, though. I don't have time and I don't have the energy to deal with online dating bullshit or meeting up bullshit or really any other type of bullshit that doesn't involve our circus." Logan's passion for her company and us was unmatched, but I knew she was lonely sometimes. Call it best friend intuition. She was the type of person who thought she could do it all until she literally collapsed on the ground from exhaustion. Even her asking to step away from duo had been huge. Normally she would power through, but it was a true testament to her own self development that she told me she needed one less thing on her plate.

Not that she needed anyone else to make her happy, but

she meddled in other people's love lives, and I knew she wouldn't mind having one of her own.

Logan was strong, smart, and stunning, but she hadn't dated anyone in a long time. She had high standards and often people felt short. She was right in saying she didn't really prioritize it. I didn't blame her either. Online dating was practically another full-time job.

"Well, I just think next time we meet up you should contribute more to this conversation," I said sassily.

"Ma'am, all you came to the table with was a make-out session. I know you can do better than that. Next time come to our chat with something that is adult only." Logan's eyes danced, and I giggled.

"Fine, fine. I'll report back the juicy details after Ozzie and I go on a date."

"Thatta girl." Logan walked over to the bar to make herself another drink. She made two and brought one over to me.

"On a slightly more depressing note, how is Myla?"

Logan groaned. "I don't know. She's been tight-lipped about her and Jake. I can't believe he's being such an ass." She tapped her fingers against the glass and scowled. "Actually, I can believe it. I just can't believe she hasn't kicked him out yet. But we all know how hard it is to end a relationship."

"Yeah, especially one that's been going on for years."

"I'm worried that she'll break up with him and he won't get his ass out of her house." Logan's eyes narrowed like she was ready to tear him limb from limb with her manicured hands.

"If or when it comes to that point, we'll be by her side."

"God only knows we've all had our fair share of moving out of places quickly." Logan shuddered like the idea brought back all her own demons. I can only imagine she was thinking of her marriage that ended almost as quickly as it began. She got married young, and it was traumatic, to say the least.

"I hope to god Genevieve gets off my ass soon," I grumbled.

"You could tell her to fuck off."

"I have told her to fuck off in more digestible terms, but she just keeps swarming around like an annoying little gnat. Plus, she's a good contact to have around and I don't want to screw over the business." It was a sticky situation that I had made even worse by kissing Ozzie.

Oof.

"The business would survive. What's more important is your emotional and physical well-being. Whatever you decide to do, I'll support you. She already knows I don't like her, yet here she is hiring us anyway because we're the best." Logan painted a saccharine smile on. It was true. Genevieve had high standards for her event planning and unfortunately, what she wanted only we could provide.

"Yeah, we are." We toasted to that.

Another ding sounded from Logan's phone, and she snatched it up. "Bex responded, and he's in! I just have to send over the contract." Logan hopped up and did a little dance, where she punched the air a few times and shook her ass.

"Well, fucking send it bitch, let's go!" I hoped for her and for our resident show that this would work out because the singer was also the emcee and it really brought the entire production together. We would have been seriously screwed to make even more major changes at the last minute.

"Should I text Aven too and see how they know each other? I'm sure everything would be fine, but you know, just in case."

I shrugged. "I think it'll be fine. Go grab your computer and send the contract and text Aven about it later."

Logan hustled to grab her laptop and began typing away,

moving between her phone and the computer at lightning speed. My best friend was a boss lady through and through. I was so proud to be a part of her company.

Ozzie and I hadn't texted or talked really since we kissed, and I wondered what I could say that wouldn't make things weird. Should I wait to ask her out in person or text it to her?

In person felt better, but I didn't know when I would see her next. Realistically, it would be in the next few days at the studio at our duo rehearsal. Maybe I would wait until then when we were alone and could talk.

Texting was always hard, too. The nuances of your voice and word choice couldn't really be found over words on a screen, and I wasn't always good at reading the virtual room.

"Sent!" Logan said proudly, closing her laptop and grinning.

"Do you think I should ask Ozzie out in person or over text?"

"In person for sure," Logan replied like it was a no brainer. "I just sent Aven a text asking about Bex."

"He was amazing when we saw him perform live. I'm sure it will be the same when he gets here."

We decided to end the evening by watching anime and sipping our drinks. Both of us were excited for what the next week would bring.

I wondered if Ozzie would be surprised that I asked her out. There was no way she was going to say no, right? My mind traveled back to earlier when our bodies pressed against one another and our tongues tangled. Warmth went straight to my inner thighs as my mind lingered on the memory of that kiss.

No way we could fake heat like that. She would say yes, wouldn't she? I guess I would just have to wait and find out.

ELEVEN
OZZIE

I was a coward. I had been avoiding Jess on purpose since our kiss. I didn't know why I had scrambled out of there so fast. Running away usually wasn't my style; I just had a mild panic attack and bolted. But I couldn't hide from her forever and I would not repeat my past mistakes. I vowed to handle this shit like an adult, and here I was acting like a little kid afraid of getting in trouble.

"I can literally see the gears turning in your head," Trevor teased as we walked around the thrift store, looking for hidden gems.

"I feel like I'm in high school right now. Why in the hell did I just run out of there like a scared little gay?" I groaned. Saying it out loud honestly made it worse.

Truly pathetic, Ozzie.

"Because you are a scared little gay?"

"Thank you for that," I grumbled as I pawed through the denim section.

"I mean, it seems like you both know each other's secrets now, so what is there to lose? You were already fake dating.

Upgrade it to something genuine. Ooh, or maybe add some physical benefits? Or would that just be friends with benefits?" Trevor tapped a finger to his chin as he leaned against the racks.

"I don't know!" I threw up my hands and hustled to a different row of clothes.

"I think you're making it more complicated than it needs to be. Go from a pretend relationship to a real one. Real dating sounds easier, honestly." Trevor trailed through the aisles parallel to mine, looking at jackets. He held up a hideous fur coat, and I shook my head and laughed.

"But what if this turns into Ozzie's tragedy 2.0?" I bit my lip, thinking about how disastrous my relationship with Sean was. The lingering effects of that experience seemed to seep into everything right now, and I hated it. Couldn't I just throw it out like yesterday's trash? Fuck.

"Those thoughts are valid. Let's not forget you dated a straight white man, which was probably doomed from the start because you, my friend, are a beautiful queer who needs someone to match your energy." Trevor picked up another jacket with alternating sequined stripes and I gave it my nod of approval, so Trevor tossed it in his basket.

"True. And Jess knows the shit that went down and doesn't give two flying fucks about it." Everything really was out in the open now. Which should have made me feel better, but instead, I was terrified.

"As she should because we all have to get the bag, girl. Life is hard out here in these community streets and we just have to work with what mother earth gave us." Trevor grabbed a few more odd-looking pieces and tossed them in his overflowing basket.

"You're a thrifting gold medalist, you know?" I said as I looked at my own basket, which was decidedly empty. My treasure finder was not on today.

"You're distracted and I just happen to be great at this." Trevor winked at me, and I grinned.

"I've been avoiding the studio times when she's been there this week because I don't know what to say or do now. I'm hopelessly lost in this weird space in between."

"I know you are," Trevor said, patting my hand and dragging my empty basket and myself up to the register so he could grab his things. "Eventually you will see each other; god do I wish I was there to witness it so I could watch the beautiful mess unfold until one of you grows some fucking balls and says how you feel. And then maybe you'll fall dramatically into one another's arms and rip each other's clothes off."

My mouth dropped open as the cashier decidedly tried to avoid our gazes. "You could have delivered that in a less aggressive and descriptive way, you asshole." I hit his shoulder lightly.

Pouting, he shoved me playfully. "And you, Ozzie, juggle many things at the same time and very well, I might add. You literally fly through the air and do impossible feats. I think you can handle having an honest conversation with Jess. This noncommunicative bullshit belongs in the past. Rise. Be reborn and tell her how you fucking feel."

"This is a lot of tough love today," I muttered as I grabbed one of his bags walking out of the store.

"Well, you don't hang out with me just because I'm pretty. I'm also honest and direct when you need someone to call you on your shit."

I rolled my eyes.

"I'm sorry, did you want me to placate you with sweet nothings?"

"No."

"That's what I thought. Now get your ass into the car and let's go hit up the next store." Trevor looked giddy as he threw his bags in the back and queued up our next stop. He wanted to hit three stores today, and who was I to tell him no and derail the fun?

He drove as I scrolled through Instagram and checked on my notifications. Out of bold curiosity, I checked my old circus company's Instagram and couldn't find it.

Did they block me? I tried to find Sean's page. Couldn't. Then Brittany and a few of the other company members until I went through every single person I could think of and could not find their accounts anywhere.

"What the fuck? Everyone from my old company blocked me."

"Seriously? That's not very sexually liberated of them."

"Let me see your phone," I demanded.

Trevor nodded to his bag, and I grabbed it using his face to unlock it and scrolled on Instagram looking up my company and some of the members. They were definitely there. I had officially been banned. For whatever reason, that stung. It was the final nail in the coffin of how grossly close minded they were. And I was a little peeved that I hadn't blocked them first. I had just unfollowed them instead.

"What assholes."

"I can't believe everyone blocked you. What kind of fuckery is going on there that Sean has brainwashed them into thinking you are some whore who eats men with her pussy?"

I blinked at him and burst out laughing.

"Amazing. Should I do a photo shoot of that for my Only-Fans? I'm kind of obsessed with the idea."

Trevor laughed too as we pulled up to our next thrifting destination.

"I'm sorry though, Oz. That still stings. I know some of those people meant something to you, even though they all turned out to be horrible." Trevor squeezed my fingertips, looking into my eyes.

"It does. But I want to forget about them and move on.

I've started fresh here and they're great at Cirque Callisto. They don't give a fuck what anyone does as long as it's not hurting anybody or ourselves. Logan created a lovely space for us weirdos, and I appreciate it a lot."

"I'm glad you found a home here."

"Me too. Speaking of, Logan is looking for some dancers for an upcoming show and to have on a short list when they get requested at gigs. Are you down? Do you have any other people in mind for who you want to dance with?"

"Yes, and yes. Shoot me her contact info and I'll share what I've got with her."

We went into the next store and Trevor continued to find amazing pieces while I found absolutely nothing. My heart wasn't in it today. I needed to figure out what I was going to say to Jess.

Like hey sorry I just made out with your face while I was doing your makeup, but I think you're super hot. And I definitely have a crush on you, even though we are pretending to date. Do you think we could go on an actual date or is that just off the table entirely?

I had no idea what she was feeling and the only way I would figure it out was if I put on my big girl panties and just fucking asked and stopped avoiding her. We had duo practice this week, and it was a guarantee to see each other and talk about it.

My phone buzzed in my pocket, and it was a group chat with Aven, Myla, Dani, Logan, Jess, and me.

> **Logan: Bex is coming in to be a resident
> full-time performer for us! Yay!**

I didn't know who Bex was, but it was nice to be in the group chat, to feel like I had another little circus family again, even though Jess was in it.

Aven: I have a sexy little secret about Bex.

I sent a question mark in response, and Logan did the same.

Jess: Do tell, I love secrets.

I tried not to read too much into that and swallowed as I fully abandoned my basket and followed Trevor around the store, validating his choices and watching him try stuff on.

Aven: Bex and I hooked up. And it was honestly the best sex I've ever had.

I laughed out loud and covered my mouth with my hand.

Me: Respectfully, this is the most sex positive space I've ever been and I'm here for it.

Logan: I subscribed to your OF Ozzie, and it's hot. We should do a group shoot sometime if you're up for it.

I nearly fell out of my chair at the idea of us all doing a shoot together.

Jess: I'm down!

My stomach nearly dropped out of my ass with that. The idea of Jess' body naked against my own just sent pleasure straight to my groin. I moaned loudly.

"Are you watching porn out there?" Trevor called from the dressing room.

"No," I replied defensively.

"Keep your sex noises to a minimum, Oz. It's distracting from my beauty." Giggling, I checked my phone again.

> *Myla: I'm a little shy about it, so maybe I can direct.*

Logan, Jess and Aven hearted Myla's message.

> *Dani: Let's get naked!*

My heart warmed at this group of wonderful humans.

> *Aven: Okay but actually, back to Bex. We can talk about Ozzie's hot pictures later.*

> *Logan: Maybe you'll have another chance at a steamy mind blowing hookup session. You're welcome. Don't be weird.*

We all responded with *hahas*, and I put my phone down. Maybe the conversation with Jess wouldn't be as weird as I thought. Maybe it would lead to something that was better than we ever imagined.

TWELVE
JESS

A surprise private gig popped up during the week, and Ozzie and I were coupled up together unexpectedly. Logan had sent out an SOS for someone to take it and they were paying big since it was so rushed. Apparently, they had booked someone else, and it fell through.

"Hey," Ozzie said as we met at this random penthouse downtown, where apparently the party was being held. Logan had some of our people come here early to set up a lollipop stand, which was basically a hoop attached to a stick that was mounted to a circular platform on the ground.

"Hey," I said, looking at her shyly. "Logan said she will be here a little later to make sure everything is going okay. It's uh... good to see you."

Ozzie gave me a tight-lipped nod and then opened her mouth to say something, but was interrupted by our contact at the event.

"Hi! You must be the performers!" said the bubbly blonde who talked a mile a minute about where we could set up, rest and grab snacks between our times. We would alternate ten minutes on and off for the gig, since it was impossible to perform for two hours straight.

She rushed us to the room, stating she would be back shortly to get us going for the event. We barely spoke as we moved about and warmed up for the set. People trickled in as Ozzie took the first round on the floor. Everyone oohed and awed as she twirled around the hoop. Her full body unitard, which was nearly identical to mine, had bold red slashes across it that accentuated her figure.

She was quite the captivating performer, and my chest warmed every time I watched her. Even though I was arguably better on lyra, Ozzie had a style all her own. It was clever and witty, with saucy hand movements and facial expressions that drew you in. She gracefully descended, and I took up my post on the lollipop.

The crowd stayed entranced for a while until everyone got pulled in by the rest of the party, where food and drink were amply available. Ozzie and I continued that way for the next hour, just nodding and walking by one another when Logan showed up.

"How's it going so far?" Logan breathed heavily and wiped some sweat from her brow. "Ozzie looks great!" She slammed a bottle of water down.

"Did you sprint here or something?" I laughed as she fanned her face.

"You could say that. I was rushing and then the elevator wasn't working, so I had to take the stairs. It was a whole thing. Did you two"—Logan gestured between me and Ozzie dramatically—"hash your shit out?"

"We're at a job, Lo."

"Still, I figured you'd get it smoothed over quickly, but from the look on your face, I'm going to guess that has yet to happen."

"After the gig, we can figure out our feelings. Right now, I just want to get this done and get paid."

"Right..." Logan drawled. "Well, I'm going to mingle. Holler if you need anything."

Ozzie and I went to do the trade again, and I nodded to where Logan was laughing with someone to let Ozzie know she was here. She looked good in that unitard. She was all curves and powerful lines. My hormones were sending all kinds of inappropriate messages to my body, and I really needed them to shut the fuck up.

Plastering a smile on my face, I mounted the hoop and began my ambient set. I tried to erase thoughts of Ozzie out of my mind and focus on the moves at hand. We had a minor break after I finished this ten-minute stint; maybe we could have a quick chat then.

After a while, Logan waved at me to come off and I took a bow to a few onlookers, who clapped sporadically. It was so weird to me that they were so desensitized to such intense physical feats at parties. Like we were decorations or ornaments and nothing more. Even though that's what they paid us for, it was still an odd feeling to be hired just to basically get ignored.

"Ozzie. Wow, what a surprise to see you here," A deep voice resonated from behind me where Ozzie stood frozen and her mouth wide open.

"Sean," she sneered. Immediately, her arms crossed, and she widened her legs like she was getting ready for battle. Why did people from her old company keep popping up out of nowhere? Heat prickled the back of my neck and I fought the urge to snarl at him.

"Who the fuck does he think he is?" Logan hissed into my ear as she came marching through the partygoers.

"Lo," I warned. Ozzie glanced over at us and shook her

head. "Let's wait and see if she needs our help. Ozzie's got this."

Logan moved us over to the side, where we could see and hear their conversation better.

"You know, I saw Brittany the other day. It's a bit odd that you're also here, considering this isn't anywhere close to where the training company is. And I would know, since I wanted to get as far away from you all as possible." Ozzie smiled sweetly, but her dark blue eyes burned.

"Well, the funny thing is, Brittany and I took a trip together here." He looked like every dumb, entitled guy I'd ever met. Like a walking Ken doll that was always looking for his Barbie.

"Great."

"Because we're dating now." He leered wolfishly at her.

"Okay." Ozzie's tone clipped.

"I'm surprised you're getting these types of gigs, considering everything about you." He raked his gaze across her body and frowned as if Ozzie was the most undesirable thing he had ever seen. My blood boiled, and I took a step forward, seeing red, but Logan hauled me back, the same fire reflecting in her eyes.

"Well, you certainly liked a lot of things about me before you found out my body wasn't yours to use and possess for your own desires." Ozzie's hands had moved to her hips, and she was right up in his face.

The surrounding party was in direct conflict with their tense hushed tones, and the guests had no idea that someone was about to go nuclear right in front of them.

"Please, you did this to yourself. I simply exposed the real you, a lying bitc—"

I stormed over and purposefully ran right into Sean's shoulder to body check him.

"I'm so sorry. But I need to borrow my girlfriend for a

moment," I said loudly. Ozzie looked like she was holding back a laugh as I circled my arm around her waist.

"Excuse me?" Sean asked. His pretty boy facade was slowly cracking to reveal the ugliness below.

"Yes, Ozzie is in high demand here as one of our premium professional performers. She has gotten more requests than anyone else in our company, plus we love to celebrate extremely talented queer women in our performances."

I swear I heard Logan snort behind me.

Sean looked ruffled and confused. "Oh yes, of course. Female empowerment is very important."

"Yes, empowering women is extremely necessary. So, if you'll excuse us." I went to shove right past him, and he grabbed for my upper arm, and I ground my molars together.

"You should know..."

"If you don't take your hand off me right fucking now, I will ruin you. You'll be lucky to ever procreate again. And if you ever so much as look at Ozzie—or even speak her name, I will make sure to ruin your company, too," I hissed in his ear and grabbed his wrist, pulling it behind his back and forcing his shoulder forward.

"My shoulder!" Sean whined.

"Touch her again and I will sue your ass so aggressively you will be lucky to work anywhere ever again." Logan was right in front of his face, which was now only a few feet from the ground.

"If you want the use of your arm, I recommend some ice and Advil." I released and patted him on his back.

"Find a reason to leave, Sean," Ozzie said it like it was a dare.

"She's a bad investment." He looked seriously at Logan as he rubbed his shoulder.

"And you're not very interesting to look at. Bye, bye!" She waved at him and motioned for security before he huffed off.

"Are you okay?" I grabbed Ozzie's hand and looked her up and down like I was checking for physical injuries.

"I'm fine, Jess," she replied softly as Logan marched after him with her security set up.

"Thank god." I pulled her in for a hug and it felt nice to feel her body next to mine. The solidness of her grounded me and made me worry less.

"He came with Brittany, apparently. And I hope they never return." Ozzie squeezed me back and I could feel her relax into me. "Thank you for having my back. I've never had friends like this before, except Trevor and I just... don't know what I would do without you all."

"Ozzie..." I started, but didn't get to finish as Logan came grumbling back.

"He's out, that bastard. Ooh, my hands are just itching to leak out all kinds of bad information about his ass. But I won't because I'm classy." She flipped her hair dramatically. "And he will be his own demise. That wasn't much of a break, but one of you will need to go back up in a second. Are you okay to do it, or should we call it a night?" Logan tapped her manicured finger on her chin.

"It's fine. Sean isn't going to ruin me getting my money." Ozzie had pulled away from me and I suddenly felt cold without her.

"Okay, if you're sure. You know I will always call this shit if it doesn't feel safe for one reason or another, okay?" Logan looked at us with a serious expression, and we nodded.

"I won't be a dumb bitch, okay? We got this." I smacked a kiss on her cheek, and she waved her hand in front of her face.

"Well, now, I'm all hot and bothered. But if you say so," Logan said as she winked and sauntered away.

"Can we talk after this?" I asked Ozzie as she got up to start the next alternating set.

"Yeah, I think we should." Ozzie's face turned into a grin, and I found myself smiling back.

Maybe this conversation will go better than I thought. After all, I told her ex to fuck off. And if I was destined to be her *actual* girlfriend, this felt like a really good place to start.

THIRTEEN
OZZIE

Logan was observing our practice today, so Jess and I weren't alone. After the surprise gig the other night and Sean's even more surprising appearance, my emotions were all over the fucking place. I felt raw and ripped open, like all my feelings and nerve endings were on display.

Jess and I hadn't spoken about our kiss yet, and after our gig, I was too emotionally spent to do it. We had agreed to talk later, but when would that be? It was the elephant in the room between us. We kept getting close to the topic and skirting away at the last minute, finding every excuse not to touch it. The tension was killing me, but I was terrified of what she would say.

I was so tired of people from my past popping up when I least expected it, especially when I was working. As a performer, I had to be on all the fucking time, and I was so goddamn tired of people testing my patience. I didn't know if I wanted to punch a wall or scream. But either way, I was ready to push my body hard.

The pinch and pain of the lyra was a welcome sensation to all the achiness in my heart and soul. We warmed up with some music and I barely said a word. I didn't know where Jess' head was at, and I was so fucking scared to know.

Right now, I was feeling too vulnerable to ask, and I just wanted to move my body. The soreness in my hip and shoulders would feel better after I moved, anyway.

"Everything okay, Oz?" Logan looked at me with care from where she sat sprawled on the ground.

"Yeah, there's just a lot going on in my head right now."

"You know, some aerialists fall or become careless on their apparatus because of a physical thing. Whether that's an injury or something else. But more often than not, aerialists' mistakes." She paused and pointed to her chest and head. "Are more likely to happen when these aren't in the right place."

Swallowing, I crossed my arms and avoided her gaze. I knew this speech had been coming. I wore my heart on my sleeve and Logan saw it all.

"For example, I bruised the shit out of my labia on the hammock when I broke up with my then-partner. Lost my focus and fell straight on my cooch, slicing both my lips in half, and then catapulted down like a fucking ping-pong ball until I was hanging upside down. Needless to say, I crawled to the ground and iced my vag and was told to take a fucking break." Logan shuddered like the memory of it brought her pain. My own nether regions had a visceral reaction to her story.

"It was bad," Jess offered from the side, and I tried not to laugh. It wasn't funny, but the mental image was a sight.

"Go ahead and giggle. It sounds like a fever dream now, but my lips still remember it, you know. They were black and blue for at least a week. Me and the hammock don't fuck around anymore." Logan smirked crookedly.

"I get what you're saying. Mentally I'm here, I promise. Things are a bit cloudy right now, but movement helps get rid of the fog, you know?"

"You can tap out at any time, okay?" Jess got into my space and reached her hand out like she was going to touch me and then didn't. Her hand fell limply to her side.

"Okay," I whispered.

"As the head coach and director and company owner here, I have the right to send you home from training at any time. If I don't believe you or see some dangerous shit, I will bench your ass for today, Ozzie. Your safety is my number one priority. Got it?" Logan took on her authoritative tone. She harped a lot on keeping her people secure and I respected the hell out of her for it, even if it was a bit inconvenient sometimes.

"Understood, boss." I winked at her. It was nice to have people who cared in my life. Who noticed when I wasn't well and listened to me when I needed it. But I could do this with Jess today.

We had mapped out most of the choreography and it was a slow dance that had yearning and a bit of unrequited love in it.

Logan started the song and Jess and I circled the hoop, our gazes pushed away from one another until the beat changed and then our eyes locked together and we circled once more. Stepping up to the hoop, we straddled and mounted it simultaneously.

From there, our bodies became much more intimate. At one point I held Jess's head in my arms, and we locked eyes as she hung from the low bar and me on the high bar. We connected our hands to then fall towards the ground, caught by our knees.

We crushed our bodies together in a dramatic embrace and then swirled open. Every touch of her skin and swell of the music seemed to clear my head. That I was here. I was alive. And I was safe.

Our sweat mingled and our breath came in and out as we fumbled through the less planned out choreography. At one point we bonked heads, and I slammed my thigh in between her legs, and we laughed. Each smile and giggle made me feel lighter and more at ease.

Her presence seemed to wrap around me, comforting me in a way I didn't know I needed after the harshness of the gig the other night. The tension from my past seemed to dissipate as we moved together.

Here, I was free and creative and strong and lovely. With Jess, it felt like I was all those things and more. Her body tethered me to this place, and I wanted to hold this moment in my heart forever.

The song ended and our final pose was sitting in the hoop, backs against one another, heads drawn down.

Carefully, we came off the lyra and looked at each other. Jess wrapped me in a hug, and I wanted to live there squished against her skin. If I had the option to melt in her arms, I would.

Logan clapped and beamed from her spot on the floor. "That was much more improved from when I saw it last! You looked connected and strong. Especially in the beginning. There are still some things to work out, but I can feel the cohesiveness whereas before, it felt like you were purposefully trying to butt heads." Logan smirked at us, and I held back a chuckle. Things had changed from when we first practiced. We were different people to one another and now we really needed to talk about it.

"Yeah, well, I thought Ozzie thought I was disgusting so." Jess shrugged, and my mouth dropped open.

"What? What did I do to give off that impression?"

"Every time we touched, you acted like I had an infectious disease!" Jess said matter-of-factly.

"Jess, I was just nervous and awkward and so helplessly attracted to you." I said in an exasperated tone, like it was so fucking obvious.

"You know this feels like something maybe you two should talk about in private?" Logan got up and gave us a little wave and blew us a kiss.

"You were just attracted to me?" Jess repeated. Her mouth fell open.

"Obviously, yes, look at you. You're so hot and strong and the most beautiful hoop artist I've ever seen. You sent my whole system into overdrive trying to figure out what to do with this crush!" It felt so good to just say it out in the open and to be honest after so much build up. Here I didn't need to hide what I felt or who I was. I needed to lean into that and say what was on my heart.

"So how would you feel about going on a date with me?" Jess was grinning goofily at me.

"A date?" It was my turn to be a little confused.

"Yeah, I know we're not actually dating, but I think you're extraordinary too and I would love to revisit our kiss from the other day. So, let's go on a fucking date." Jess stepped into my space and my face went blank for a moment before I grinned stupidly back at her.

"I would like that very much." Giggles erupted between the two of us.

"Okay, well, let's work out the kinks in this routine and then set a date and then get the fuck out of here." Jess ran through our to-do list like it was the simplest thing in the world.

Nodding, I let the words sink into my skin. Maybe it could be that easy?

For the rest of rehearsal, I felt stronger and more capable—like the heaviness in my heart had lifted and I could do anything and everything. Our routine got better as we worked through the messier parts. Slowly, we reduced the number of collisions and sloppy transitions. It wasn't perfect, but it was getting there.

Logan popped in and out to make sure things were running smoothly. Over time, we became more graceful, our bodies telling us what needed to be done.

We laid down on the mat, our chests heaving and sweat sticking to every part of exposed skin before Jess was the first to talk.

"How do you feel about dinner sometime soon?" Jess rolled on to her side, so she was facing me. I mirrored her and did the same.

"I love it."

"Great, let's do it in a few days. This time I will pick you up now that my eyeballs have adjusted to their normal-ish state." She hauled herself up and offered a hand to help me up.

Her palm felt solid in mine, and I groaned as she lifted me up. We cleaned up our stuff and finished saying goodbye to the few stragglers in the studio. Logan gave us an encouraging note about our progress, and we headed out.

Jess and I had parked right next to each other, so we walked out in a comfortable silence. She stepped over to my car and we stood there looking at each other. Heat curled in my belly from her icy blue eyes trailing against my skin.

"I would very much like to kiss you again, Ozzie." Jess's eyes twinkled with mischief... and something else. Warmth went straight to my belly button as she shifted closer and pressed my back up against the car. I let my bag thump to the ground as she caged me in with her arms.

"I think you should," I whispered as her mouth was inches from mine and she smiled. It was a flash, something I would have missed if I wasn't paying attention.

She moved assuredly toward my mouth, her lips meeting mine in a gentle brush. I leaned into her and that was all the encouragement Jess needed as she pressed her body to mine, and I molded into my car.

Her kiss commanded me as she sucked and nipped at my lip and ran her tongue along the seam of my mouth. I groaned as I opened myself up to her and she slid her tongue in, and I sucked gently. It was her turn to moan as I pulled away and started trailing kisses along her jaw and neck. Licking the sweat there, I inhaled her scent as I continued the journey across her collarbone up the other side.

She hungrily found me again and our bodies were smashed together, but still not close enough. I wanted fewer clothes and more skin, but I settled for hurried hands in her hair and her wrapping her arms around my low back, so I arched further into the car.

Wetness pooled between my thighs, and I thought about how much I wanted her mouth on me everywhere and how badly I wanted to taste her and explore her body.

"Oh, hell yes!" Logan yelled from the door of the studio. She whistled at us, and we jumped apart with swollen lips and messy hair.

"Don't stop on my account. I love the show!" Logan clapped gleefully, and we both blushed.

"Fuck off, Logan!" Jess hollered, throwing up a middle finger, which seemed to delight Logan even more, as she headed back inside.

"Well, on that note. I'll send you the details of our date and we can revisit this later." She slid her hands down the front of my chest, scraping her fingers against my nipples.

"I can't wait." I pulled her in for one last smacking kiss on the lips and moved my hands down her ass and squeezed.

"Oh Ozzie, we're going to have a lot of fun." Jess swatted at me playfully and skipped to her driver's side seat.

Sliding into my car, I exhaled loudly. I was already in deep for Jess, and we had just fucking started.

Screw this pretend dating. I was ready for the real thing.

FOURTEEN
OZZIE

"You look nice," Trevor purred at me as I sat jittery on my couch. I wasn't sure why my nerves were on fire, but they were. Jess and I had hung out before, but now it was official. What if I royally fucked this up? What if we were only destined for this farce and not the real thing? Or what if I just spontaneously burst into flames because of how weird and awkward I was?

"Thank you." I looked down at my black satin joggers and black cropped halter top which I paired with combat boots and some random jewelry.

"What time is the date?" Trevor asked.

"6:30."

Trevor lifted one eyebrow at me and made a pointed stare at the clock in our living room. "Girl, what? It's 5:30!"

"I have entered into waiting time and cannot be pushed out of it. The only logical thing was to get ready and wait." It was my anxious curse. To be doomed to be in waiting time purgatory because what if it took three times as long to get ready as it normally would and then I was late?!

"Neurodivergency at its finest," Trevor said and winked at

me. I laughed. I couldn't help it; this is what my mind and body did. Unfortunately, I was incapable of doing anything else in the meantime, so as soon as Trevor stopped harassing me, I would pretend to watch T.V. while mindlessly scrolling on my phone.

The longer I sat and waited, the worse my anxiety got and at some point, I ended up pacing the room until I got a text from Jess saying she was five minutes away.

"Your waiting time is almost over," Trevor sing-songed from another room in the house. He had checked on me intermittently and gave me little words of encouragement.

"Thank god," I grumbled as I checked my hair, teeth, and armpits one more time. "SHE'S HERE!" I yelled like I was an announcer at a football game. Ugh, why was I being so strange already?

"Go get her!" Trevor cheered for me as I headed out the door. She was standing outside in a cute, flowy light blue dress that showed off her strong arms and muscular legs. She was stunning. My breath caught in my throat as I tried to form a coherent sentence.

"You look beautiful," I said quietly as we hugged, and I held her at arm's length. Her long hair was curled and swept back away from her face. The sun caught the strands of teal, making them shine and sparkle around her face. Just the lightest touches of makeup dusted her cheeks, lips, and eyes. She was like a magical fairy coming in to grant all my queer dreams tonight.

"Thank you, so do you Oz." A blush crept up on her cheeks as I felt her eyes roam across my body. Now that we weren't hiding our attraction to one another, it was almost shameless how much we seemed to be devouring one another with our gazes.

We interlaced our hands together as she led me over to her car and it did funny things to my heart. This was the first time we were being intentional about our time together and how we felt about one another.

Honestly, it felt really fucking good. My nerves were starting to fade, seemingly replaced by butterfly wings brushing against my navel.

We hopped in her car, and she handed me the aux cord. "Passenger princess privileges." She winked at me, and I laughed.

"I'm honored. What kind of music is normally your vibe?"

"I'm an angsty dark music kind of gal."

"Same, the scarier and weirder the better."

"Exactly." She drove with ease as I picked a song from my favorite duo, Neoni.

"So, where are you taking me this evening?" I leaned back, enjoying the view of her profile. Her full lips and sharp cheekbones were on full display and practically glowing in the sunlight. Jess was stunning; there was no other way to put it and her commitment to her art made her practically shine.

"My favorite poke bowl place, as long as you like poke. I wanted to share it with you. But I have other options if you hate sushi, or fish, or maybe a general distaste for sesame seeds?" She smiled shyly at me as she rambled on. Her nervousness was unexpected. But adorable all the same.

"Lucky for you, I like all the above." I reached over and stroked her thigh, letting my hand feel the warmth of her skin.

"Great."

I swear I saw a pink blush start to sneak up on her neck and cheeks.

We drove the rest of the way in comfortable silence, with my hand gently stroking her exposed thigh. I wanted to see her squirm just a little bit, a crack in that composed facade. I really wanted to know what her face would look like, flushed with arousal and climaxing around my mouth, but that could wait.

Things were just getting started between us. There was no need to rush.

"Respectfully, if you don't stop doing that with your hand, I may have to pull this car over." Jess's voice was strained, and her posture was rigid as she continued to keep her eyes on the road.

Laughing, I pulled my hand up a little higher, pressing the hem of her dress up, exposing even more leg. She gasped and then I slid it away. "No need for that. I'll try my best to keep my hands to myself."

"You're naughty, Oz," Jess purred as we pulled into a quaint little restaurant.

"You haven't seen anything yet."

She giggled, and it went straight to my heart. I wanted to make her laugh more. Each smile she gave was like a fucking ray of sunshine, and I was desperate to feel her warmth.

We headed inside and requested a table on the patio where we both ordered drinks and several appetizers to share before we chose what bowls we wanted.

"We aren't going to start with, so tell me about yourself, right?" I sipped on my drink and looked at her with an eyebrow raised.

"I would prefer we start literally any other way." She cackled, throwing her head back and exposing the column of her throat.

"Let's start with how you got into circus?"

"I got into it pretty late, honestly by society's standards, I was in my early twenties." She tucked a flyaway piece of hair behind her ear. People liked to think that if you didn't start something as a child, you missed out. But in reality there was no age limit for new things, especially circus. You could choose a different life at any time. All it took was a first step.

"What was your first class?" I asked, wanting to know all the details.

"Silks, I was convinced it would be my thing."

"Amazing, happens to the best of us. I bet you were brilliant in your first class."

She chuckled. "I don't know about that. I was a runner and track star throughout my childhood, so the athleticism was there, but everything else needed some work. My quads and hamstrings were so fucking tight when I started, and I wasn't anywhere near my splits when I first began. But I did love to spin and so spin I did."

"Aw, I love a good origin story." I took a bite of the spring rolls that were delivered to our table.

"From there I fell in love with the lyra. And I started getting into every circus camp and class I could. I worked from home as a marketing specialist and would sneak off on trips to travel around to different circus training facilities." The corners of her mouth tipped up, and she sighed. "Then Logan started getting into it too and asked if I would do a duet with her because she wanted to start her own company. I said yes and then the rest is sort of history." She grabbed a bite of tofu in front of her.

"That's amazing. We love a non-traditional life."

"What about you, Ozzie?"

"I started circus when I was young, but juggling is new within the last few years. I think in my teens is when I got really into it and it was kind of on and off through college. I got a business degree and realized it wasn't my dream. So, I went back to the circus to train and start performing. I moved around a little, kind of making it work at random circus places, guest artisting and then finally settling into my last company, which was near where I grew up."

She reached over and placed her hand over mine as I inhaled sharply.

"We all know how that went, so no need to revisit it, but

then I obviously needed something new, so here I am with you all."

"And we're so glad you're here." She beamed at me, and it made my heart melt.

"What else are you into besides circus-ing?"

She giggled at my made up verb. "Hmmm, well, I like to play video games, drink tea, eat sugary things and knit."

"You knit, huh?"

"What? It's not just for grannies!"

"I think it's cute." I squeezed her fingertips and went to grab another spring roll.

"And you? Do you have any other hobbies outside of all this?" Jess wavered her arms around in an over-exaggerated manner.

"Obviously. I love reading all things fantasy. Books, movies, you know, all that nerdy stuff. Big fan of video games as well. Maybe we should play sometime?"

"I will say I'm a girl who games, not a gamer girl. And I like cozy games." Jess hummed while she sipped her cocktail.

"Got it, so if we're competing, I would probably win?" I teased.

"Ah, very confident, I see. I'm sure I could kick your ass at something. But probably not at something that involves shooting, aiming, and running around at the same time."

"I look forward to it." We toasted to that and made it through the rest of our meal easily with conversation flowing about our families, world views and all the quirky things in between.

"You know it's funny because when I've dated men, I usually always have to worry about their political views or other misogynistic capitalistic white supremacist bullshit because you just really never know what will come out of their mouth."

"I have a simple solution for you." Jess's mouth quirked up in a slight grin.

"What's that?"

"Don't date men." She shrugged her shoulders like it was that easy as she devoured the last few bits of her meal.

"Easy for you, a lesbian, to say to me, a bi woman." I pointed my chopsticks at her accusingly. "Unfortunately, I'm still attracted to them."

"Truly tragic, honestly. Women are just better." She smirked smugly.

"Noted."

We finished up and went halfsies on the bill and it felt nice. There was an electricity in the air that kept me on my toes but a comfortability that settled into my bones.

"How would you feel about coming over to my place to hang out for a little bit?" Jess tapped her fingers on the table and rested her chin on her other palm.

"I like it. It sounds delightful."

We got up and left. Our hands easily found one another again and I couldn't help but feel like whatever had happened here tonight was changing our relationship for the better.

Fifteen

Ozzie

We entered Jess' place, and it was exactly as I remembered. Cozy and warm, smelling just like her. She shut the door behind us and looked at me with heat in her eyes.

"I'm not going to lie, I'm ready to escalate some things." She stalked over to me and grabbed my hands, dragging me to the couch.

"Is that right?" I smiled.

"I've been tested since my last partner and everything came back clear." Jess shoved me down on the couch, and I realized I liked it when she was bossy.

"Me too," I breathed as she slowly slipped off one strap of her dress. My eyes tracked her movements as she slid the other strap off and the dress pooled at her feet. Her body was a work of art. Muscles and smooth skin everywhere. She had a smattering of moles across her abdomen and a small tattoo on her hip.

Her breasts were petite and perky as her dark pink nipples peaked, begging to be sucked. Just a sliver of rose-colored panties hung low on her sharp hips. I took my time taking her body in, all the long lines and corded muscles. She had slipped off her shoes and then she did a little spin showcasing the globes of her ass and I was nearly salivating.

"Jess, you're breathtaking." I watched in awe as she prowled towards me, her body moving like a predator stalking her prey. As she straddled my lap with her tits right in my face, I ran my hands up and down her sides, dusting her ribs and hips. She caged me in with her arms and leaned forward, so I was forced to tilt my head up to look at her.

"Ozzie, I want to fuck you."

I shivered at her words.

"Your wish is my command." I dove right in, grabbing her hips and pulling her hard against me. She gasped as our lips smashed together and we tangled our tongues. She made little groans that had me getting wetter by the minute. It was like our bodies were made to be pressed up against one another with no space in between us.

I plunged my tongue into her mouth, and she sucked generously as I palmed her ass and pulled her even harder against me. I needed fewer clothes on, and I needed her thong off.

Pulling away, I moved to her beautiful breasts and took one nipple in my mouth, sucking gently while I kneaded the other. Jess arched against me, groaning and reaching down to her panties. She ground against her fingertips as she played with her clit. I could literally die here with my mouth on her skin and I would perish happily.

"Yes Ozzie," she moaned as she chased a release at the mercy of my mouth on her hard peaks and her fingers at her wet pussy. Jess's first orgasm crashed against her as she gyrated against her hand and shoved my head against her boobs.

Women's bodies were the fucking best.

She breathed heavily as she finished her last wave of release and slipped her hand out of her panties. I grabbed her fingertips and sucked at them, my eyes nearly rolling back in my head at her rich taste. I was desperate for more.

"Well, that's fucking hot." Her chest was moving up and down.

"I need to taste you." I moved her off me and stood in front of her. It was my turn to be naked. I stripped off my top and slid my boots and pants off, so I was standing in just a lace bandeau and a black thong.

"Ozzie!" Jess pleaded, licking her lips and practically eye fucking me. She opened her legs wide, and I kneeled, sliding her panties off and exposing her wet folds. I kissed along her inner thighs and sucked at her hip bones, and she pulled at her nipples as I made my way up to her throbbing clit.

I took a long lick along her seam, and she groaned. Sliding my hands underneath her ass, I pulled her all the way to the edge of the couch and threw her legs over my shoulders as I dove into her dripping cunt.

I sucked and licked at her clit, using my fingers and my mouth, moving to her groans as she grinded against me and fucked my face. She chased her own release as I gripped her ass harder and kept my steady pace on her clit. I pumped two fingers in and out as she breathed and arched. She was glorious as she found ecstasy. No sight would be as thrilling as watching my girl chase her own orgasm. It was forever imprinted in my mind: the sounds, the way she moved, the taste of her on my tongue.

"Ah, Ozzie!" she whimpered as she came on my face, and I felt the contractions of her pussy around my fingers, as I milked the waves of pleasure while she panted against me.

"Fuck, Ozzie." Jess's hair was rumpled, and her mouth hung in a loose smile. I crawled up her body and found her lips again as we mingled her taste between our tongues. It was delicious and intoxicating, sharing her release.

"Mmmm," I hummed against her, and she wrapped her body around mine.

"Now tell me, my sweet Ozzie. What do you like?"

"What kinds of toys do you have?"

She stood up and pulled me towards her bedroom. She was naked and enthralling to look at. Sliding her hands against my skin, she tossed my panties and bra to the floor.

"You're extraordinary," she said, pushing me into the soft sheets of her bed.

"How do you feel about a vibrating strap on?" She opened a drawer and pulled out a long vibrating dildo with a harness. This was a dream. It had to be. Never in a million years had I thought we would end up here at this moment. The harness fit snugly against her skin and I desperately wished I could take a picture.

"I like it," I giggled as she put it on and squirted a generous amount of lube on it and put some on her own fingers. She slid two into me and finger fucked me, moving against my clit and my inner walls.

"Come for me once and I'll give you my cock, Ozzie," Jess said, her tone authoritative and bossy. It made my insides turn into liquid heat.

I groaned as I pressed against her hand as pleasure and warmth started to build and lick up my spine. The orgasm crashed into me, and I cried out as Jess smiled down at me with a satisfied grin.

"Awe what a good girl," she said as she came over to me and turned the dildo on and lined it up with my entrance. Moaning her name, I shivered at her words. It was like she knew exactly what to say to make me boneless. Jess slowly slid in all the way to the hilt, giving me a moment to adjust. The vibrations hit all the right spots as she leisurely took it all the way in and all the way out.

"More on my clit," I panted as she circled my throbbing

center with her thumb and continued to move in and out of me like she had all the time in fucking the world. She wrung it out until I was writhing against her and calling her name. The waves of bliss just kept coming until they crashed into me and shoved me under as my second orgasm pulsed through me from my fingertips to my toes.

Jess rocked her hips until I was fully spent and then she slid it out from me and off her own hips and laid down next to me.

"Fuck my face, Ozzie. Climb on top and show me you can do one more." Jess smiled mischievously and the way she bossed me around had me getting wet all over again.

"Yes, Jess."

I straddled her, and she ate me out like a fucking queen. Licking and sucking as I held on to her headboard and rode her face as she used her tongue and fingers, making me feel things that I hadn't felt in a very long time. My body and heart could hardly take it as another orgasm crashed into me and I milked it out on her tongue. She spasmed underneath me as she stroked her own clit and chased one more release. I couldn't remember a time I had come that many times with a partner.

Carefully, I came off her and laid beside her as we exchanged kisses, tasting myself on her. Our kisses were softer and sweeter, taking our time to explore one another after we had been completely satisfied. My mind could not think of another time that I had been so content in bed.

"You're sensational." I rubbed my nose against hers. She started to trail kisses down my neck and suck at my collarbones and then took my nipple in her mouth.

"Jesus, Jess."

She laughed as she moved to the other one and I squirmed against her, wetness pooling at my thighs almost immediately.

"I need some water. No more," I croaked out, and she giggled, pulling away from me.

"Is three the max?"

"It is tonight." My body was incapable of moving right now, so all I could do was smile.

She laughed. "I think we both need water and some snacks." She sauntered off her bed fully naked and went into the kitchen. She returned with some drinks accompanied by chips and candy. She popped a piece of chocolate in her mouth as she lounged against her pillows.

"I don't think my legs will be working properly for a minute, seeing how hard you made me come."

"Same. This was enough exercise for me today." She winked, and I laughed.

"This was amazing." I grabbed my underwear and slipped them back on and grabbed my top, sliding it over my head to lounge next to her. Taking another drink, I exhaled loudly.

"It really was. Ozzie, I really like you," she said, her icy eyes sparkling. My heart seemed to expand at her words.

"I like you too."

Jess chewed her lip nervously. "What if we took a pause on the pretend dating and tried something real?"

"I thought you would never ask." Grabbing a handful of chips, I smiled sillily at her.

"Great! On the bright side, the only people we have to tell are Logan, Aven, and Myla, since they were the only ones who knew it was a ruse."

"I'll have to tell my roomie Trevor, but he already knew the vibes were happening here." In fact, he would have a huge I told you so for me, but I didn't mind. I was happy to be wrong about pretend dating being the way to go.

"Amazing," Jess said as we snuggled into one another, munching on our snacks as we shared casual touches and kisses.

"We're so cute," I hummed against her skin.

"So, what do we do from here?" she asked playfully, trailing her fingertips against my thigh.

"Uh, want to watch a movie or something?"

"I didn't mean literally but figuratively." Jess rolled her eyes, but her smirk gave away her mischief. "I also want to be transparent that I'm only into monogamy."

"Same. I'm a one-person kind of gal. So, I would say we're dating... maybe not to girlfriends yet, but definitely dating." I pulled her thigh over mine.

"Okay. Now we can watch a movie. You can choose."

The rest of the right we shared giggles and more touches where we explored each other's bodies. Exhausted, we fell asleep tangled in each other's arms. It was the best night's sleep I had had in months.

Sixteen

Jess

Ding.

What was that annoying sound, and why was it invading my dreams?

Ding.

Was I imagining things or was something going on? Did I leave the microwave on or something?

Ding.

God damnit. I groaned, opening my eyes to a passed-out Ozzie. I smiled, looking at her spiky blonde hair and her rumpled shirt snaking up over her soft belly. Her lips looked a little swollen and idly, I wondered if my lips looked the same way. Last night had been absolutely perfect. Images of Ozzie mounting my face and my dildo disappearing into her cunt flashed in my mind. I wanted to see all the ways she would respond to my words and my toys.

Ding.

"Okay. Who the fuck's texting me?" I grumbled and Ozzie stirred, mumbling and turning away.

Myla: SOS. I ended it with Jake, and he won't leave.

Myla: He could stay with his brother but refuses to leave saying he has a right to live here.

Myla: He's also months behind on paying his half of the mortgage.

Myla: I own the goddamn house and I want him OUT.

Rage made me wake the hell up really quick. I knew that asshole would make this breakup a shit show.

"Mother fucker," I said cursing Jake. I looked over to where Ozzie was sleeping soundly. "Hey sleepy head." Mumbling in her ear, I then took her lobe into my mouth, sucking gently, so she groaned, her mouth falling wide open. I really wanted to eat her out again. My body was practically screaming for it.

"Ozzie, open your eyes," I whispered, and she shook her head, throwing her arm across her face.

"Tsk, tsk. If I must, then." I slid down her body and snaked underneath the cover to where her cunt was on full display. I snuggled between her legs and licked her fully as she arched and moaned. If this was the only way to wake her up, then so be it. I smiled against her. What a way to get ready for the day.

"Jess," she breathed, and I went to work, making her wetness drip into my mouth. I sucked on her clit and dipped my fingers inside her, stretching her and moving to different rhythms as she writhed against me. I felt her orgasm building until her thighs hugged my ears and she shook around me.

Ozzie convulsed around my fingertips and her clit throbbed in my mouth.

Flinging the comforter over my head, I peeked out, looking at her lazy smile.

"You awake now?" I teased, and she nodded.

"I sure am." She giggled, and I smacked my lips loudly. I let this moment of bliss hold us for a few extra seconds before I changed the trajectory of our day because Myla needed us.

"We have a situation." I pulled my phone over and showed it to her.

"Fuck. Okay, let's go then." Ozzie hopped up and pulled her pants and shoes on. My heart nearly burst out of my chest for her sense of urgency. Ozzie was a part of our group now but there was something wildly attractive about the person you were dating showing up for the people they loved and cared about.

"Breakfast on the way?" I asked, doing the same, and she nodded. Why the fuck couldn't Jake just make this easy for everyone? Why did he continue to be a dumb fuck face?

Ugh.

"I'll drive." Ozzie hustled through getting her stuff together, and I gave her Myla's address.

Me: Ozzie and I are on our way.

**Logan: Roger that. I'm bringing snacks
and my big strong muscles.**

Dani: I've got a taser just in case.

Aven: Be there in 20 minutes.

My people were the best. We showed up for one another

and Jake wouldn't even know what hit him when we got there.

> *Myla: Thank you, friends. He just*
> *stormed out. What if we just moved*
> *all his stuff to the front lawn and then*
> *he would have to leave? I'm not even*
> *kidding.*

> *Me: Let's fucking do it. You still have his*
> *location, right?*

> *Myla: Right. I'll keep tabs on him while*
> *we get all his crap out.*

> *Logan: I called more reinforcements. Bex*
> *is on his way too.*

> *Aven: Let's fuck it up.*

Ozzie and I quickly put ourselves together and then sped towards Myla's house. Jake was in for a rude awakening. He should have never messed with Myla, and now he would pay the price. In two hours, his shit would be out on the lawn and so would he.

We pulled up to her home a little way out in the suburbs. It looked like Logan was already there, barking orders while Aven held Myla's hand. Her purple hair was up in a very sad looking messy bun that drooped heavily to one side. Her cheeks looked pale, and she was gazing at nothing like she was seeing right through the world around her. I wanted to slap Jake across his stupid face.

Dani and Bex were spotted marching in and out of the house with boxes that had already been packed up. Logan seemed to be leading the charge of what to get put out in the yard.

Both of us hopped out of the car, ready to go.

"Put us in, coach, whatchu got?" I hustled towards Logan, who smiled at us knowingly.

"Feels a bit funny that you two would be together so early in the morning?" Logan smirked at us, and we both stopped abruptly.

"Uh." Nothing else came out of my mouth. Ozzie blushed a little, and I gripped her hand tight.

"Almost like your date last night was a real success?" Dani hummed from behind us. We all laughed, even Myla. "Logan already told me that your cute little make believe relationship plan turned into something genuine. How adorable, honestly."

My mouth dropped open, and I looked at Logan, who just shrugged. Myla's smile quickly disappeared and my heart ached for her.

"Anyway. How you doing, Myla?" I went over to her as Ozzie raced inside to help with the removal of all his garbage.

"I feel like a weight is gone from my chest, but at the same time I can still feel the pain of all that baggage. That doesn't make any sense, but I don't know how to explain it." Myla's eyes were watery as she watched the little parade of cardboard leave the house.

The boxes weren't neat. He didn't deserve it. It truly was a free for all, shoving everything you could into one container or another. Most of them had random objects sticking out of the top and he was lucky we didn't just dump everything in the trash. Instead they were not so gently being carried straight to the curb so he could just drive by and get them. It was more than he deserved in my opinion, but who was I to argue?

"How's his location looking?" Logan came over and held Myla's hands.

"Still not here. I bet we have an hour or two left."

Logan nodded as Aven headed in to do more damage control in the house. "Alright tell us what else has to go."

On the bright side, almost everything in the house that was used for living, like kitchen utensils, furniture, and decor, were all Myla's. It was her house before Jake had moved in and it still would be after he moved out. We mostly just had to get his shit out of the bathroom, closet, and storage rooms. There were some miscellaneous things strewn around the house, but we made quick work of it with the entire team.

I saw Myla kept looking at Dani with a weird misty look in her eyes and I wondered if something was going on. Meanwhile, Aven was pointedly avoiding Bex's mischievous grin, and it was hilarious to watch.

Ozzie worked efficiently and without groaning and griping. She kept purposefully seeking me out to add touches and tickles. My face was constantly split into some silly ass grin.

"This is very fun for me." Logan mused as she observed all the odd relationship dynamics going on.

"I'm glad we can be your entertainment," I replied.

We swept the house once more, gathering every tiny thing and combing each room for any last little remnants that he may have left. It took two and a half hours. Smugly, Logan walked around and looked triumphantly at the space.

"Amazing, he won't be bothering you anymore, Myla." Logan's voice softened as Myla sat and looked around the house, a bit dazed and confused.

"Hey, what's going on in that pretty head of yours?" Dani approached Myla and squatted in front of her.

"I just can't believe he was wiped away in a few hours. Like it's good but weird and sad, you know? It was a long time coming, but I just... I don't know. Now that it's happening, I'm a little overwhelmed with the emptiness."

"Are you going to be okay living here by yourself?" Aven asked, walking over and sitting beside her.

"I don't know."

"Well, I can move in for a little bit?" Dani offered. They had just moved here, and I think they were living with a friend, but it wasn't a permanent situation.

"Would you?" Myla's cheeks flushed slightly.

"Sure, Myla." They got up and went to make some arrangements.

"Did you hear that?" Ozzie leaned towards the door.

Car tracks sounded outside, and we all looked wide eyed at each other, waiting for what was about to happen next.

"What the fuck, Myla?!" Jake came storming in and we all formed a ring around Myla, waiting to step in if necessary.

"You need to get out, Jake. Don't make this any worse than it already is," she said with an edge.

"You put all my stuff on the curb outside?!" His face was beet red. Spit was flying out of his mouth and he shook an angry finger at us.

"I suggest you go outside and pack up all your shit from the lawn and leave before we carry your ass out," Logan hissed. She would do it too. I had no doubt in my mind that Logan could drag his ass out all by herself, despite her petite size.

"I would be more than happy to help put stuff in your car, mate. But you're done here," Bex said forcefully; he stood tall and looming next to us. I think he had just gotten into town and was immediately ready to get into a fistfight for Myla. He would be a wonderful addition to our little family if Aven could ever move on from their one-night stand.

Jake looked around in disbelief and must have thought better than to argue with all of us standing there, ready to fight with all our awesome circus muscles.

Silently, we followed Jake out and, without exchanging any words, we made quick work of putting boxes in his car. He grumbled and groaned the whole time, complaining about anything and everything.

Unfortunately, not everything fit. There were still a few boxes left sitting there.

"Where are you staying? We'll get your boxes there, so you don't have to come back," Dani said, looking at him with narrowed eyes.

Jake looked at Myla once more and then listed off the address. He drove off in a huff and Dani, Bex and Ozzie packed up the rest in Dani's car.

"I'll go with Dani to drop this shit off." Ozzie pulled me in for a toe-curling kiss that earned wolf whistles and hollers from everyone.

Wow, I could get used to this.

"I'll text you later." I blushed slightly as they drove off. Bex followed separately just to make sure everyone was safe.

"Didn't Bex just get in?" Aven asked.

"Pretty much. I got the text while we were talking at the studio and he said he wanted to come help if it was okay." Logan smiled at her, and Aven scowled.

"Let's go see how our girl is doing." I ushered them both back towards where Myla was hovering just inside her front door.

"Well, that was... something." Myla cleared her throat and took a look around her. Aven, Logan and I all went back inside, where we popped a bottle of wine. "Isn't it too early to drink?" Myla asked.

"Not for something like this, babes." Logan poured us all a glass, and we sat down.

"Cheers to saying fuck you to Jake and hello to a new chapter! Thank you all for being here. I appreciate every one of you. I-I couldn't do this without you." Myla raised her glass with a sad smile and we all gulped down our first sip.

Men really were the fucking worst.

Seventeen

Ozzie

Jess's long hair fanned over my lap, and I stroked through her strands. "How's Myla holding up?" Jess turned her bright eyes to me and smiled sadly.

"I think as good as you can be after having to forcibly shove your ex out of your house. But Dani moved in, and things have been going well, I think. Myla feels better having someone there, and Dani is a gem. They're getting along just fine, I suppose."

It had been a couple of weeks since we had kicked his ass out. It wouldn't be the first or last time I would have to help a friend get the fuck out of a bad situation, but it always sucked, nonetheless. Breakups were messy, even if they were necessary. Healing couldn't be rushed, and I knew either way Myla was taking it one day at a time.

"Are you excited to meet Trevor?" I asked Jess. She fully sat up and looked at me with playfulness in her eyes, her hair slipping through my fingers.

"Yes, I cannot wait to meet this infamous best friend of yours who apparently deals out massive shit to you."

"Okay, well, he should be home in a bit and then you both

can talk all the shit you need." I snickered. It had been a long time since I really wanted to introduce someone to Trevor. He and Sean had accidentally met at one of our shows, and it was weird. Plus Trevor immediately hated him, which should have been the red flag to end it all, but it wasn't.

Tonight, I was desperate for them to like one another.

"What should I start with? Your most embarrassing moment? How bad is your morning breath? How long do you leave the dishes in the sink?" Jess waggled her eyebrows at me.

"You're enjoying this far too much. I can answer all of those. I leave the dishes in the sink anywhere from zero minutes to several days. I try to do them every night. Try being the important word there. Don't hold it against me. My morning breath isn't any more heinous than anyone else's. And my most embarrassing moment is parallel parking in front of a friend's house with Trevor and slamming into both the front and the back car in a panic."

She busted out laughing, looking absolutely delighted.

"Well, damn, I'll have to think of some more questions."

The plan tonight was to have a relaxing evening where Jess and Trevor would meet. I was feeling a little nervous since our real dating hadn't been going on that long, really just a few weeks. But we had technically been pretending for a lot longer. So maybe it all evened out in a weird way.

Trevor, of course, knew all the juicy details, but it was strange to start introducing someone you were dating to your people. Fortunately for Jess, most of her people were in the circus and only her mom lived semi close, so all of her friends were already very well acquainted with me.

Additionally, my family lived far away, so Trevor was like my found family here. We had been through thick and thin together, moving as starving artists but making the most of wherever we were because, hey, at least we had each other and everyone else could just fuck off.

"Honeys, I'm home." The front door burst open, and Trevor stood there in all his glory, holding takeout bags from our favorite Chinese restaurant.

"Trevor, Jess. Jess Trevor." I did a quick introduction, standing awkwardly between them, suddenly unsure of what to do with my hands at this exact moment.

"You went to the show with Ozzie that night," Jess said matter-of-factly.

"I did. And you were the sexy little hoop siren." He winked at her, and she offered to grab the bags from him and set them on our dining room table.

"I'll grab some drinks," I blurted out as I hustled to the kitchen. Why was my weirdness coming out now?

Ugh. Breathe Ozzie. These are your people. Everything is fine.

Gathering the drinks, I stepped back into the dining room. We settled down and popped open some seltzers to enjoy with our food.

"Is it true that Ozzie's most embarrassing moment was when she gave all the cars around her fender benders when she was trying to parallel park?" Jess asked casually. My nervousness fizzled out at her playful tone.

"Oh, it's true. That must be in the top five most embarrassing things for sure." Trevor looked delighted that this was the direction that the conversation was taking.

"You're really not holding back at all, are you?" I scooped up some fried rice and looked between them, feeling the tension leave my shoulders as they smiled at one another.

"Why would I do that? This is fun!" Trevor clapped his hands together, and we all laughed.

"Ozzie says you're a dancer?" Jess asked.

"Yes, I am."

They dove into talking about dance, which Jess knew surprisingly a lot about. I found out that she had a sister who was a professional dancer, but she was living abroad doing shows in Europe. Apparently, she had been a dance recital groupie for quite some time growing up.

"I really loved watching her on stage. When I was younger, I was a runner, so moving to music and making shapes with your body because you wanted to was something I couldn't even comprehend. I was jealous because it felt like the sky was the limit. You could be angry, sad, scared or whatever character you wanted and show it through your costuming, your song, your movement quality. I was great at running, which was why I stayed with it, but goddamn it's boring."

"I dated a cross-country runner in high school, and I had to sit through his races," Trevor confessed.

"And I'm sure it sucked." Jess giggled.

"Oh yes, and then he had to suck to make up for it."

I nearly spit out my food at that as Trevor cackled and Jess nearly choked on her own rice. Okay, apparently we were already comfortable enough to make sexual jokes around one another.

"What?! Don't act like that's a surprising thing to say." Trevor raised his eyebrows and dared me to argue.

I rolled my eyes as Jess smirked. The rest of the evening flew by as we finished our food and chatted for several hours. The conversation seemed to flow easily, and without pause between the three of us. I could tell the two of them liked each other and enjoyed one another's company by the way I kept getting booted out of their chatter.

Trevor had despised Sean, but he seemed to be delighted in Jess's demeanor. Sean was a very typical man. Lots of brawn and minimal brain. I wasn't even sure why I liked him in the first place.

Eventually, we all made it outside, to our patio, to sip the last of our drinks and enjoy the sunset.

"So, does this mean we aren't pretending anymore? Is it officially done? Now it's real?" Trevor asked.

"I would say so. I don't think we're labeling anything just yet, but I'm happy with where this is." Jess squeezed my hand, and it sent tingles along my skin.

"So adorable. I just want to throw you off this porch." Trevor grinned cheekily at us. Soon the sun disappeared completely, and we moved back inside, where Jess said her goodbyes. She had an early morning private lesson that she had to do so her evening couldn't last forever.

We walked out holding hands.

"Thanks for doing that," I said, my voice breathy and low. I pressed her against the car and let my hands find her hips, gripping her hard.

"I think it went well," she replied, her own voice throaty as her chest rose and fell. She looked at my lips and chewed on her own.

"It did."

I leaned in and captured her mouth with mine and slowly moved my hands to cup her face as she wrapped her palms around my ass and pressed me even closer, so our nipples were practically touching. Soon things got heated, and we were pawing at one another with nips and kisses.

"Okay, if we don't stop, I will never make it home," Jess panted, and I nuzzled into her neck, inhaling her scent.

"You're right." I placed one last smacking kiss on her lips.

"Bye, Jessi girl." I kissed her knuckles and walked backwards toward my place.

"Bye, Ozzie babes." She blew a kiss my way and slipped into her car.

I waited until she was fully backed out and off into the distance before I went back inside.

"Well, you two are fucking cute as can be," Trevor said as I walked in a little loopy from the feeling of Jess's lips on mine.

"We are, aren't we?" My head felt like it would float away if it wasn't attached to my body.

"I really liked her, Oz. Much better than that meathead Sean." Trevor pulled me in for a hug and I squeezed him back.

"Unfortunately, I like men even though I should probably stay away from them." I sighed.

"Preaching to the choir, Ozzie." Trevor laughed.

"Thanks for giving your stamp of approval. It means a lot to me that you both got along so well," I said and meant it. If Trevor and Jess hadn't gotten along, I don't know what I would have done.

"You didn't need my approval, but you're welcome, none-theless. I'm highly cultured and a grade A classy bitch." Trevor popped his lips.

Rolling my eyes, I headed to my room where I messed around on my phone waiting for Jess to text me, letting me know she made it home okay. No one had reached out since my run in with Brittany or Sean. Maybe I would finally be able to put that all in the past.

I had a fun idea that I wanted to slide by Logan to generate some extra revenue and say fuck you to him and all the people who thought what he did was okay.

Jess: Home! Thanks for having me over.

Me: Glad you made it.

I had a moment where I almost wanted to type "I love you." Shocked, I thought about what that really meant. Did I really love Jess? I mean, in some ways, yes. I loved her when we became friends and when I saw her on the hoop.

But was I in love with her? I felt like I was getting there. But it was way too soon to put that on the table. We had only been really dating for barely any time at all.

*Jess: I had a lot of fun. I like being a part
of your life.*

The message caused a funny sensation in my belly, and I made an effort not to overanalyze every word she said. Did she feel the same way? Did she love easily? How many people had she said it to? Shit. How many people had I said it to?

For a moment, I let my thoughts spiral rapidly before I took a deep breath and reined it in. This wasn't weird. People fell in love with whoever they were dating. This was normal. No need to let it get out of control in my head and then word vomit it on to her.

Exhaling, I realized that I needed to respond back to her message.

*Me: I really like being with you. Playing
pretend just wasn't doing it for me.*

Jess responded back with a haha.

*Jess: Okay Ozzie babes. I'm headed to bed.
Goodnight.*

Me: Goodnight.

I set the phone down and, for the first time in a long time, I allowed myself to think about the best-case scenario where Jess and I would be together. We could perform together and be an incredible duo inside and outside the circus. Everyone would be happy for us, and our little circus family would be even more tight-knit.

It seemed lovely. Almost too good to be true. I hoped that dream could become a reality as long as one of us or our exes didn't fuck it up.

EIGHTEEN
JESS

"What's the emergency?" Ozzie showed up, appearing disheveled and concerned at my doorstep. It was really unfair how much I wanted to fuck her every second of every day.

"I have a sex emergency." I pulled her into me and smashed our lips together.

"Jess, are you fucking kidding me?" Ozzie looked at me incredulously and then started laughing.

"No, yeah, I'm so serious." I smiled.

"Don't do that again." Ozzie ran her hand through her hair. "You nearly gave me a heart attack telling me you needed me to come over asap." I felt a little bad about making her so nervous. My intention wasn't to scare the shit out of her. My body simply craved her and my mind was desperate for her attention.

"Okay, if I promise not to do it again, then can we have sex?" I grabbed her hands and started walking backwards towards my bedroom.

"Fine, it's a deal." Ozzie smirked and shut the door behind her.

"Promise you aren't too mad?" I teased.

"No, but you should probably be extra nice to me to make up for it," Ozzie said, letting me lead the way.

"You're so fucking hot." I was practically salivating, looking at Ozzie's body. I wanted to explore every inch of it and wrap myself in her and then drown in the taste of her.

"Want to have a little more fun today?" Ozzie asked sassily, running her fingertips across my skin.

"What do you mean?"

"How do you feel about some light bondage and noise canceling headphones or something?" Ozzie looked at me with hunger. Wetness pooled between my thighs and I nearly shivered.

"I would like to try all that very much." Goosebumps erupted over my arms, and I wanted to know what this would feel like with Ozzie in full control.

"Do you have some scarves we could use?" Ozzie walked over to my closet and looked at it intently, like she was trying to imagine what she could do with all my clothes hung up. "I've got some noise canceling headphones in my backpack."

"Ma'am, did you come prepared to do naughty things to me?" I asked dramatically. "And how many scarves do we need?"

"At least two, and I always have headphones when I get overstimulated and need less noise. They just happen to also work for other things." Ozzie lifted her brows at me, and I chuckled. We loved someone who was exceptionally prepared.

Walking over to my closet, I dug out some supplies and handed them over.

"Clothes off, princess," Ozzie whispered in my ear, and I shivered from her words as she left to get her headphones. I could get used to this. Ozzie made me feel things that no one else did, it was intoxicating.

"Yes, ma'am." I threw off my shirt and shorts. I had nothing underneath.

"Jess, you're magnificent." Ozzie ran her fingers up and down my sides, tickling my ribs. She ran a hand on the inside of my thighs and pressed my knees a little wider. She gently slipped one finger inside of me. I clamped my hands on her shoulders and threw my head back, groaning as she stroked my innermost walls.

"So responsive." Ozzie snickered and led me to my bed, where she tied the scarves to each of my bedposts and commanded that I lay down. She tied my wrists gently, her fingers dusting over my skin. They were just tight enough for tension, but not enough to hurt by any means. My body was hers to play with.

"I'll place these around your ears and you think about just relaxing. Anytime you need something different, or it doesn't feel good, you just say so, okay?" Ozzie kissed along my forearms and up to my shoulders before she gently placed the headphones around my ears. I was plunged into silence.

"Okay. I promise to communicate what I need from you," I said, but it didn't come to my own ears the same way. It felt natural to let my eyelids close and breathe deeply. All I could feel were Ozzie's light touches and her weight shifting around on the bed.

Suddenly, I felt very vulnerable, spread open and tied here with no ability to hear or move. But then Ozzie's fingertips trailed up and down one thigh and then the other. Pleasure pooled low in my belly as I relaxed more into the loss of control. It was nice to have her take care of me. I trusted Ozzie fully and knew that she would give me exactly what I needed.

Ozzie's mouth journeyed across my collarbones, tickling my skin and making me shiver. I felt the bed dip, and I wanted to just sink in and let Ozzie work magic on my body. Her touch came back as her lips left little zaps of electricity along my skin. Everything felt more heightened with my eyes closed and the headphones on, my wrists bound.

She nibbled and bit at all the sensitive parts of me. My ears, my neck, and my hip bones. I groaned and arched, trying to fight for more contact, but she kept me guessing going from one part of my body to the other.

She came up right next to me and gently moved one of the headphones. "Doing okay, princess?"

"Yes," I practically panted. My eyes searched hers as she gently tickled my skin with her fingers.

"Where do you want me to touch next, Jess?" Ozzie purred and I could feel the wetness soaking the bed beneath me.

"Please put your mouth on my tits and your fingers inside me," I begged, hardly recognizing my own voice. But the need for more of her touch and for more friction was so bad I thought I might explode. She slid the headphones back in place and all her touches felt charged.

Ozzie's mouth closed on my hardened peak, and I groaned as she gently pulled and sucked there. She could do anything she wanted to me, and all she wanted was to see me cry out in ecstasy. I desperately wished I could sink my hands into her hair. The need grew even more because I couldn't do a damn thing without her allowing me to do so. It was absolutely delicious.

Her fingertips took a slow journey down my abdomen, and I tried to lift my hips to meet her, and she chuckled against my skin as she moved to my other breast. Agonizingly slow, Ozzie parted my wet folds and sunk a finger inside me as I groaned.

"More please," I found myself begging despite not hearing my own voice and Ozzie added another finger, curling inside. My eyelids squeezed tighter as I focused on the intensity of each movement and sensation.

"More," I begged as Ozzie added one more and I thrust against her. Ozzie's thumb started circling my clit and all the sensations paired with the addition of all the toys sent me careening over the edge.

"Ozzie!" I cried out as the orgasm ripped through me. Pleasure rolled through my body, and I gasped as another wave hit me. Ozzie stroked me all the way to the end as I squirmed and wiggled underneath her skilled hands. My eyes flew open, and I looked at her.

"Good girl," Ozzie mouthed to me as I moved my hips against her fingers, milking out every drop of the warm deliciousness of my orgasm.

I knew I had soaked Ozzie's hand; I was so wet and wound up. Ozzie's mouth continued the journey down my center until I felt her breath right over my mound.

"Ozzie, please," I pleaded, wanting her mouth there more than anything. She nipped along the insides of my thighs and kneaded my ass with her hands. "Eat me out, I'm begging you."

Ozzie's mouth was on me in a second and I moaned, wrapping my thighs around her head as she licked and lapped against my wetness. Her mouth went right to my clit, licking and sucking against the sensitive bud.

Another orgasm roared forward as Ozzie used her mouth and her fingers. The second orgasm hit me like a freight train as Ozzie's tongue worked magic on my clit, hitting the perfect spot for me to cry out again.

It was like I was flying off the edge, seeing stars burst in front of me as pleasure rushed all the way to my toes. I quivered around her fingers, and she continued to stroke me through my spasms around her. She gently removed the headphones from my ears and sucked each lobe.

"Wow, you're good at coming for me," Ozzie mused as she

kissed up along my body, giving special attention to my nipples and slipping another finger inside me.

"Oh," I said as she continued to play with my wet pussy.

"Will you eat me out, Jess?"

"Yes, please." My voice came out needy, but I didn't care. I wanted to taste her and make her see stars the way I did when she was nose deep in my cunt.

Ozzie moved to mount my face. It was even more erotic for the fact that I was at the mercy of her body, fucking me with my arms tied up.

I could smell her essence and it made my mouth water as she settled herself on top of me and I licked her greedily, wanting to slide my tongue inside her so badly as she ground against my mouth, and I lapped and licked at her clit.

"Yes, baby girl, just like that," Ozzie commanded as I reveled in the taste of her and how perfectly her pussy fit against my tongue.

Ozzie continued to move until she called out my name and shook around me, her thighs quivering and her breath coming out in pants. I ate every drop of her pleasure until she gently came off me and her mouth was on mine. Our tastes mixed together and it sent more heat to my belly button as our tongues danced.

Ozzie pulled her lips away and pressed something else against my mouth. "Suck," she instructed, her voice low. My eyes flew open, and she thrust her nipple against my lips.

"That's it Jess. You suck while I finger fuck myself."

Holy hell, I was so turned on.

Ozzie used my mouth for both of her tits until another gasp and groan came from her and what I assumed to be her second orgasm from playing with herself. It was glorious to watch and feel her come apart. Carefully, she untied my hands. Ozzie kissed the insides of my wrist and I lay there limply, fully spent and feeling absolutely blissed out.

"How was that?" Ozzie asked as she settled her body next to me. She pulled me close so that our noses were only inches apart from one another.

"Amazing. I've never experienced something like that with headphones before. It made everything so much more intense. At first it was sort of scary and vulnerable, but then fuck me if that wasn't the hottest sex I've ever had." I leaned forward and pressed my lips to hers, feeling like I just wanted to melt into her.

We tangled in each other's arms and held one another for quite some time in silence, just reveling in each other's presence.

"Next time you have a horny emergency, just say that instead. I'm more than happy to oblige." Ozzie kissed the top of my head and I laughed.

"Yeah, I get it. Don't cry, wolf, just say what I want." I rolled my eyes, and it was Ozzie's turn to laugh. The sound of her joy was one of my favorites. She was quickly becoming someone I couldn't imagine my life without. When the hell had that happened?

"I was worried! Your pussy is good, Jess, but do it again and you'll see what happens when you're bad." Ozzie nipped at my ear and I yelped.

"Got it. I won't do it again." Snuggling deeper against her firm body, I let myself relax and drift off into sleep where my dreams included Ozzie on her knees, face buried between my thighs, and I thought I could finally die happy if that were the case.

Nineteen
Ozzie

"Ozzie, this was the best fucking idea you've ever had. Why didn't I think about doing something like this sooner?" Logan grinned proudly at the crew we had around us.

"Because you were missing someone like me who already has a good following and knows what the fuck they're doing. But my followers and patrons really like the nude shots of me doing anything circus related. Just be mindful of all your bits you know when you're on the apparatus... Not every trick is meant to, or *should* be done naked you feel me?" I shivered; there were too many times when I first started where I did not heed my own warning.

"Do you say that from experience, Ozzie dearest?" The corner of Logan's mouth quirked up.

"Yes, and let me just say it was not worth the pain. My labia and nipples did their best to recover, but they won't ever be the same." I pouted and then winked, which sent Logan cackling.

I had the idea to do a naked circus photo shoot and then put it up on my OnlyFans. My hope was that we could donate whatever the profits were to our scholarship fund so people could take part in the circus for free. Especially because we were an adult only studio. it was a no-brainer.

"I'm pumped for this." Our photographer Micah was a good friend of Trevor's and had done some of my own photo-shoots. He was lovely, bubbly and kind. Not to mention, nudity didn't faze him. He was an excellent professional and a lovely human being.

"Okay, so I'm thinking we do some individuals if you're comfortable, then small pairings or couples, then full group photos?" he offered. I knew everyone would have different comfort levels, and that was totally fine. There was no pressure to do anything except what you were comfortable with.

"I want to go first!" Logan sang and hopped right in there. In a dramatic wave, she whipped off her robe and stood there in all her tattooed and pink haired glory. Her confidence was flowing off her as she strutted her way to the apparatus completely in the nude. There wasn't a stitch of shyness in her as she sauntered off.

She was a natural and moved gracefully in front of the camera like she was born for it. Logan did a few shots where she was hanging underneath the trapeze in some splits and straddles and one arm hangs. There was no fear as she moved around.

"My coochie is beautiful and deserves to be worshiped," Logan purred while spinning slightly upside down with every-thing on display.

"Honestly hot," Aven commented. She was standing in a robe off to the side, admiring her best friend.

"I don't know about this," Myla said, looking a little nervous. I couldn't blame her. Logan was wide open for the world to see and did not give a single fuck. Not everyone had that kind of conviction. It wasn't exactly my style either, but Logan was absolutely killing it.

"You don't have to do it. This is all up to you. At any time, you can opt out. Today if you decide to take photos and then later realize you want to keep them for yourself, that's great. Wear as much or as little as you want, this is for you to feel powerful. There are no rules except whatever feels right for you, Myla," I said. I wanted to reassure her that this was meant to be empowering, not weird or uncomfortable. "Consent can be revoked at any time, and we can stop immediately. You just have to say the word."

"Okay." She bit her lip, fussing with the bow around her waist. All of us were hanging out in our robes until it was time to step up.

Logan took more time making fun shapes and blowing kisses to the camera. "Logan, why the fuck don't you have your own website? Your tattoos and ass would be making all kinds of people drool," I teased. She really seemed more free without her clothes on.

"Great question. I don't know. I haven't given it much thought, but maybe I should. I'm just so fucking busy. No time for anything fun." She pouted. Finally, she hopped off and smiled at Micah, thanking him for the photos. She walked over to us and slipped on her robe, looking as poised as ever. Like taking naked photos was the most natural thing in the world for her.

"Who's next?" Micah asked, looking around at us.

"Meeee!" Aven popped up and released the fabric around her. Her poses were artistic and poetic, whereas Logan's were sultry and sexy. It was so cool to see how personalities came out and what that meant in terms of how it looked in photos. Aven did some hand balancing and splits that would be divine on camera. She had a tattoo that lined her spine, and her hair was in its naturally curly state today.

Her poses made me think of photos of naked people in museums and fancy artistic cocktail bars. She was less blatantly open with her poses and instead found ways to keep every-thing tucked away with small teases here and there. A true work of art, Aven was stunningly beautiful and elegant.

"Okay, hot stuff." Logan clapped as Aven rolled into her middle splits. Aven smirked and popped up, covering herself as Micah praised her athleticism.

"You're so imaginative," I complimented.

"Thank you, thank you." Aven bowed. "No autographs today, please!"

Logan rolled her eyes.

"I'll go next." Jess waltzed forward and untied her knot. I tried not to stare. I had seen her naked body at least a few times now, but the view never got old. Her shots were powerful and strong. Every line she made exuded that she was the one in charge, except when she was writhing beneath me.

It sent pleasure down my spine to think about how she had begged me to eat out her pretty pussy just nights before. The way my tongue had glided against her nipples and how she felt coming around my fingers, it was magnificent. It was nearly impossible not to think about all those moments as she sent glances my way. I swear to god she stuck her tits and ass out just for me.

"Ma'am, stop objectifying your girlfriend please," Logan said, stuffing her face with a granola bar.

"You don't know that I'm doing that," I scoffed. What had my face been doing that gave me away?

Ugh, Ozzie, keep it together.

"Oh yes, I do." Logan giggled while Aven's mouth quirked up.

Jess carefully draped herself over her hoop and took a few photos like that. God damnit, I would need a set of my own photos to keep. Her nipples were tight little peaks as she arched and lifted her chest up towards the sky. My feelings for her were blossoming with each and every sultry gaze.

Jess caught me practically drooling and winked at me.

"Jesus, you're going to be the death of me," I whispered.

Jess cackled.

I had the urge to take her right then and there in front of her friends and claim to the world she was mine and I was hers. But I didn't because that was not what today was about and fucking your girlfriend at your place of work, in front of everyone, was probably not the best idea.

"Okay, I need to look away from you." I tore my eyes away from her strong thighs and locked eyes with Myla's worried eyes. "Myla, do you want to go or want me to go?"

"I can do this." Myla took a deep breath and tentatively released her robe. She opted for some nipple pasties and a nude thong with clear straps on the hips.

Jess had already hopped off her hoop and was popping grapes in her mouth, looking at me and licking her lips. How the hell was I supposed to control myself when she was doing bullshit like this?

"This sexual tension is fun," Logan mused.

Turning my attention back to Myla, I tried to get Jess's tits out of my mind. Myla began by using the silks to cover some of her skin and it made for a shy, demure vibe. It was lovely and perfect for her as she used the silks like a sheet and let them drape over her as she wrapped herself up.

"Myla, this is a beautiful shot," Micah exclaimed. You could see her getting more comfortable as she adjusted the fabric to show more of her and her shoulders began to relax.

"Sorry I'm late!" Dani walked up next to us, tying a robe around their waist. Their eyes zeroed in on Myla and their pupils blew wide.

"You're just in time, I think," Logan teased.

Damn, nothing got past that woman. Myla smiled shyly at Dani as she continued to find shapes where she had just a hint of skin and a sly gaze. We all threw out encouraging words.

Cheeks flushed, Myla quickly gathered her robe and pulled it tight around her, her eyes shining.

"That was exhilarating, if not a little terrifying." She breathed heavily, and Dani avoided her eyes.

"You were fantastic. Truly," I reassured her, and then Dani stepped up. They shed their robe and went over to their straps where they tangled themselves up in kinky poses seemingly unbothered by the amount of skin that was being pinched by the apparatus.

"LOOK AT THAT NON-BINARY BADDIE!" Jess yelled excitedly.

"Jesus," Logan said as our rigger pulled Dani up and they did some spins and splits that left little to the imagination, but it was like watching a magical being. Everything was precise and languid like they oozed cool competence and confidence. It was like a spell had been cast and we could do nothing but watch in amazement.

Jess slid her arms around me and nuzzled into my neck. My heart fluttered, and I turned to kiss her cheek. "You were stunning up there. Truly breathtaking," I whispered against her skin.

"Thank you. I wanted to put on just a little show for you." She nipped at my ear.

"I'm sorry, ma'am. Are you an exhibitionist?"

"Maybe," she purred.

"Okay, we should revisit this later, I think." Jess was just full of surprises that I was dying to discover.

"Do you think Dani has a crush on Myla?" she whispered, tickling my ear, making me squirm. The change of topic taking a little edge off the nagging lust in my lower belly.

"Absolutely. Do you think Myla has one back?" We all continued to watch as Dani basically did their whole straps solo naked. Their orange red hair was flying around them like a halo as they spun rapidly, making beautiful shapes in the air.

Everyone was transfixed on the spot. Myla gazed in awe, but I wasn't sure there was anything else there.

"Not sure. Myla is queer, so who knows since she left that shitbag Jake," Jess said quietly.

I giggled, and the spell was broken as Dani carefully descended and tied the robe around their waist. They were a force to be reckoned with, and I was sure that was the vibe the camera got as well.

"Dani, you're fucking hot." Logan fanned herself and pretended to swoon.

"I need a drink after that, you sexy thing," Jess purred.

"Oh thank you, I always love performing for my fans," they teased.

Myla said nothing as a blush crept up on her cheeks and she excused herself to go grab something from the other room.

"Ozzie, are you the last individual one?" Micah asked, and I nodded. Slinking out of the silky fabric, I opted to use larger juggling rings to pose with for my shoot. I moved and danced around with my juggling props, contorting, and stretching into different shapes that would provide an aesthetic that would leave little to the imagination.

Aven whooped while Myla hollered on her way back in. They gassed me up while I danced across the studio and then finally sweaty and out of breath, I called it a day for my individuals.

"Thank you for sharing this with us." Aven squeezed my hand.

"You're a talented model and creative, Oz. We're lucky to have you." Logan gave me a crushing hug.

"Now, we're going to do some group and couple shots." I smiled, looking at each of them. Myla blushed as Dani squeezed their shoulders.

"Me and you first?" Jess asked as she grabbed my hand and

led me over to the hoop. We posed with arms wrapped around one another and started to find a natural rhythm and dance of our bodies being flushed together, foreheads touching, hands wandering and lips trailing each other's skin. Nothing too scandalous but enough to start to feel the tension build again. I tried to keep my lewd thoughts away, but it was nearly impossible with Jess's naked body slathered up to mine.

"I'm getting hot from just watching this," Dani commented. Dani and Myla paired off to try some photos where Myla kept up her demure facade and Dani exuded confidence and dominance. It was a lovely dynamic as Dani guided Myla to different shapes where she could use fabric to conceal and hide in a way that was teasing and flirty.

Logan and Aven paired off and performed acrobatic feats. Soon we all swapped in with each other, seeing where we could create teasing images and powerful ones and everything in between.

We were at it for several hours before we called it quits, all exhausted and sweaty.

"I think that's a wrap, Micah. Thank you." I gave him a quick squeeze as we all finished and headed to put our regular clothes on.

"Who's ready to get the fuck out of here and go celebrate of all of us being sexy mother fuckers?" Logan asked, pumping her fists into the air.

"Hell yes," Jess said, doing some kicks.

"I love this enthusiasm," I laughed. "You know I'm in."

"Fine," Myla said.

Dani and Aven shrugged in agreement. We headed out and celebrated the fact that we were in control of our bodies and there was nothing anyone could do to take that away from us.

TWENTY
JESS

Tapping my phone impatiently, I waited for my mother to show up at my place. My phone finally dinged, and my mom's clipped tone came through, stating that she was, in fact, here.

Shielding my eyes, the best I could, I met her outside. Her attire was exactly what it always was, a clean, crisp white button-down shirt and dark slacks with sensible shoes.

"Thanks for coming, mom." I nodded as I ducked in and readjusted my glasses.

"I'm surprised you called me," she said as she took off from my driveway. The only reason I called her was because everyone else was busy doing a show today. Unfortunately, she was my best option outside of a Lyft or Uber to go to my regularly scheduled eye treatment.

"Well, truthfully, there weren't very many options today," I grumbled, and she grunted in response. Ugh. It wasn't that my mother was the worst, she just wasn't the best. She had never really got what circus meant to me and she rarely watched my shows. Which was fine, considering I would rather have her not watch and keep her comments to herself than show up and share her annoying takes of what she did and didn't like.

"How is work going?" She attempted small talk as we drove the twenty minutes to my doctor.

"Good, busy this performance season...." I stalled, wondering if I should tell her I was seeing someone.

"And Genevieve?" she asked in her monotone voice.

"We, uh, broke up a while ago." I forgot that I hadn't told her. It felt like eons ago that Genevieve and I were together. In fact, I had several messages from her that I'd been ignoring. I didn't know how to reply to her telling me she was so excited for Ozzie and me to perform at her event in a month or so. Instead, I had just liked the messages and then gone on with the rest of my day.

"Oh, and you didn't think to tell me that?" my mom scoffed. I couldn't tell if she was actually hurt or not.

"I'm sorry I've just been really busy, and I actually—I'm seeing someone new."

"And what's their name?" she inquired as we pulled into the parking spot in front of my doctor's building.

"Her name is Ozzie, and we're partnering in some acts as well."

"What happened to Logan?"

"She's so busy running the company that she doesn't have a ton of time for us to be duo partners anymore."

My mom sighed. "That's too bad. I love Logan. You must tell her I say hi." Logan had a weird way of worming herself into everyone's heart. Even my mom's heart wasn't immune to Logan's charm when she turned it up.

"I will. If you want to come in and sit in the lobby, I should be done shortly." We walked in together and I was called back quickly, where they numbed my eyes and started the treatment.

Twenty minutes later, I was out in the lobby with super

cool shades walking towards a blurry vision of my mother. I grabbed some Advil from my bag and popped a few. When the numbing wore off, my eyeballs would be grumpy, and I still had to get through my day.

"Thanks." I nodded at her, and we walked back to the car.

"Will I get to meet Ozzie soon?" she asked. Genevieve had dinner with her a few times, but considering I barely saw my mother, it wasn't a huge deal to have her meet the people I was dating. We weren't close, and I was okay with that. I had come to terms with that a long time ago. My mother was who she was, and I didn't have the emotional energy to try to convince her to be anything else.

"Sure, if you want. I'll set something up."

"Send it to my assistant's account and she will look at my calendar."

Instead of replying to that, I directed her to go back to the studio so I could stay there until someone could take me home later.

"Well, let me know if you need anything else."

"Thanks mom, I'll see you later." Then I popped out of the car, relieved that I didn't have to endure any more small talk with her. Immediately, she pulled out her phone and began barking at someone while simultaneously peeling out of the parking lot.

Jesus, I hoped she wouldn't hit anyone.

Someone's car I didn't recognize was at the studio, but everything was a bit fuzzy, so I couldn't be sure.

"Hello?" I walked in wondering who it could be since most of the professional company was at some gig today.

"Hey Jess! Nice shades," a smooth, deep, accented voice said.

"Bex?" I asked as a blurry figure emerged and his form came more into focus.

"Hi darling!" He came in for a hug and I accepted it warmly.

"Logan said I could just pop in since everyone's out at that corporate event today." He flashed a dazzling white smile at me, and I smiled back. Bex's hair was dark and unruly today, curling at the ends, his earrings catching little flashes of light and his hot pink nails splashing against his tanned skin.

"It's so good to have you here!" I squealed. "Are you performing drag anywhere locally while you're here?"

"Oh, you know I have a few things lined up, J," he said and my heart felt fuller knowing he was here.

"I heard you and Aven had a moment..." There were hardly any secrets around here and Aven had already spilled the beans.

"Well, Christ. Yeah, we've hooked up. I hadn't seen her in a long time before Myla's boyfriend takedown a few weeks ago and I haven't been in the studio since I was trying to get settled. So..." I swear he blushed a little.

"Don't worry about it because if you must know, my new duo partner and I are dating. Her name's Ozzie and she can juggle, too." I bragged a bit. Ozzie was becoming more and more a piece of my everyday life. It was terrifying, but I loved it.

"Oh, so a woman who is good with her hands," Bex teased, and I laughed. "We like that. I figured something was going on between you two when we rescued Myla from bro-dude Jake."

"Thank you for helping with that. I know that's a weird way to get started here, but we're a family and your backup was appreciated."

"Of course. I'm happy to be here. You all are one of my favorite groups of people."

We caught up the rest of the time until the gang came stumbling in with hair and makeup in various states.

"How did it go, Lo?" I asked as Logan came in, looking especially messy.

"Good, glad that shit is done, because ambient performing really just takes it out of me sometimes, you know?"

"I'll go do a coffee run if anyone wants anything?" Ozzie offered, walking in, looking fresh and ready to go. It made my stomach flutter looking at her bright blonde hair and full lips. She walked over and slid an arm around my waist. I was absolutely enamored with this woman in front of me.

"Want to come with?" she whispered in my ear, and I nodded.

"Text me what you all want." She waved her hand around as Myla entered, with Dani mumbling about caffeine deprivation.

Aven was last to enter and time seemed to hold still for a moment as Bex and Aven's gaze collided and there was a zap in the air. They barely had anytime to connect with the mess at Myla's. He had just showed up like the glorious person he was ready to put on his man privilege with his hot English accent and get Jake the fuck out.

"I'm Bex by the way." He stepped up and shook Ozzie's hand, peeling his gaze away from Aven.

"Nice to meet you officially, Bex. Thanks for answering the SOS call the other day. I'm sorry we didn't get to chat much then. Feel free to text Jess if you want anything, my treat."

"Bex, you also missed out on our hot nude circus photo shoot!" Logan exclaimed from where she was now laying down on the floor.

"Well, that sounds like my kind of fun," Bex answered, looking directly at Aven, who stood frozen in the doorway.

"Aven," I said. "Ave," I tried again.

I finally reached out and shook her shoulders, and she whipped her head around, mumbling something incoherent about a cold brew. She stepped forward and smiled sheepishly at Bex, whose eyes bore into her as she walked further into the studio.

"Okay, well, let me know," Ozzie said loudly and dragged me out to the parking lot, where she pressed me against her car and attacked my mouth with hers. It was fast and furious, our tongues tangling together and our bodies melting together. Hands grabbing and bodies grinding.

"Hi Jess," Ozzie whispered against my skin.

"Hi." I ran my nose along her cheek.

"How was your mother and how are your eyeballs?" She peppered kisses across my nose and brows.

"Oh, my eyes are pretty much the same. And my mother... apathetic as usual."

"Hmm, okay, an interesting way to describe your mother, but I'll take it."

"She wants to meet you," I said as we pulled out and headed to the closest coffee shop.

"Okay, if that's what you want. I'm in." Ozzie ran her fingers up and down my thigh.

"It would bring her an iota of joy, so I think we should do it."

"Let's bring her that iota of joy then." Ozzie squeezed my knee. "And I want to take you out on a special date sometime this next week if you're okay with that and have time."

"Oh, hell yes! I absolutely have time," I said as we pulled up to our favorite local spot. Spending my days with Ozzie sure beat the hell out of enduring it any other way with my mother. She was exactly what I needed and wanted; I couldn't wait to see what our date would entail.

TWENTY-ONE
OZZIE

"Are you ready?" I asked.

Jess looked stunning in her cut-off denim shorts and cropped white tank. I had told her to dress casually, and the way clothes seemed to hug her body nearly sent me to my knees.

"Yes! I will say I don't normally like surprises, but you make everything a little better, so I'll deal with it." She wrapped her arms around me and pulled my lips to hers. She tasted sweet against my tongue, and I let my hands roam down to grab her ass.

Giggling, she pulled away and looked at me lovingly.

"Okay, let's go before I get too caught up in the way your ass looks in those shorts."

"Ozzie, do you like my butt?" She strutted over to my car and bent over, exposing the muscles in her hamstrings and practically folding in half.

"Ma'am, get the fuck in my car," I demanded as we hopped in. "How much of a surprise do you want this to be?"

"What do you mean?"

"Well, you can close your eyes until we get there if you

want, or you can keep them open. It's up to you." I inter-twined our fingers together and kissed her palm.

"I'll close my eyes. I trust you," she said softly and rested her head back. Her dark hair came down in loose waves and I had the urge to take a picture right then and there if I wouldn't have been driving.

Slowly, we made our way to our special date spot in comfortable silence.

"Okay, we're here. Eyes stay closed if you want it to be a really big surprise." I carefully helped her out of the car and placed one hand on her low back and clasped her fingertips in mine.

"If I trip and eat shit, I'm going to be fucking pissed," Jess mused, the comment lacking any real venom.

"I'll keep that in mind." Slowly, we made it through the garden pathway in front of us and we stood in front of a picturesque picnic all set up ahead of time.

"Okay, you can open your eyes." I folded a pair of sunglasses into her hands and waited for her to put them on.

Jess gasped and pulled a hand to her mouth. "Ozzie..."

We both gazed upon the picnic setup, which was top-notch. I would have to tip the party company accordingly. There was champagne chilling in a bucket on top of a small table with a blanket. The spread was decorated with flowers, a plethora of food and a little sign that said *Happy Date Night*.

"What did you do?" She walked around and looked at it in disbelief.

"Just a fun little date night surprise for you." My insides warmed as tears sprang in her eyes.

"You did all this for me?"

"Well, I hired a company to come get it set up, but yes, I got it all taken care of for you, Jess." This was the moment I had thought about saying I love you, but I wasn't sure it was the right time. I didn't take that term lightly, and I wasn't sure

Jess was on the same page yet. Wringing out my hands, I tried to swallow the weird lump in my throat.

"This is the nicest thing anyone has ever done for me." She walked over and flung her arms around me, wrapping me up in a tight hug.

"I like you... like a lot," I whispered into her hair, nuzzling her neck.

"I like you too. It sort of freaks me out how much," she confessed, tightening her grip on my hips.

"What do you mean?"

"Well, I just struggle sometimes to fully let myself be in a relationship and fall into something true and meaningful because a lot of my past relationships have been surface level. The depth just wasn't there. With you, it's different. I'm afraid the depth we have might swallow me whole sometimes." Tears slipped down her cheeks, and I wiped them away.

"We can navigate it together. One step at a time. Nice and slow." I put my fingers underneath her chin and brought my lips to hers in a light kiss. It sent heat to my core as the kiss deepened and turned hungry. We were running our hands over one another until Jess finally pulled away.

"We should, however, enjoy this lovely picnic because I would hate for this to go to waste," she said.

I nodded in agreement as we sat on the ground and snuggled up to our table.

"How are you feeling about our gig coming up with Genevieve since she's the event planner?" I poured a glass of champagne for both of us and looked into Jess's no longer watery eyes.

"Sort of weird. Why does she have to be even more in my business post break up? Especially since we're dating now. She's always working at some weird angle. I don't know. I've been ignoring her messages, but I won't have a choice but to talk to her obviously when we get there. But fuck, the money is good." Jess took a long sip, and I tried not to stare at the column of her throat as she swallowed.

"Messages? Does she text you a lot?" A small curl of jealousy started in my veins, making me feel a little hot and possessive.

"Yup, see?" Jess showed me her phone and scrolled for a few moments where Genevieve's *just checking in* messages seemed to go on forever.

"Jesus Christ. Would you be mad if I said I was a little jealous?"

"No, I think it's kind of hot, honestly." Jess bit her lip and lowered her eyelids.

"Oh, you like people who are possessive, do you?" I raised a brow at her.

"I think a healthy amount of jealousy is fine as long as you don't move to controlling and manipulation. I don't mind a bit of protectiveness over what's mine, you know?"

"Hmmm," I hummed, tapping my glass, and standing up and walking over to her.

"What are you doing?" She asked, her pupils going wide as I stood over her.

"I think I want to show you that you're mine and only mine." A slow smirk creeped up on me. There wasn't anyone here, and it was a pretty private area of the garden.

"Ozzie..." Jess warned, but her breath was coming in pants.

"Take off your shorts, Jess," I commanded and her mouth formed a little o as she looked around quickly.

"What if someone sees us?" she whispered, but her glass was already coming on to the table and her fingertips fumbled with the buttons on her shorts.

"I rented out the space for a few hours. No one should be coming this way and it's exclusive back here." I looked around at the stone walls covered in shrubbery and the stone fountain in the middle of the water pool across the way. There was only one way into this section of the grounds, and we would be able to see anyone who came in before they saw us through all the blooms.

"God damnit," she swore as she slipped off her shorts and revealed a black thong. The globes of her ass looked good enough to bite.

"Thong, off," I ordered as I stood above her and she smiled quickly, sliding the straps off her hips and exposing her already wet pussy.

"Yes, ma'am." She sat there waiting for her next instructions and it sent wet heat straight to my thighs.

"Lean over the table, princess. Ass up." She did as she was told, and I widened her legs so I could get access to her pretty wet folds.

"Ozzie," she panted as I saw her arousal waiting for me.

"Don't be too loud," was all I said before I got on my knees and started eating her out from behind. She groaned as I took her sensitive little bud in my mouth and sucked on her clit. I dug my fingertips into her ass and hips as she rode my face, and I lapped her from front to back, wanting to drown in the taste of her as I tongue fucked her.

"Ozzie," she groaned out as her legs started to shake and I curled two fingers inside of her while sucking on her clit.

"Come for me, Jess," I instructed before I dove in and spanked her. Hard.

"Ahhh," she squealed as her legs shook and she spasmed around me, climaxing all over my face and riding out the waves of pleasure by rocking her hips against my mouth.

Releasing her, I sat back as she panted on the table. I pulled her to me, and she smiled, her face flushed and her hair wild.

"Ozzie," she whispered as our lips collided and she licked her own arousal off my tongue and started to slide her fingers down towards my own pair of shorts. I let her hands find my center, and I groaned as she finger fucked me while I feasted on her beautiful tits.

We were drunk on the sounds and feelings of one another. I groaned as pleasure licked against my spine and her fingers found the perfect spot on my clit and I squeezed around her hand.

"Jess," I moaned as I came on her hand and rode her fingertips until the last wave of pleasure left me.

We sat there panting and grinning like idiots at one another. The words were at the tip of my tongue to say I love you, but something held me back.

"I've never fucked in public before." Jess finally broke the silence and slipped back into her bottoms.

"I'm glad to be your first. Any other kinky firsts you want to explore?" I said as I reached for a grape and my glass of champagne.

"Well, let's see." She threw her head back and let the sun warm her face as she proceeded to list all the deliciously dirty things she wanted to do together. The rest of the day, all I could think about was how much trouble I was in because if I ever lost Jess, I didn't know what the fuck I would do.

Twenty-Two
Jess

Myla walked around and poured champagne for all of us. We huddled into her living room where Ozzie was getting the laptop set up.

"This reveal is going to be absolutely stunning," Dani said as they tucked their legs underneath them. I watched as their eyes trailed Myla around the room.

"This spread is impressive, you all." Aven looked lovingly at the food on the table that consisted of fancy jams, fruits, meats, and desserts.

"We're just trying to be good hosts." Myla blinked at Dani, who smiled slowly back at her.

"Everyone shut up, it's ready!" Ozzie practically squealed, and it made my chest warm.

"Me first!" Logan purred, and I rolled my eyes.

"You were already first at the photo shoot, you know." I pushed her playfully, and she lifted a dramatic hand to her mouth.

"Are you saying I'm an attention whore?"

"I think you're the one who said it," Bex teased, and we all laughed.

"You hush because you weren't even there!" Logan flapped her hand at him.

"It's too bad too because I would have been an absolute star." He popped a strawberry seductively in his mouth.

"Are you all done?" Ozzie clapped her hands and looked around as we settled in.

"Logan's up first! And let me say, her tits and tattoos are absolutely stunning." Ozzie had put music on to set the mood. We watched in awe as Logan's photos popped up and her muscles stood out against the artistry on her arms and legs. She looked powerful and sleek on the trapeze; her expressions practically sinful.

"Jesus, I'm so not straight," Aven mumbled.

"None of us are, thank god." Myla watched as Logan's demeanor consumed the screen.

"God, my ass is great." Logan toasted herself and took a huge swig of champagne.

"Now, Jess!" Ozzie waggled her brows at me as my figure popped up on screen. My hair hung dramatically over my body as I draped myself over the hoop. I looked hot and sexy, like I could bend the world to my own desires.

"Is that the look that made you fall in love, Oz?" Logan teased as the strong lines of my quads and abs flashed on screen.

"Something like that..." Ozzie trailed off, looking at me for a minute and then peeling her eyes back to the screen.

Heat rushed to my cheeks, and I squeezed my thighs together. We hadn't talked about the love word yet. Even though my heart and my body were unequivocally hers. Anxiety fluttered in my belly. This was not the time or place to unpack it either, so I stuffed some crackers into my mouth instead.

"Keep track of what photos you want to donate to the site for people to view. There are numbers in the bottom corner,"

Ozzie said, pulling me back to the present moment. Hopefully, everyone would just move on from Logan's love comment.

"Oh, I mean, all of mine can be used. People would be so lucky to see this body." Logan's confidence was unbreakable.

"I will keep that in mind, Ozzie. Thank you." Myla narrowed her eyes at Logan, who just shrugged.

"Myla, you up next?" Ozzie asked gently.

"Yeah, let's see what's going on here." She fumbled with her hair, hugging her arms around her body protectively. This had been way outside of her comfort zone, as modesty was usually more her style.

Her photos weren't as revealing as mine or Logan's. The fabric draped over most of the important bits as opposed to Logan's, whose photos were fully exposed to her tits, ass, and every crevice in between. Mine were somewhere in between.

"These are positively poetic, Myla," Dani said, placing a gentle hand on Myla's twitching fingers. Dani seemed to have a special way of calming Myla's nervousness.

"These feel like photos that would be in a magazine, Myla," Aven said quietly.

Myla's high cheek bones took on a pink sheen. "Thank you, everyone. I'm glad I did it, even though it was absolutely terrifying."

"Aven?" Ozzie flipped through the rest of Myla's that were the epitome of beauty and grace.

"Let's see these beautiful titties," Aven purred and Bex gave her a funny side eye.

"The acro is hot, Aven. Damn, I'm surrounded by some sexy sluts." I smirked at the photos flowing on the screen.

"I'd prefer the term whore," Bex teased.

"Maybe a harlot?" Dani added.

"Noted." Laughing, I looked at Dani. "You ready?"

"Let's fucking go." Dani's confidence was steady and calm. Not as aggressive as Logan's, but immovable and unshakeable.

We all gasped as Dani popped up, doing the wildest things in their straps while fully nude. Their athleticism was unmatched, and I could not even wrap my head around doing what they did on my apparatus. My nipples, labia and asshole could never. But here Dani was like a goddamn superhero doing things that would be extremely hard under any other circumstance and especially difficult without any clothes.

"You're my hero." Ozzie looked in wonderment at what Dani did. With each new photo, we all continued to ooh and ahh.

"I do what I can," Dani shrugged, and we continued to fly through the photos until we had Ozzie left for the individuals.

"Ozzie, let's see this model behavior of yours," Logan demanded. Ozzie's body popped up, and I had to refrain from releasing the pressure in between my thighs. Ozzie's were artistic and delicious. Like nothing I had ever seen before. Ozzie was truly gifted in finding angles and movement that captured beautiful energy and made you feel something. Her body was a work of art, a juxtaposition of hard and soft, capturing moments that you didn't even know existed in time.

Everyone's eyes seemed to glisten, and no words were spoken as we flipped through. Ozzie bit her lip and looked around at all of us.

"Jesus, is it that bad?" Ozzie's eyes filtered back and forth across the room.

"It's glorious," I whispered and got up. Before she had time to respond, I launched myself at her, tackling her to the ground and smashing my lips to hers.

"Fuck! Fuck! *Fuck*!" Logan cheered, and we broke out into smiles.

"Not everyone's a voyeur, you feral woman, you," I said as we sat up and snuggled close. What an intense thing to share with the people in my life, but I wouldn't have it any other way.

"That was beautiful. Ozzie, you're so talented. Thank you for letting us do this together." Aven wiped at her eyes.

"I never thought I could do something like that, but that was really empowering," Myla agreed.

"Well, tell me which ones you want to put up and get donations for and then the rest are yours to keep and do whatever you want with," Ozzie said, looking proud of the artistic project she created. "Let's go through the group photos."

We all threw compliments on the way our art seemed to come to life with our bodies on display. It was amazing to see how powerful vulnerability was. Micah had done a fantastic job.

Eventually, we all broke off, deciding which photos to keep and which to donate as I whispered into Ozzie's ear. "I know what I want to do with some of those photos."

"What's that?" Ozzie licked her lips.

"How about I show you instead?" I bit her ear, and she shivered. That night after we went home, I showed Ozzie exactly what her photos did to me.

Again.

And again.

And again.

———

Ozzie's hair was all ruffled, and she looked positively lovely lying-in bed next to me. I wanted to run my fingertips all over her body and soak in the smell of her skin. God, that was a wild thought to think about.

We had only been dating for a few months, and I was already falling hard. It felt like love was in the air, but I didn't know if Ozzie was in the same place. I was a little worried too about how intertwined our lives were. We worked together and were duo partners, which was a lot of time with one another. It sounded cute in theory but, it could be disastrous for the company if something happened to us.

Chewing my lip, I tried not to think too hard about it.

"You're going to bite your lip off if you keep at it like that." Ozzie cracked one eye open and smiled lazily at me.

"Thank you for that astute observation, Oz." I playfully shoved her shoulder and snuggled down into the sheets with our eyes locked together as we both reached out to stroke one another's skin.

It was like we had to be touching, no matter how close we were, physical contact wasn't a want but a bone deep need.

"What are you thinking about so hard in that big, beautiful brain of yours?" she asked, propping herself up onto her elbow.

"Oh, nothing much. Just how much it would suck if something happened to us, and the company would be ruined and it would probably be an absolute disaster." I winced as it came out of my mouth because it really did sound dramatic and like I was overthinking it. But I wanted to be honest and even though the words were brutal, it was what kept swimming around in my brain.

"Jesus, Jess, that's intense," Ozzie laughed, and I shoved her again playfully.

"I'm an over-thinker and it would! You can't deny that." It was sort of a legitimate concern, even if it didn't feel super appropriate for us at the moment. There was no reason to think this wouldn't work out. We were taking things nice and slow. There was no rush for us to commit or do anything more than what we were comfortable with.

"Everything will be fine. Plus, I think I'm going to buy a house here," Ozzie said casually.

My brain seemed to short circuit on her words. What happened to nice and slow with no added pressure?

"What? A house?" I looked at her quizzically. This was the first time I was hearing this. Nervous energy started to skitter across my skin. A house was a huge commitment. Like a gigantic financial commitment that said I would be here for a while, no matter what. If Ozzie bought a house and then something happened to us, she would be shit out of luck. So much money would be sunk into this thing and then she would be stuck here and unable to leave. The idea was ridiculous.

"Yeah, I mean you're here and I love the company. I think I want to set up some roots here, plus it's a good investment and Trevor and I would love more space."

My anxiety spiked at the thought of Ozzie buying a house and making this permanent for me. Oh no, no, no. If Ozzie was making this decision because of me, I couldn't let her do that. I just confessed that I thought us breaking up would be a train wreck for the company, not to mention how much it would absolutely destroy Ozzie's house plans.

"You're not doing this for me, right?" My voice was pitched high. Ozzie's face crumpled. This was the exact type of thing that I was worried about. How could she not see that? She had been worried about the same thing because of what happened at her last company. I thought we were on the same page.

"I mean, I'm not doing it just because of you. But I'm not going to pretend like you aren't one of the reasons I want to be here." Ozzie's voice was strained and I could see the hurt in her eyes, but how could she think about doing this right now when we only just started dating?

"You shouldn't do that for me, though." My fight-or-flight response had suddenly kicked in and my heart was beating wildly. How could I get it into Ozzie's head that this was a bad idea?

"Jess, people buy real estate all the time. And taking your relationship status into account is a normal thing to do." Ozzie sat up and frowned.

"But I don't want you to regret being here if we don't work out. This is exactly what I was just worried about." I got out of the bed and started to pace the room. Why now? Couldn't Ozzie just wait awhile and then decide? This felt like boarding a speed train with a one-way ticket into a danger zone.

"You don't think we're going to work out?" Ozzie asked incredulously.

"I don't know!" I shouted hurriedly, wanting to snatch the words out of the air as soon as they left my mouth. I didn't want Ozzie to regret making a decision like this if we didn't work out. No one knew what tomorrow would bring and investing hundreds of thousands of dollars into something because of that seemed like a really, really bad idea.

"You really don't know? Come on Jess, you can do better than that. Set aside the overthinking for a second here." Ozzie crossed her arms over her chest. Was she angry at me? How could she not see what was happening!

"We don't know what's going to happen and I can't commit to all of this right now." My brain felt like scrambled eggs as I tried to organize my own thoughts, even though the only thing I could feel and hear was my racing heart.

"I didn't ask you to commit to anything. It's not like I'm asking you to move in with me. I just said I wanted to be more rooted to this place, which means that I will be more devoted to this relationship. I'm a big girl who can do what I want with my life. I'm not asking for anything more from you. I thought you would be happy! Nothing has changed in terms of our commitment to one another." Ozzie's eyes were watery, and I wanted to scream.

"This changes everything!" My voice sounded strained and childish. I didn't want Ozzie to make huge life decisions based on me. I wasn't ready to think about that yet. I wanted more time and more space to figure out what the fuck this was. A house felt like an extension of how Ozzie felt about us. What if I wasn't ready to do this yet? What if I couldn't be what Ozzie needed?

"Jess, breathe. This isn't a big deal. I haven't even bought anything. I've just been talking to a realtor."

"Ozzie, this is a *huge* deal! You're buying a house because you want to settle down here with me. We haven't even been dating that long." Sweat formed on my brow and I needed some air. My body was going into overdrive, and I wanted to flee, fast.

"Are you serious? I'm making this decision with you in mind, as well as a lot of other things. I'm allowed to do what I want with my fucking money. And you know this is more than just a fling, Jess. I care about you a lot! I lo.." Ozzie cut herself off, and I shook my head.

We both looked at each other, chests heaving, almost daring the other one to say the words that seemed to be at the tip of both of our tongues. I couldn't do it though. My chest felt like it might cave in on itself and my throat was begging for air. My fear of commitment was snarling and rearing its ugly head.

"Ozzie, I can't do this," I panted.

"Don't you fucking dare do that, Jess. You know this is an overreaction! Just talk to me!" Ozzie practically growled and took a step towards me, but I backed up.

"Don't tell me I'm overreacting!" I snapped.

"Then don't freak out!" she threw back at me.

"Stop, I can't have this conversation." I shook my head

and closed my eyes. Nothing was coming out the way I wanted it to. I needed a moment. A fucking second to figure out what the hell I was trying to say.

"When you can start thinking about this rationally, you can call me Jess. And when you can admit your feelings to yourself and then me, then we can talk. In the meantime, I'll see you at rehearsal." Ozzie gathered her things and stormed out the door.

I watched her go and immediately wanted to run after her and tell her not to leave, but I couldn't. I sunk down to my floor and tears slipped out of my eyes.

"What did I just do?" I sobbed into my hands and wanted to curl in on myself. *No, no, no...* This wasn't how today was supposed to go. I should have never confessed my fear to Ozzie because the world thought it was a funny joke to throw them back in my face only a few moments later.

My phone dinged, and I looked at it and saw it was a text from Genevieve.

"Oh, fuck off." I threw it across the room, where it hit the wall with a loud thud. Why did this have to happen after our wonderful date and photo shoot reveal? I felt like I was living in a fairytale, one with orgasms that made my toes curl. But now that blissful moment is gone. I walked over and picked up my phone and called Logan.

"Hiya!" she answered cheerily.

"Hey," I responded, my voice trembling. Tears started to slide down my cheeks, and I wiped at them aggressively.

"What's going on?" Her voice was laced with concern.

"I don't want to talk about it," I said quietly. My voice barely audible to my own ears. Silence followed, and then my short sniffles turned into a full-blown sob.

"Jess." Logan's voice pulled me back as I tried to get ahold of the hurt in my heart.

"Logan," I replied, not knowing what to say, like my

thoughts were running chaotically through my brain and my emotions seemed to be wreaking havoc in my body.

"I know you don't want to talk about it, but here you are... calling me to... do what exactly? What can I do for you right now?" Logan asked. I could feel her cheeky smile through the phone.

"Will you come over and just watch a movie and eat junk food with me?" I didn't know how to explain my nuclear reaction to her about Ozzie. It was like I wanted to express my feelings in a calm and collected manner, but instead I flung words out like a sword and watched them cut up the woman I loved.

"Sure, babes, and then you can continue to not talk to me about it. I'll be there soon." She hung up, and I sat there on the floor wondering what had happened exactly.

What was I so afraid of? I had fulfilled mine and Ozzie's worst fears. What the fuck was wrong with me?

I didn't have an answer for it right now, but sooner or later I would need to confront myself and then Ozzie.

Fuck.

I was great at messing shit up.

Twenty-Three

Ozzie

J ess was on the other end of the warehouse training with her headphones in and I was staring at her very obviously, even though she refused to meet my eyes. I lurked around the space, trying to get her to at least look at me, but she pointedly avoided my gaze.

I still didn't know what happened. Why did the idea of me buying a house send her spiraling into space? It was perfectly normal for people to buy fucking real estate in their adulthood. It was also very normal to consider your relationship status while making large-scale decisions. I thought we were having an open and honest conversation after she confessed her own fears, and I thought the idea of me buying a house would comfort her.

Obviously, I had been very wrong.

This house wasn't even for us. It was for me and Trevor. Why the fuck did she lose her shit over something that wasn't even about her explicitly? It was meant to be a *hey I want to stay here no matter what, so this thing between us whatever happens I still care about you,* but instead it seemed to make her feel scared and angry. I grumbled around the studio until, finally, more people started to trickle in and notice the obvious tension in the air.

"So, what is going on with you two?" Aven asked, standing next to me. She looked between me and Jess, tilting her head like she could puzzle it out right then and there.

"I really don't know." I crossed my arms over my chest, hoping to catch her eyes so we could talk this out.

"Did you have a fight or something?" Myla walked in, rolling her shoulders and shaking her head from side to side.

"Kind of. I told her I was thinking about buying a house here and settling in." Was there something else I wasn't seeing here? Maybe her friends would be able to add some more context clues, because I still didn't understand why things exploded that way.

"That sounds great! We would love for you to stay. You know, like forever." Aven gave me a quick squeeze and my heart broke a little. That was the reaction I had been hoping to get from Jess, however, I had gotten panic and avoidance.

"Well, apparently not because it was very triggering for Jess, because the idea of me staying apparently contributes to our inevitable doom of breaking up. And me having a house here adds to the pressure for this to work out and if it doesn't, it will fuck everything up. So fuck me and my idea to buy some real estate and make decisions for myself and my own money!" The words tumbled out of my mouth. I said them while looking at Jess, but she continued to spin and twirl on her apparatus, ignoring us all.

God damnit, if she would just look at me.

"Whoa," Myla whispered. Her and Aven looked between where Jess was floating around in the air and me. The silence felt heavy and thick on my skin.

"Did you all break up?" Logan walked over and pulled her long, pink hair up in a ponytail.

"I don't know." I threw my hands up in the air, frustrated

that this was even happening in the first place. Did we break up? It felt like a fight, but there were more words to be said and I was confident that we could work it out if she would just talk to me about it. If we both had clear and calm minds, I was sure we could understand one another more and move past this.

"I just kinda asked that." Myla widened her eyes.

"How can you not know?" Bex joined our conversation and suddenly everyone was standing there, including Dani.

It wasn't my intention to have an audience, but these were her people. They knew her better than she probably knew herself. And they loved her. God, I did too, and all I wanted was to say that and for this to be joyful. Not the complete and literal opposite.

"You will have to ask Jess because I don't know what the fuck happened, but maybe she does." My mood was slowly deteriorating since I had walked in. I moved away from the group to the opposite corner where I put on my headphones and began my juggling warm up trying to pretend like this wasn't a giant fucking mess that was fissuring my heart into pieces that I wasn't sure I could pick up.

"You two need to figure this shit out, okay? Because I can't be managing your relationship while I also run this company and take care of all you assholes." Logan waved her hand around in a no nonsense type of way.

"You're her best friend! You talk to her!" I said, realizing how childish this all sounded. This was never meant to be bigger than me and Jess.

"Seriously, Ozzie?" Logan raised an eyebrow at me.

"She won't even look at me, let alone speak to me." Now I was starting to feel out of control. My emotions were like a giant swirling tornado, ready to consume whatever it needed to in order to feel better. Collateral damage be damned.

"Fine, you know what? I want to see the routine you have

for Genevieve's event. How about that? If you can't speak to each other. That's fine by me, but you signed up for this event and the money. And I will be damned if I let you all ruin it for yourself, so get on the damn hoop together," she commanded. I immediately regretted asking for Logan's involvement. Because she would get this shit solved for us, even if it was a painfully awkward process.

"Mother has spoken." Dani chuckled, and Myla held back a laugh.

"Jess!" Aven screamed and Jess furrowed her brows, looking around.

"Jess!" Myla added, flailing her arms, and she finally took one of her air pods out.

"Why are you yelling?" Jess said, tilting her head to the side.

"Logan wants to see the duo act you and Ozzie have been working on." Aven didn't even try to hide her big ass grin.

Jess's cheeks turned pink, and she gazed down. "Right now?"

This was not going to be good.

"Yes, right now!" Logan snapped, and I gritted my teeth, walking over to her.

"Why does it have to be right now?" Jess grumbled.

"Because I said so, and I'm in charge. I pay you and tell you what to do for your job," Logan said sweetly. "Is there a problem or something? Should I call a therapist to mitigate?" I swear to god Logan's eyes shone with mischief. This was bad. Very, *very* bad.

"No problem. No therapist either." Jess crossed her arms over her chest.

"Avoidance isn't cute, you know?" Logan purred, looking at both of us. I rolled my eyes and Jess looked down at the ground. "If you didn't want to get me involved, then you shouldn't have asked. But now you did so, do as I say."

"You know, the drama is kind of fun," Bex commented, looking around at us and smiling.

Scoffing, I marched over to Jess with my head held high and looked at her fully. She avoided my eyes and looked over to where Logan was strutting over to the stereo with all her power and purpose.

"I don't know what happened between you two, but you better figure it out," she snapped, getting her phone set up. This no nonsense *figure your shit out* Logan was kind of terrifying.

"Are you ready to talk, Jess?" I asked, looking her up and down, waiting for her answer. I wanted it to be a yes, but I knew it wouldn't be. Things were still too fresh and now the emotions had just gotten dialed to eleven. I just wanted to move past this as quickly as possible.

"Uh, not yet. Maybe we can just run the piece?" Jess asked quietly.

My eyes practically rolled out of my head. Walking over to the hoop, I got into my starting position without saying a word. Now I was the one whose emotions threatened to make this shit even worse than it already was.

"Roll the music, Logan." I motioned for Jess to come over and she pushed her shoulders back, her performer mask slipping into place.

"3... 2... 1..." she whispered as we walked the hoop around and mounted it in perfect synchronization. I tried not to think about her body being pressed to mine or my hands wrapped around her waist. Or the sweat sliding down her back and her muscles straining in her arms as we moved and danced in the hoop. Or how this could be the last time if things didn't get figured out.

At one point, we grabbed each other's necks and connected foreheads. She swallowed loudly and closed her eyes as we continued to move and brush past each other like we were in a tango. How was it possible to be so close physically but so far away emotionally?

The song ended, and we breathlessly dismounted the hoop and took a bow.

"That was actually really beautiful." Logan had tears slipping down her cheeks as the rest of the group clapped and hollered. The emotional wave that had knocked everyone around earlier seemed to dissipate and all that was left was a weird, hollow silence. It felt like it reached into my heart and squeezed, making it hard to breathe.

"Thanks," I said crisply and walked away from them back to my juggling corner and picked up all my shit, and headed out.

"Ozzie, you don't have to leave," Jess called out.

"Yeah, I do." I texted Trevor and asked him to meet me for a drink. I couldn't get the feeling of her skin out of my head, and I would lose my mind if I was near her in this state.

So, I left, hoping I could think about anything else with my best friends. Tequila and Trevor.

TWENTY-FOUR

JESS

Ozzie sat there with her slicked-back bright blonde hair, deftly applying the final touches of her lipstick. Logan lounged in a chair, glancing between the two of us occasionally. I felt like a complete asshat.

I hadn't talked to anyone about what had happened between me and Ozzie, including Ozzie herself. Even when Logan came over to console me, I had just been vague and sad as we binge watched trash t.v. It had now been over a week of this shit and the further we got away from it, the worse it seemed to be getting.

God, I just needed to fucking muscle-up here and talk to her. We had practiced for this huge event and Logan confirmed that it was up to par. Then Ozzie had reiterated that I could call her when I was ready to talk. And I had done nothing.

The whole studio was buzzing about it because there were no secrets, and I was pretty sure someone had pushed Ozzie into sharing some of the details. It wasn't like we were broken up, but we weren't exactly together, either. This terrible limbo had made my stomach hurt and heart ache for the past week, and I had only myself to blame. After our show, I wanted to talk. To clear the air. To explain that the idea of setting up roots made me nervous, but if I was going to find it with anyone, I was glad that it would be with Ozzie. I practiced what I wanted to say to myself at least fifty times and I was just hoping I could do it without being a total trash show.

"Call time is in thirty minutes for your duo opening act. Then a short break. After that you each will alternate fifteen minutes on and off so someone is always on stage," Logan prattled off the details from her itinerary. She seemed to be extra annoyed with both of us since this happened. Neither one of us was handling this very well right now, and Logan was clearly over it. As long as we did our jobs, though, she wouldn't be able to complain too much.

Tonight, we were both in dazzling leotards that reminded me of disco balls. There were cut outs throughout, but the leotard clung tight to my skin and my whole body was glittered out.

"Are you all so ready to dazzle the party goers?" Genevieve purred as she walked in, looking like the exuberant host she was. She was even more antagonizing now that the rest of my life was going up in a ball of flames.

Ozzie rolled her eyes, and I stifled a dry laugh.

"Oh, they're ready. If you wouldn't mind giving them a little privacy to warm up, we're right on schedule for your timeline, Genevieve," Logan purred back, blinking at her innocently like she hadn't just dismissed her from the space. Genevieve was on everyone's last fucking nerve.

"Well, it's so great that you two are performing as a couple since this charity is all about family and love," Genevieve bristled, and I avoided Ozzie's eye contact. Genevieve didn't need to know we were fighting; it was irrelevant. We could still show up and do our jobs for this event. Pretend to be in love. At least maybe Ozzie would be pretending. Mine would be real and painful.

After this, we could go home, and I wouldn't need to take any more events from Genevieve ever again with the money she was dolling out for this shit. Which was the thing that was getting me through this evening. After this, Genevieve would be out of my life and Ozzie and I could figure this out. I was sure of it.

"Thank you, Genevieve. It was kind of you to think of us." Ozzie smiled without teeth and tilted her head to the side.

"Right." Genevieve looked uneasy. Clearing her throat, she blew a kiss at me and stalked out of the room.

"Christ, she's irritating," Logan grumbled as she straightened her black dress and nodded at us.

"Start warming up and we go out in five. I'm going to go find myself a snack." She sauntered out of the room and the silence felt loud. We both got up and started doing jumping jacks and squats. Stretching into our legs, both breathing heavily as we moved through our individual warmups.

Ozzie barely looked at me and it nearly severed my heart in two. Had I fucked up so bad that there was no coming back from this? I hoped to god we could survive it. Because I didn't know if I could on my own.

Logan came back shortly with a small plate of food in her hand and stuffed the appetizers in her mouth.

"Damn if she doesn't know how to throw a good party with great food, though," Logan said with a full mouth.

"Chew your food before you choke," I teased, and Logan smiled at me, showing all the food in her mouth. Ozzie laughed, and I giggled, the tension in the room breaking for just a moment as our eyes connected and heat slid across my skin. My heart felt so loud in this quiet space, but then the moment was gone.

Shattered into a million little pieces, unable to be put back together again, so we continued in our silent warm up until it was time to walk out together. We had planned our entrance to be hand in hand as we walked in and our piece was basically a love story acted out by us on the hoop to a romantic song.

The announcer started our entrance and Ozzie's hand came in mine.

"We've got this," she said and squeezed my palm, making the knot in my stomach loosen just a little bit. It was the first supportive thing we had really said to one another in a week or so. We strutted in with the lights on us and our costumes created a kaleidoscope of colors on the audience. They were all seated at tables with lavish foods in front of them. We walked to the middle of the room where our hoop hung ready for us to hop on and move above everyone's head.

The song started, and we danced around the hoop to only meet in the middle and hook a leg on the apparatus together. The crowd oohed and aahed as we spun and clung to one another. After our embrace, Ozzie dropped from the center to below the bar where I caught her hand and foot to keep her from plummeting to the ground.

We played the part of star-crossed lovers on the lyra. Emotion poured from my heart like this was my apology. Every touch and contact was a sorry that I wished I could whisper out loud, but instead, my body tried to do the talking as we continued to dance in the air for claps and hollers.

Finally, the song was coming to an end, and we ended on the ground as the crowd roared. We bowed, and I snuck a smile at Ozzie. Her strong body glistened in the spotlight; her hair was sticking up in funny places, but she smiled happily at the audience around us and then me. I wondered what this felt like for her. Was it her way of saying she still cared?

We interlocked fingers once more and walked out breathing heavily and the announcer had everyone clap again. Genevieve stood off to the side with a sour look on her face, even though this whole fucking thing had been her goddamn idea.

"I honestly want to stick my tongue out at her, but I think that might be childish," Ozzie said through her full smile, her lips barely moving. I whipped my head and chuckled.

"I would love to see the look on her face." I smiled back at her. We slid back into our easy teasing cadence. And god, it felt good.

"That was amazing, you two. Truly brought me to tears." Logan handed us each water as we walked back to the room we got ready in.

"Jess, I have you up first. You start in fifteen minutes, okay? Then Ozzie will swap out or if you get tired before that, just give me a little signal, as I'll be around." Logan left to go get us some food, and we both stood there with so much hanging in the air.

"Ozzie, I..." I started, and Ozzie shook her head.

"Let's get through tonight and then we can talk, okay?" She looked hopeful and I would be lying if I said I didn't feel the same.

"Okay," I whispered and Ozzie pulled me in for a full body hug where all parts of our exposed skin connected and touched with the other. I wanted to sigh and hide in that embrace.

"Oh, sorry, I didn't mean to interrupt." Genevieve's high shrill pierced my ears, and I practically snarled at her. Ozzie jumped back, and the moment broke again. What was with my ex killing my dreams tonight?

"It's fine, Genevieve." Ozzie's voice sounded tired as she went to smooth down the edges of her hair.

"Well, the crowd loved it! You two looked very enamored with one another. Thank you for doing this." She beamed like we were doing her a favor.

"Well, thanks for paying us," I said, as uncouth as I could

manage, and her smile only faltered a little despite her best efforts.

"We love supporting local queer artists. Hopefully, we can all work together in the future even more. Maybe even hang out outside of business. I would love for you to meet my new girlfriend." Genevieve's eyes blazed into mine and I didn't have the fight in me anymore to be pleasant. Why was she like this? It was like a weird game of chess, except she made up the rules and controlled all the players.

"Did you tell your new girlfriend that you text me almost every day? Maybe you should check in with what boundaries are okay with people Gen before you start adding people to your fucking roster," I snapped and stomped out of the room, looking for Logan.

The shock on Genevieve's face was enough to know that I should have kept a lid on my emotions, but I didn't care. I was done with her, and I was going to go out there and do my piece and then block her fucking number. This was the last time I wanted to see her face.

"Jesus, Jess, why are you stomping to your spot?" Logan looked at me funny and handed me some food that I tore into, like a ravenous tiger.

"Genevieve is pissing me off. You may have to do damage control because I lashed out."

Logan narrowed her eyes. "I'm on it. You okay to go out with this much emotional turmoil?" Logan gave me that look that said, *don't let your emotions get the best of you.*

I breathed in and out a few times and closed my eyes. "Yes, I won't throw anything too tricky. Just the ambient shapes. No hard splits, spins, or drops tonight. I got this."

"Don't get hurt out there or I will be pissed. Okay?" She lifted her eyebrow at me.

"Yes, ma'am." I saluted her, and she rolled her eyes, heading back to the room where I had left a shocked and fuming Genevieve with an unsuspecting Ozzie. Ugh, that probably wasn't my best move. Hopefully, she would forgive me.

All I had to do was get through the rest of this set unscathed. Then Ozzie and I could finally talk, and I could tell her what a dumb idiot I was and how I felt. I only hoped she felt the same way in return.

TWENTY-FIVE
OZZIE

"Last set, Ozzie." Logan gave me a squeeze, and I nodded as I headed to switch out with Jess. We each had several solo acts after our partner piece. I had taken the last shift of the night.

Jess was smiling and twirling around on the hoop in graceful, long movements, and I swallowed, trying not to think about how much I fucking loved her. Things weren't exactly great, but I felt like maybe she was finally in a place to talk about what was going on. Walls had been built up between us. We had barely said two words to each other since our fight. But it seemed like she was ready to talk, and I was ready to do a better job of listening and understanding.

"Ozzie! That was so great. You and Jess are just such an attractive couple." Genevieve had popped up out of nowhere through the throngs of people. Jesus, she was pesky.

"Thank you, Genevieve." I wanted to talk to her as much as I wanted to step on a Lego especially after Jess had laid into her earlier.

"I mean, Jess is sort of a hard person to be with, so kudos to you for putting up with her." Genevieve twirled a finger in her hair and smiled innocently at me. My mouth dropped open. She truly had no limit to the bullshit she would spin around Jess. Did she think that she would find a friend in me by trashing the person I was dating? What was wrong with this woman?

"Seriously?" My hands clenched at my side, and I tried not to lose my shit right then and there on her. How fucking dare she act like she can talk about Jess right now?

"Yeah, she is such a tough girlfriend, you know?"

I looked at her in fuming silence, clamping my mouth shut. This was not a time to cause a scene. I had one set left to finish and then we would go. We would take our money and leave. Hopefully, that meant that I would never have to see Genevieve's stupid face ever again. Jess and I would make up, and this whole thing would be behind us.

"Like she is such a weird commitment-phobe in relationships. But kind of suspicious that she is so committed to Logan and the circus. Your partner should be more important than your friends, obviously. Her circus stuff always got in the way. I guess she did need someone like you to be with her who just gets this life, because I just don't understand why everyone is so obsessed."

Clearly, she misread my bubbling, silent rage as an invitation to keep going because it seemed like she was just getting started.

"I could never date a performer who is too busy for me. My girlfriend now just dotes on me and acts like I'm her whole world. Thank god Jess and I broke up, otherwise I would have never met her." She flipped her hair like she wasn't setting a land mine of anger off in my body.

"Get Jess's name out of your mouth, Genevieve," I snapped, cutting her off.

That's it. I didn't fucking care about this job anymore. Logan was great at picking up the pieces and so help me god if

I had to stand here one more minute and listen to the vile disdain dripping from her lips, I would punch her in the face.

"Excuse me?" she gasped.

Jess's eyes zeroed in on us and she wrinkled her brows from where she continued to perform on the hoop. Good god, I hadn't wanted a scene, but goddamnit, I would give one to Genevieve.

"Stop talking about her like that and for god's sake stop texting her. Thank you for hiring us for this event, but you've got to get the fuck out of her life." I thought I heard an audible gasp from Jess on the hoop, but maybe I had imagined it.

"Who are you to talk to me like that?" Genevieve's eyes widened, and she looked around as if someone would come and rescue her.

"How dare *you* talk about Jess like that! Did you even care about her? Because I can't imagine talking about someone like that who was once my girlfriend," I hissed. I was trying to keep my voice down, but what I really wanted to do was scream in her face. Genevieve's audacity seemed to have no bounds, and I was sick and fucking tired of her bullshit.

"You cannot treat me this way. I paid for you to be here, and you are working for me today," she practically spat at me.

"And that doesn't mean I deserve this bullshit. Don't fucking hire me again, then." My voice was getting higher and louder by the second. Soon we would have a full out brawl if she didn't step the fuck down.

"The check has already been cashed." Logan appeared out of nowhere and linked her arm in mine. "Additionally, I already requested that we work with one of your other team members for future events, since they seemed to have more knowledge and understanding of our needs. So you can go ahead and leave Jess and Ozzie alone for the rest of the evening," Logan said, her voice dripping with venom. She plastered on the most devious of smiles. The message was clear: *back the fuck up.*

"Fuck you guys," Genevieve hissed, looking between the two of us.

"Careful, I would hate for your boss to know that's how you conduct yourself at these expensive soirées," Logan crooned as Genevieve stomped off.

"What a bitch," I said as I walked toward the stage.

"Ozzie, we can cut the set. You know bad things can happen when your head isn't on the hoop." Logan looked at me seriously.

"Logan, I'm fine. I could do this in my sleep," I said, wanting to just do my job and then be done.

"Are you sure?" Logan looked at me with a hard stare.

"Absolutely. Jess's probably getting tired. Let me go relieve her." I appreciated Logan's concern, but it was fine. I was fine. Genevieve hadn't gotten under my skin that much.

Logan nodded, her expression still reading unsure, and I headed over to where Jess gracefully dismounted, and took my turn. Logan was always harping on safety, but I was trained for this. A dumb little argument where I wanted to throw hands wasn't enough to knock me off my performance game.

My skin still tingled from my verbal spar with Genevieve, but I would let it fuel me for an excellent last set. The fire in my veins would make me more confident and daring, not careless. I saw Logan talk to Jess, and she pointed to where we had stood and argued. I knew she had heard some of it, but probably not everything. I couldn't even imagine what it must have been like to be in a relationship with Genevieve. Just a working relationship with her was a nightmare. That woman was beyond infuriating. We all had baggage, and it didn't give you permission to shit on your ex about it.

Breathing deeply, I plastered a smile on my face and tried to use the anger in my body to find shapes that stunned the crowd. I continued to spin and twirl around the hoop. The more I moved, the bigger my emotions got.

I was so sick and fucking tired of people like Genevieve butting into people's lives. That was exactly how it had been at my old studio. Everyone had stuck their nose in everyone else's business.

I mean, Sean had made it his business to discredit me and tell everyone about it, but that didn't make it okay. My head was spinning at how much frustration seemed to go through me between Genevieve and my own hang ups. Usually, movement helped me dispel it, but it felt like it was consuming me, and I just wanted to scream.

Genevieve had just made me so fucking furious. I clenched my teeth and continued to move through my routine. Out of the corner of my eye, I saw her looking at me with her hateful eyes and I had half a mind to flip her off. Not that I needed any more reason to blow this situation up, but if we were already going to avoid working with her in the future, maybe it wouldn't hurt?

Instead of telling her to fuck right off, I decided to throw my hardest tricks to show her I was unbothered by her constant nagging and ripping. It was the more mature way of getting my message across.

That being a performer was amazing and wonderful. That performance artists could have love lives that were vibrant and strong with other people, and that our community was beautiful and commitment to our community was magical.

At least in my head, that's what I was saying as I threw my body into my art. How dare she act like this wasn't important to Jess? That our creativity and passion weren't inexplicably drawn from who we were in our most vulnerable forms.

Genevieve could go fuck herself.

That was my last thought as I flung myself into a trick. An audible pop pierced my ears and then searing pain shot through my shoulder as I gasped and tried to make a graceful descent on the ground.

My body flopped down in an uncharacteristic way, and I looked to where my shoulder seemed to be hanging way too low on my body.

What the fuck?

My brain scrambled as I tried to understand what happened. I took a clumsy bow that was barely noticed by any of the partygoers. They were all absorbed in their cups and were fully pulled elsewhere.

Maybe my arm wasn't that bad. Maybe this was all a bad dream. The pain seemed to come in waves of agony as nausea threatened to overtake me.

"Ozzie." I could hear Logan's voice weirdly above the rest of the murmuring crowd and music. Stars filled my vision as I stumbled once more and looked at my right arm again. My shoulder was definitely not in the right place anymore. This was bad. This was very, very bad.

"Fuck." My balance was off as I tripped looking for a familiar face. My head swam and hot pain laced along my side.

No, no, no, no.

"Ozzie!" Jess called out as I lurched forward and hit the ground with my knees. Darkness swallowed me whole as Jess's voice echoed in my head.

Twenty-Six
Jess

"Fuck!" I spat out as I watched Ozzie get wheeled away on the gurney. Logan stood next to me with her arms crossed, her face giving off *I told you so,* energy at about one thousand percent.

We had tried to be as discreet as possible, dragging Ozzie's body carefully to our prep room. Truthfully, not many of the guests gave us a second look as they were all too drunk and absorbed in their own shit to notice us carrying a limp Ozzie through the crowd. I couldn't decide if that was a bad or good thing. Right now, I just wanted Ozzie to be safe and healthy.

Her mumbles and groans were barely audible over the pounding music. Her shoulder was unquestionably dislocated from the looks of it. She was getting erratic towards the end of her set, moving aggressively like she was working out her feelings.

An artistic choice that did her no fucking favors.

"Fucking hell, I knew she shouldn't have gone up there. I should have stopped her." Logan paced around, biting her lip. I had called Bex and Aven to come get the rest of the stuff for the gig as we followed Ozzie to the hospital.

Thankfully, Genevieve had made herself scarce after Ozzie's set and hadn't been around when she collapsed. The other members on her team had moved into a flurry until Logan told them we would handle it and that Ozzie would be fine once her shoulder got put back in place.

Logan had tried to play it off as cool and collected, but now she was losing her shit. Her carefully crafted boss bitch attitude was slipping now that we were at the hospital.

"It's not your fault, Logan," I said even though I knew it wouldn't help her own guilt because it sure as shit wasn't helping mine.

"I know it's not my fault, but I should have checked her ass after the smack down her and Genevieve had." She pulled at her hair and closed her eyes, her chest rising and falling quickly.

Logan had already told me about the details of the conversation that happened between Genevieve and her. I heard snippets while I was performing, but most of it was me inferring from body language what the hell was going on and knowing that it could not have been good.

"It's partly my fault for having such an annoying ex," I grumbled, and Logan forced a laugh.

"It looked just dislocated, right? Ozzie's hypermobility makes her even more at risk of dislocations. Shit," Logan muttered as we got settled in the hospital waiting room.

"This is her livelihood, and it all got fucked up in one night because of Genevieve riling her up." Shame and guilt riddled me the longer we sat, both of us not doing a great job of staying calm now that we had a moment to think.

"Ozzie's head hasn't been in it since you two have been bickering, you know," Logan said. "I'm not blaming you, just stating that as a fact in our reality right now."

"I know, I was scared. And now she may not be able to perform because of me." I swiped at the tears on my cheeks.

Tonight was supposed to be the night we walked away with a huge chunk of money and then made up with one another and lived happily ever after.

"Don't be ridiculous. She will perform again. Plus, she can juggle one handed and if it's dislocated, they will put it back and she will do PT. She can and will perform again. It will just take time. The pain will fucking suck. The rehab will be brutal, but Ozzie can do this," Logan said quietly, not sure if she was convincing me or herself. "It's not the first dislocation I've seen, and it certainly won't be the last." Logan sighed, rubbing her temples.

Hours started to creep by, and we hadn't heard anything. When I asked if we could go back and see her, they refused because we weren't family.

"But I'm dating her," I pleaded.

"Sorry, unless you're married, there's nothing we can do until she wakes up." The nurse gave me an empathetic look, and I groaned.

I had texted Trevor and asked about looping in her family, but he had said they were too far away to do anything. Realistically, she would update them when she was awake. No need to worry them in the middle of the night. He was on his way as Logan and I passed the time in the waiting room.

"Did you all ever make up, then?"

I tapped my foot restlessly. "Not necessarily. We hadn't really hashed things out yet. I just got overwhelmed with the idea of Ozzie staying here for me."

"Why? That's a normal thing to do, Jess," Logan whispered.

"I know."

"People decide all the time they like a place and its people and then stay there. Not that I want you two to break up, but you both will survive if you don't last." Logan looked at me, her expression serious.

She would know. She had been through worse when she divorced from her high school sweetheart. But I didn't know if I would survive this. If I could live through seeing Ozzie every day and not being with her and not feeling the touch of her skin or hearing her laugh.

"It just felt like a huge commitment at the moment. Now it feels fucking stupid." I wrapped my arms around my torso and closed my eyes.

"I know it probably was surprising, but it's also not all about you. Ozzie can make decisions about how she wants to live her life and take into account whatever she needs to make that choice." Logan squeezed my arm.

"You're right. I know. I jumped the gun when I freaked out," I mumbled. I couldn't help the way I felt, even though logically I knew it wasn't the mountain that I had made it out to be.

"Hey, Jess. Logan." Trevor walked in with gas station coffee in hand. "This is the best I could get at this time of night." He shrugged and smiled softly.

"It has to be better than the coffee here, so I'll take it." Logan snatched it and inhaled deeply.

"How's she doing?" Trevor sat down next to me as I took a scorching sip from my cup.

"I don't know. They won't let us see her until she wakes up. They said she had passed out from pain probably or her body going into shock. Hopefully she wakes up soon," I said, wanting her to just be alright.

"I know you two are at odds right now, but she really does care for you, Jess. She isn't always great at articulating her feelings and I get the feeling that sometimes you aren't too. Go do the queer thing and make up already," Trevor teased, and I scoffed.

"I know," I grumbled.

I stood up and paced around the waiting room as Logan and Trevor chatted.

What if I would have never had the opportunity to tell Ozzie how I really felt? How fucking shitty of me after everything we've been through together that I couldn't get the words out of my face to say how I fucking felt.

"Jess! She's awake!" Trevor hollered at me, and my heart stuttered. I wasn't ready. I needed to re-practice what I was going to say first. I couldn't just wing it, now that so much more had happened. What if I said the wrong thing and that sent her careening further away from me? She just dislocated her shoulder because my ex had fucking butted into our business. Oh my god, this really was all my fault.

"Okay, you should go first," I swallowed loudly, and he tilted his head and stared into my soul.

"Are you sure about that?" Trevor asked, looking a little confused.

"Yeah, I just need some air." I watched as Trevor walked down the hallway with the nurse and tried to calm the nerves in my belly.

"Don't be a coward, Jess. Fight for what you want." Logan stood up and shook her head at me like she was disappointed.

"Don't do that to me," I pleaded.

"Don't do it to yourself! Go in there and tell her how you feel. You're better than this. Don't lose your nerve now!" Logan placed her hands on her hips.

"What if she doesn't feel the same way?" The anxiety plowed into me, scraping against my throat and ripping into my heart.

"And what if she does?" Logan shot back.

"Logan, I'm scared," I whispered. My stomach suddenly twisted up with the sudden urge to throw up.

"Love is scary, Jess. But it's worth it." Logan was practically begging me to do the right thing.

"Is it though?" My moment was now and I couldn't do it. Ozzie was in here because of me. Why would she want to see the person who was responsible for all this?

"Yes"—she dragged her hand through her hair—"I know better than anyone that love can rip you to fucking shreds, but this kind of love. The kind of love that you could have with Ozzie. It's fucking worth it."

Tears started to fall, and I didn't know why. I couldn't go in there like this. Not right now. I was too raw and vulnerable. The words wouldn't come out right and after all this time and after everything that had happened, I didn't know if I could survive Ozzie turning me down. Surely she would understand that I needed a little more time? She would appreciate some more space because I was partly to blame for this horrific accident, right?

"Maybe I should wait until she has rested some..." I found myself stepping back towards the exit as Logan scowled at me. I knew this was an excuse. Running away was easy. Staying was the hard part.

"Don't walk out of here, Jess. You're just digging a bigger fucking hole. You're worried you might be rejected and you're a self-fulfilling prophecy if I ever did see one. Leaving now might seal the fate that you're so afraid of! Don't run away!" Logan called after me, and I didn't know what to do or say as I took off through the hospital doors, taking big gulps of air. But it was too late. Her words stung even though they were the truth.

Disappointed with myself, I called an Uber and wallowed all the way home wondering what the hell I was going to do to clean up this fucking mess.

TWENTY-SEVEN
OZZIE

"Wow, you look like shit." Trevor sat on my hospital bed, and I rolled my eyes.

"Thank you for that you, asshole," I groused. Logan slinked in and looked at me sympathetically.

"Ozzie, I'm so..." she started, and I held up my hand.

"If you act like this is your fault, I will throw this water in your face." I would do it too. She had tried to warn me and I was too stubborn to listen. I wouldn't be making that mistake again, as this one was going to be a costly bitch to get through.

Her mouth dropped open in an O and then it bled into a smile.

"It wasn't your fault. I should have listened to you." That was the simple truth. If I had just gotten out of my head, I would have realized that too. But lingering in the past wouldn't help. All I could do was learn from it and move on, hoping I didn't fucking wreck myself again in the process.

"Yes, I love being right." The corners of her mouth tipped up and the tension eased from her brow.

"Instead, I let my pride get in the way and acted like an

idiot, putting my body at risk. Even though I would like to put at least a little bit of the blame on Genevieve, but as a whole, I take responsibility." I looked down at my shoulder, which is now in a sling.

Right now, I couldn't feel much pain at all since I was hopped up on pain meds. This shoulder had been dislocated before and was prone to getting spicy with me in training whenever I pushed it too far. Thank god it wasn't the rotator cuff because I had that surgery on the other arm and that was a real bitch to heal from.

God, I was usually so fucking careful to keep my body in safe tricks because of my hypermobility, and it just took one dumb bitch with a bone to pick to get me off my game and hurt myself. Those tricks would have been fine if I was paying closer attention, but tonight my mind was completely else-where, and these were, unfortunately, the consequences.

"We can all collectively put some blame on Genevieve." Trevor crossed his arms and scowled.

"Too bad she won't be footing the hospital bill," I complained.

"Cirque Callisto will help take care of that. Don't worry about it, Oz. However, next time when I suggest taking a break and clearing your head, you will take it. Do you under-stand?" Logan put her hands on her hips like she meant busi-ness. She was back to head bitch in charge mode and it made me feel a little better, like things were sort of normal.

"Yes ma'am," I replied, and Trevor giggled.

"I haven't told your family. I thought you would want to text them about, you know, you breaking things or dislocating things. Since it isn't new to them, I figured you would want to handle it." Trevor looked over at where my phone was sitting on the table next to the bed I was in.

"Yeah, that can wait, honestly. They'll be fine." They knew

I could take care of myself and that I would do what I needed to do to heal and recover appropriately.

A nurse came in and looked at the two of them with their scowling faces and cleared her throat. "Ozzie, you're cleared to leave. Here are your follow-up instructions for PT and to make a follow up appointment with your regular doctor."

"Thank you." I nodded as I swung my legs over and stood up.

"How do you feel right now?" Logan asked.

"Right now, with the pain medication coursing through my veins. Like a million bucks!" I joked.

"Right, well, that won't last forever. Did they call in another prescription for the medication? Let me see your follow up stuff," Trevor said, snatching the follow up directions out of my hand and reading through them like the overprotective best friend he was.

"Um, did Jess not come?" My heart thudded in my chest. I knew she saw me, and I was pretty sure she had called my name.

Did she really not care at all? We had plans to talk as well. The least she could do was show up and at least see how I was doing.

"She did. But she left..." Logan trailed off.

"She left?" I asked, baffled. Why the fuck did she just leave without saying a fucking thing?

"Yeah, like the spineless coward she is." Logan's eyes narrowed, and she pursed her lips.

"Oh, okay." I tried not to let that crush my chest. Maybe we were done with one another if she couldn't even bear to face me.

"She cares. Jess is sadly stuck in her own way and unfortunately, easily overwhelmed with feelings. I promise you, at some point she will talk to you... I just don't know when that is. The guilt was heavy for her and you know how she gets in her own head about things." Logan's features softened.

"Okay, if you say so." I felt like my heart was broken all over again. I had been waiting for her to come to me so she could tell me how she was feeling. I wasn't the one who had lost my shit over the possibility of me buying a house here.

"Her commitment phobia reared its ugly head and then so did her relationship insecurities. She *will* talk. I promise. Don't give up yet, Oz. You two have just gotten started." Logan patted my uninjured arm.

I choked back a sob and swiped at my face.

"Let's take this party back to the house," Trevor said, ever so gently.

"Text me with what your regular doctor says, Oz. Don't worry about money and performing and shit. We'll take care of you, okay?" Logan gave me a little side hug and headed out with us.

Walking out of the hospital, I wondered what my fate would be because right now it felt like my body was being broken all over again. Maybe this was for the best. Maybe I would wake up tomorrow and be okay with the way things were. Or maybe I would grieve something that never really was.

———

My follow up happened shortly after I left the hospital. I was put on bedrest for the next week or so, and then I could gradually add movement, like walking around with my sling. The pain in my arm was now dull and throbbing thanks to regular Advil coursing through my veins. However, training was to be put on hold at least for another month. I would go back in a few weeks to get evaluated. They seemed optimistic about my recovery, which was great. There should be no reason I wouldn't be back juggling and circusing in no time.

That news should have brought me lots of joy, instead my heart ached. I still hadn't heard from Jess, and I tried not to let the ache in my heart get me down. Logan, Aven, Myla, Dani and even Bex had all come to visit. They brought food and shared the latest drama. Sometimes they weirdly handed me things from Jess like flowers or my favorite snacks, but she never came of her own volition. I didn't understand. Why didn't she just come by?

I was tired of being angry about it, instead I was just sad. I'd been avoiding the studio as well. I mean, I couldn't train, and I didn't want to face Jess randomly. She needed to make her intentions clear, that she wanted to fix what she broke. We were on her schedule, not mine.

Logan told me to come back when I was ready and hopefully in the next few weeks, I would be approved for gentle physical therapy so I could start to get my life back on track. Laying around and healing was hard enough without my thoughts and feelings running wild trying to figure out what to do about Jess and I's relationship.

Currently, I was holed up in my room trying to decide if Jess and I had broken up without actually making it final. Maybe I should start the journey of moving on since she had practically ghosted me. My phone dinged, and I looked at it and nearly dropped it.

> **Jess: Hey, I know I'm a piece of shit for taking so long. I needed to sort some things out and go to therapy a few times. Logan said you're healing nicely and that your shoulder isn't bothering you too much. I'm sorry that I haven't been there to help you**

through it. I've been thinking about
you a lot. And I'm ready to talk
whenever you are, so just let me know
when you're available.

I reread the message at least three times.

"Are you fucking kidding me?" I snarled and wanted to throw my phone across the room, my anger flaring up.

"What's happening?" Trevor ran in with a kitchen knife like he was ready to fight someone.

"Put the knife down and read this bullshit." He snatched it from me as his eyes darted side to side, taking in Jess's words.

"Well, it's not the most eloquent, and it certainly is very late, but it is an effort. Better than sending little gifts through her friends. What are you going to do about it?"

"I thought I was done being angry, but I'm pissed again. Why has she waited so long?! And why the fuck did she run away at the hospital? Can you believe this shit?" If I didn't love her so much, I would give her a piece of my mind and tell her to fuck off. But I was so mad because I cared so much.

What a fucking hard juxtaposition.

"Ozzie, you have every right to be mad. But ask yourself what you want. Do you want to hold on to anger and hurt or hear Jess out and maybe figure things out?" Trevor handed me back the phone and picked up the knife in a non-threatening way.

"I want answers and ideally, I want her," I confessed. It was true. What I really wanted was for us to figure this out. I didn't want to run away screaming at the first sign of a fight. We could do better than that. *I* could do better than that. Relationships were hard sometimes, but I knew if we could get past this, we could get through anything.

"So, text her back and tell her you're ready to talk." Trevor started to walk away.

"What were you going to do with that knife?" I snickered.

"Honestly, I don't know, but I felt better with it." He cradled it in his hands and walked out. Sighing, I replied.

Me: I'm ready to talk now. When and where do you want to meet up?

Her three dots popped up almost instantly.

Jess: Tomorrow? The studio at 2pm?

Me: Sounds great.

It was a date.

TWENTY-EIGHT

JESS

I was regretting my decision to have us meet at the studio. Maybe I should have had her come to my house instead? It just felt like the studio was a neutral spot. One of our places felt oddly intimate and might feel aggressive if this conversation were to go south.

Hell, I had really fucked it up.

My past relationship trauma had clouded my judgment and instead of talking about it like a normal person, I ran. My fight or flight took over, and I just got the fuck out. I mean, would Ozzie even be able to forgive me after leaving her at the hospital? What kind of asshole does that? I would beg on my knees if that was what it took to get her back. I was ready to do whatever it took to fix this.

Breathing deeply, I tried to get it together. I had rehearsed what I was going to say and hoped that it wouldn't come to intense groveling, but I would do it if I had to. Ozzie was one of the best things to happen to me in a long time.

I wanted what we had. The love between us was special. Unlike anything else I had ever experienced with anyone else. But I needed to tell her that and convince her that I wasn't a flight risk for the future. I could have tough conversations and be a dedicated partner if she would let me.

But if I blew it forever, then I would have to deal with the consequences of watching her move on and find someone else. The thought made me sick to my stomach of her touching or kissing someone else. My head started to feel fuzzy as an image of Ozzie kissing a faceless person popped into my head.

Stop it, Jess.

This is not helpful to this conversation. You need to be calm, collected, and kind. Not inducing a jealous haze after a made-up scenario in your head.

Tapping my toe, I paced the space, waiting for her to come in.

Maybe she wouldn't show? I checked my watch for the hundredth time and chewed on my lip.

Fuck. I was about to send her a text when the front door opened and there she was.

My heart clenched at the sight of her. She wore a cropped tank and high-waisted biker shorts. Her hair looked a little messy, with little blonde spikes sticking out at random angles.

My god, she was a work of art. Her athleticism was apparent even as she stood tall and locked me in her gaze. A sling hung on her shoulder and cradled her arm to her torso. I nearly choked on a sob at the sight of it. Why had I waited so long?

"Hi Jess." Her face gave nothing away as she spoke softly, like I would run off again. Like she was scared that I would flee from this conversation, too.

It wasn't unwarranted considering I dragged my feet for weeks to just get to the point of being able to look her in the face again.

"Hi Ozzie." Tears threatened to slip down my cheeks at the sight of her. "How's um... your shoulder?" I swiped at my eyes. That was a dumb thing to say, obviously not great.

She tilted her head as she took in the movement. "It hurts like a bitch sometimes and then it's fine other times. Not the worst I've been through, but not great. I can start physical therapy soon and eventually I will be back in the air and juggling with two hands again."

"I'm so sorry..." I whispered, still stuck in the same spot I was in when she walked in. Ozzie took a few steps forward.

"Don't do that," she commanded.

"Do what?"

"Act like this injury is your fault." She waved at her arm.

"But it is. Genevieve would have never been on your ass if it hadn't been for me!" I threw my hands up in the air and finally could move my feet as I paced around.

"Genevieve is her own person, and I should have been more careful." Ozzie ran her hand through her hair.

"Don't you do that!" I called back to her.

"Do what?" Ozzie furrowed her dark brows.

"Try to make me feel better about this whole situation! When we know that, I'm the one who needs to take responsibility here. I ghosted you for weeks because I couldn't have an adult fucking conversation and then my weirdo ex pissed you off enough that you had a career altering injury!" My voice pitched high, and I was breathing hard.

"Jess..."

"No Ozzie. Don't try to placate me. I need to say this. I'm sorry."

Ozzie's eyes looked watery.

"I'm sorry for freaking out and not being able to handle you being here permanently when, in reality, I'm terrified. I'm scared of losing you and messing shit up like I did anyways. I'm scared of how much I want this, and you and us. I'm scared of hurting you even if it is the last possible thing I want to do..." I chewed on my lip.

"I'm sorry for not telling you sooner that commitment is

hard for me and that I want you to be here despite me acting like I don't. I'm sorry for having an ex who can't leave me the fuck alone and I'm sorry for not telling you sooner that I love you and I don't want to do this with anyone else." I choked on the last few words and looked at Ozzie, who had a small smile on her face.

"Are you done, Jess?" She asked as tears poured down my face. Her own features softening.

"I'm just so sorry for running away at the hospital and not being able to get this out of my face faster. I know I don't deserve your forgiveness, but I want it. I want you. And I will do whatever it takes to prove it to you again and again." Could she see how much I meant it? How fucking ready I was to fall at her feet and do whatever she needed from me to prove that I was in this for the long haul? That I wanted to be together despite my mistakes.

Ozzie raised her brows and her eyes widened.

"And I promise from now on I won't run away, but I'll tell you what's going on in my head and we can work it out together. That is, if you take me back..." I trailed off.

"Is there anything else you want to say?" Ozzie asked gently.

My bottom lip trembled. "No. Will you say something now?"

"No," Ozzie said and strode forward, her legs eating up the space in between us as she smashed her lips to mine. I gasped as her tongue dove in with a punishing force as I let her hand tangle in my hair. Was this really happening right now?

My hands landed on her hips, being mindful of her arm as we both kissed like we were starved for one another. All lips, teeth, and tongue as we said all the unspoken things between us these last few weeks and I let her take control to show me exactly how she felt.

Ozzie pulled away aggressively, leaving my head spinning

and my cheeks still wet from my tears. She wiped them away with her fingertips.

"Does this mean you forgive me?" I asked, looking into her eyes.

"Yes. I forgive you. I was really fucking pissed at you when I got your text. Jess, you waited too damn long to have this conversation!" Ozzie practically scolded me and I deserved it.

"I know." I hung my head, but Ozzie's fingers grabbed under my chin and pulled my eyes to her.

"But my love for you is bigger than my frustration." She smiled at me as I grinned stupidly.

"Your love?"

"Yes, Jess. I love you. I love how creative you are and your loyalty to your friends. I love your sense of humor and the way you take pride in your work. I love when you get snarky and how your hair looks right after we have sex. I love you even when I'm pissed off at you. I love being with you and performing with you.. And I just love you like I've never loved anyone else." Ozzie reached down and linked our fingertips together.

My stomach was fluttering and my heart threatened to beat out of my chest as I brought her knuckles gently to my mouth and kissed one at a time. "I love how weird and clumsy you are sometimes." *Kiss.* "And I love how confident and authentic you are." *Kiss.* "And how passionate you are about community and art." *Kiss.* "And I love how you fight for what you believe in." *Kiss.* "And... I just really." *Kiss.* "Love." *Kiss.* "You." *Kiss.* "Ozzie." *Kiss.*

Tears started to fall from Ozzie's deep navy eyes and I pulled her in for a gentle kiss. A brush of our love across one another's skin.

"I'm still going to look at buying a house, because I want to be here. But that doesn't change anything about what I'm asking for from you, you know that, right?" Ozzie said carefully, like the words might send me spiraling again.

"I know. I want you to be here, Ozzie. I want us to be committed to one another here."

"And I also want Genevieve to leave you the fuck alone." Ozzie squeezed my fingertips and smirked.

"Don't worry, I'll handle her." I stood up a little taller and felt like a weight had been lifted off my shoulders.

"Since you didn't come and visit me at the hospital, I feel like you owe me some extra love," Ozzie teased.

"Oh yeah, and what does that mean?" Giggling, I placed another kiss on her soft lips.

"Well, I'm not supposed to lift my arm above shoulder height, so I'll probably need some help with a shower." Ozzie's eyes crinkled, and I fought the urge to shove her playfully.

"Fine, it's the least I could do since I haven't been there the last few weeks. I want to be there for all the other things. For whatever life throws at us in the future, I want to be by your side." I would no longer let my own head trash rule my relationship. This was scary and hard and worth it because Ozzie was worth it.

"And to save water for the environment, you should probably just also take a shower with me. I would hate for you to ruin your clothes, or anything else so better just take it all off you know?" Ozzie dragged her fingers down my arm, leaving goosebumps along the way.

"Ozzie, are you just trying to get me naked and wet for your own pleasure?" Gasping, I fanned myself with my hand.

"That's exactly what I'm trying to do."

"I'll allow it on one condition."

"I don't think you should be making demands here, Jess..." Ozzie teased.

"You'll like this one, I promise."

"Okay, let's hear it," she sighed, raising one brow.

"You have to say I love you at least a hundred more times," I giggled.

"I'll even spell it with my tongue on your skin." Ozzie whispered in my ear, and I blushed.

"Ozzie!"

"I love you, Jess." She beamed widely.

"I love you too, Oz."

"Now take me home and fucking show me," she hissed.

"Yes, ma'am." We left the studio and got into her car. I would spend the rest of my life showing her exactly how much she meant to me until the only name that was on her tongue was mine for the rest of our lives.

Epilogue: One year later...
Ozzie

"Remember how this house sent you into a tailspin at just the mere thought of it?" I teased as Jess and I sat down on the couch, snuggling into one another. We had been through a lot this past year, but like anything else, we made it work and we were still here figuring it out together. It was hard to even conjure up the remains of the anger I had felt at the time. It had been difficult for both of us, but we made it through.

"Remember how you fought with my ex and ended up being so caught up in it that you dislocated your shoulder?" Jess replied in a sugary tone. She was lucky we were at a point where we could joke about it.

"Okay, first of all..." I started, but she shut me up with a kiss. Her mouth ignited a heat deep in my core that could only be fed by Jess's touch. God, I loved this woman. Even though our path hadn't been perfect, it had been ours. Hopefully, there would be no more exes, dislocations or any other hospital visits in our near future, as I think we could both use a break from the intensity of it all.

"But now I'm as good as new." I grinned, pulling away

from her. Many months of rehab and physical therapy and taking extra care of myself had allowed me to go back to what I loved in no time.

"Logan would have been really pissed at Genevieve if your shoulder didn't make a full recovery," Jess said, her face scrunching up.

"It wasn't really anyone's fault per se, just a collaborative effort of me, you and Genevieve," I teased. We intertwined our fingers together and her hand felt so right in mine.

"I think that's a fair assessment," she cackled, throwing her head back. "But now you're stronger and more focused than ever. You're great at doing your overall physical therapy to keep your whole body healthy and happy."

"Well, I can think of another reason I'm so happy," I purred. Things had settled into a comfortable rhythm between us and I couldn't be happier.

"Fuck, I love you." Jess pulled her hand away and then straddled my lap, my hands easily landing on her hips.

"I love you too." I pulled her in and nipped at her nipple through the thin fabric of her top.

"Hey. We have company coming over soon!" she said as I began to snake my hands up her shirt and palm her breast and suck the other nipple through the fabric. She arched against me as she slid her fingers into my hair. Her body always seemed to call to me no matter how many tastes I got. It was never enough with her.

"We have time," I said against her skin, inhaling her scent and sliding my hand into the waistband of her shorts so I could tease her clit and slide my fingers into her wet pussy. The way her inner walls hugged me and arousal coated my hands, it was absolutely addicting.

"Ozzie," she breathed as I slid one finger in and sucked harder. She rode my hand, letting all her wetness coat my palm as I added my thumb to her swollen clit. Her body started to move faster, and her breath came in harder. The groans and moans she made had my own pussy dripping as she clenched around me and rode her climax. She was devastatingly beautiful. I would never get tired of this with her. My hunger for her only seemed to grow and expand the longer we were together.

"Goddamn," she mused as I slipped my hand out and she licked my fingers clean.

"You're definitely not party ready now," I teased, the wetness on her shirt and in her shorts obvious. Her hair was untamed and her eyes wide. She looked thoroughly fucked and I would be lying if I said it didn't make me a little smug to know that this version of Jess was all mine.

"This is our first housewarming party together and everyone is going to know we just banged on the couch," Jess said, laughing, but there was no real venom there. It wasn't like it was a surprise that we had a healthy sex life. After all, these people were our friends and we all probably knew more about each other than most people did. We were a close knit family, and it was sometimes hard for us to keep our hands off each other.

"Trevor will be scandalized. This couch was his favorite," I said, giggling at the thought. Trevor had moved out just a few months ago to let us lovebirds have our own place. It was a sad and happy moment. An end of an era for us besties but a new chapter for Jess and I's relationship. I think Trevor would have been more upset if he hadn't snagged an absolute hell of a deal on an apartment with an excellent patio and city view.

"Well, prepare to be even more scandalized," she said as she slid off me and grabbed my own shorts, and pulled them off aggressively. Yanking my legs, she dragged my ass to the edge of the couch.

"Grab your pretty tits for me, would you, Ozzie?" Jess commanded and said little else as she dove in with her mouth to my aching center.

Jess

I loved the taste of Ozzie on my tongue. She groaned as I licked and lapped, and tongue fucked her. Her hands worked on her own nipples as I nipped at her inner thighs and hip bones. She was so good at following my directions, especially in bed. I wanted her to feel as good as she made me feel. My orgasm still sang in my blood as I continued to devour her.

I used my mouth and fingers to bring her to orgasm just the way she liked. Her hips lifted as she cried out my name and I didn't let up until she was panting quietly, looking at me in between her strong thighs absolutely spent from writhing against me.

Licking my lips, I came back up and kissed her passionately so she could taste herself on me.

"You're delicious," Ozzie said against my lips as she wrapped her arms around me, and we snuggled in together.

"And don't you forget it," I teased and pressed myself against her. It was funny to think that not that long ago the idea of Ozzie and me being in a house together had sent me into an absolute emotional garbage can. Now it felt like the most natural thing in the world. We had worked through that sticky part, as I had tried to navigate my own baggage and come to terms with what I really wanted from us.

"We really do have to get ready to have everyone over, though." Ozzie didn't make a move to get up to do anything.

"Just a few more minutes." I burrowed deeper into her arms. I didn't really want to leave this spot, but we would have countless nights here together. Especially since we were the ones who invited everyone over. Feels like it would be a bit rude to turn them all away now.

"Fine, just a few more minutes," Ozzie conceded, and we just breathed together, savoring this time with one another.

It wasn't long before we both got up and got ourselves ready to receive our guests. Many bottles of wine were opened to celebrate living together and passed around. We were surrounded by our friends, great food, and music, as we giggled into the night.

Ozzie gazed over at me at one point during the evening and winked.

"I love you," I mouthed as chatter filled the air.

"I love you too," she mouthed back.

Happily, ever after did exist, after all, and I fucking found it. I would be damned if I ever let it go.

THE END

ACKNOWLEDGMENTS

Thank you first and foremost to Circus Scorpius, my own circus company. A special shout-out to Elena and Kelsey for being wonderful coaches, mentors, and friends. This book has so many real elements (safety of artists and athletes, how the heck you do anything in the air, how to do an act, etc.) because of the beautiful space CS and GPCC provides for us to be weirdos. Another thank you to GPCC, the rest of the community, and all the professionals. You all make my day every day.

Thank you to my parents, who continue to support the ups and downs of an author daughter who writes queer smut. You all are the real MVPs.

Thank you to my friends, who continue to shout from the rooftops that I'm a published author even when it makes me want to fold into myself to be perceived.

A special shoutout to my DFF family, as many places would not be as excited to have a queer author ranting about queer sex on social media, but you all holler louder than anyone else I know.

Thank you to all the queer, BIPOC, trans, fat, and disabled humans who made writing things like this even possible and continue to fight for equity, diversity, and inclusion.

Thank you to Gretchen, who is not only my circus bestie, but read this story in the beginning and offered love and support. You're one of the reasons I love going to the studio day in and day out.

Thank you to my cover designer Amanda at Eternal Geekery, who made my book come to life. I said muscle mommy juggler, and you said let's goooo.

Thank you to my amazing editor, Rose, having your help, expertise and support on this book has truly made it shine. You have no idea how much I have appreciated your kindness and care throughout this entire process. You're spectacular.

Shout out to my betas Heather and Sonya, who were so lovely and kind as I sent them things in weird chunks.

Thank you to my fellow authors who have offered advice, love, and care through this process. I like to think of self publishing as a team sport and when one of us wins, we all win.

Thank you to my booktok, bookthreads, and bookstagram family. You all are the reason that I can do this.

Thank you to my wonderful pupper, Brulee. She's a star and I love her so much.

Finally, thank you to my readers for giving me a chance to share the weird and wonderful. This would quite literally not be possible without you. I am humbled and honored to be your storyteller, if only for a day.

Author's Note

This book would be nonexistent without my actual circus. They inspired this book because we are all just a bunch of weirdos doing fun stuff in the air and rolling around on the ground. Having a community of people that hold you up and support who you are as an adult is amazing and I'm so grateful for them.

The circus has been a wonderful space to explore what it means to be a beginner as an adult. To be vulnerable and creative. Safe spaces to have community and growth are essential not only for the queer communities but other marginalized communities as well.

If you care about the arts and are interested in our performances, Circus Scorpius is real and wonderful. You can find them on Instagram and subscribe to their patreon if you are a patron of movement art or make a one time donation.

You rule, and I am so glad that I walked into my first aerial class years ago. I still can't believe that you wanted me to be a part of the professional company as the weird clown-y juggler that I am. Thanks for celebrating what makes me, me.

A special shout out to one of my friends (you know who

you are) who shares Jess's eye condition and inspired the meet cute of this story. Thank you for being excited when this idea came to light and telling me to go for it. You're one of my favorite people I've met in my circus journey. Thanks for bitching and moaning with me through conditioning and classes. Not to mention, all the ups and downs that come with working with bodies that don't always function the way we want (looking at you eyeballs, joints, muscles, etc.). I am grateful to train and create art beside you.

Additionally, I also struggle with hypermobility like Ozzie and not seeing so well like Jess, but in different ways. Their experiences are based on some of my own, as well as outside research and consultation with some others. It can be exhausting to deal with symptoms of any kind and navigate life when there are many days that feel overwhelming and hard.

Disabilities and conditions can be visible and invisible, and we each have our own experience. The experience of these characters is only one facet of what living with these things can be like. Everyone's journey is unique and different and the stories in this book are only one small part of that and not meant to be a one size fits all experience.

Treat people with care, love, and accommodations when they ask. The world will be a kinder place because of it.

Reviews

If you want to share your thoughts and feelings about *Tangled Encounters* please consider leaving a review on Amazon or Goodreads or both! It helps independent authors find their audience. Additionally, feel free to send an email to info@madisonnicolebooks.com. I would love to hear from you!

Social Media

If you would like to stay updated on all the new book things, you can see my shenanigans here:

TikTok | Instagram | Threads
@madisonnicolebooks

Or get signed copies here:

Website: www.madisonnicolebooks.com

ABOUT THE AUTHOR

Madison Nicole is a queer author who currently lives in Kansas where she teaches dance, fitness and circus arts. You can catch Madi playing video games, reading dark romance books, and juggling when she is not writing. Her favorite indulgences include iced coffee, tequila, and dark chocolate. She is excited to continue to explore her writing career and bring more stories your way!

A sneak peak into book two, Unexpected Attachments...

Myla & Dani's story

CHAPTER 1

Jake screamed at the TV, something about a random person being an asshole for killing him in his game. His dark hair was messy, and his sweats hung low on his hips, exposing the tanned skin of his muscled abdominals and chest. Once upon a time, he had been a dream—the epitome of what a woman should want. Of what I'd thought I wanted.

A knight in shining armor, except I had never needed one. My independence was always more important. I was the one who had a house, a thriving career, and a beautiful group of friends. It seemed all that was missing was a handsome suitor at my feet. The picture of a perfect life, I just needed a love interest to complete my happily ever after. There was a time when I'd thought he was the missing piece.

Even thinking those things made me cringe. I felt stupid and naive for falling into the trap of thinking I needed a partner to make my life fulfilling. Now, it felt like Jake was all that was wrong in my life. Maybe that wasn't fair, but it held a decent amount of truth. He wasn't what I wanted anymore. The emotional and mental labor needed to keep him alive felt like I signed up for a child instead of a partner. The urge to

strangle him was way more present than the desire to be intimate with him. My daydreams were about being alone now,
without the weight of an absent, pretty-boy boyfriend.

I watched him, engrossed in his game, and felt nothing but
annoyance and irritation. There was a time when I loved him.
We had years together where I'd thought he was the one, but
then I realized I was queer. He had taken it in stride, acting
like it wasn't a big deal even though I was grappling between
the identities of bi, pan, and queer. It didn't really matter to
him because we would be together forever, he'd said. As if that
didn't fundamentally exist in my DNA—as if the suppression
of it for years was no big deal. It was difficult to explain how
momentous it was and how I was a changed person because of
it. But he didn't really understand.

That was the start and end of that conversation with him.
Otherwise, he liked to pretend I was who I always was: a
straight, half-Korean, half-Russian girl, who was only interested in a hunky, straight, white, handsome bro-dude. That
the evolution of my identity didn't matter to our everyday
lives.

How do you explain that to someone who has no idea
what it means to be confused by the things they think and
feel?

My whole friend group was queer, and it was celebrated
and normalized in a way I seemed to be missing in my intimate
relationship. I couldn't put my finger on exactly what was
missing, but I knew for certain this wasn't actually supporting
my individuality.

It made me think of my parents and their own love story.
My heart ached in the best way. I remembered asking them a
million times when I was a small child about how they'd met.
It was like a fairy-tale story coming to life—a beautiful circus
love story that was basically meant to be a movie.

They both worked on a show overseas together. Two

acrobats who fell in love from two different places. A match made in heaven. Now they were retired and came to shows when they could, but mostly they traveled the world, still obsessed with each other and lending support when I asked for it. Neither one of their families were excited about the circus, despite both Russia and Korea having deep roots in performance arts. It had always just been the three of us growing up in the States. They had settled down here after their amazing career. My parents had gone out with a bang, making their last shows a dedication and homage to their story. I cried every time I watched their final performance, and then still shed a few tears when I would replay some of their acts in my head.

They were, of course, not surprised at all I was queer. The circus fostered deep-rooted inclusion for everyone, and that's what they'd grown up in. They loved me no matter what and just wanted me to be happy. After I was eventually set up with Cirque Callisto and had bought my house, they took off on their own adventure, wishing me well and chatting when they could. Even from miles away, I could feel their support, which was why it didn't make a damn bit of sense that Jake was feet away from me, yet I didn't feel shit from him.

My heart yearned for a love like theirs. Was that really too much to ask for?

The last few months, Jake's effort in our relationship had taken a magnificent cliff dive and somehow was now buried six feet underground. He stopped showing up for me in the ways I needed him most. The house was mine, but he lived here too, and I was sick and tired of being treated like someone's maid, chef, and unlimited money supply. He had no inclination to help with anything, and I didn't know why I tolerated it. Sometimes it felt like my fault, like I had allowed it to happen, but he had made those choices. My mind was a mess, vacillating from blaming myself to putting it all on him.

I felt like his freaking caretaker, and it made me want to light something on fire.

"Hey." I interrupted my thoughts as I stood in the doorway. He didn't hear me, so I walked closer to the TV, but he barely spared me a second glance. Was I just invisible? So easy to cast aside when all I wanted was to have a genuine conversation? It felt like I didn't matter, and that was like a punch to my stomach.

"Jake," I said, projecting confidence into my voice even though my insides felt like Jell-O. The urge to scream or cry hit my body like a tidal wave and threatened to knock me over. I needed to have this conversation without emotionally melting in front of him.

I can do this. Deep breaths. In and out.

"Myla, I'm in the middle of a game!" he whined before cheering about something that happened with his buddies in his headphones.

"Yes, I can see that it's very important," I drawled sarcastically, but it barely registered for him. My belly started to heat with rage, and I ground my teeth together. I could fucking do this. I didn't want to be a coward. Today, I would not let him walk all over me.

"We can talk later?" He grinned at the screen, and it made me want nothing more than to rip the cord from the outlet and stomp on his headphones, wiping that smug smirk off his face.

"No, we can't. I have a performance tonight. You know, with the show I've been doing for the past month you *still* haven't bothered to see." He became uninterested in my shows a while ago. Even though my parents weren't here, they watched every recording they could get their hands on. He couldn't even do that, let alone show up in person. I couldn't remember the last time he had championed my art. This was my life, for god's sake. I liked to think I was an interesting person. Circus was fun and exciting! Most people would be delighted to support their partner's creativity, but not mine. Mine would rather sit on his ass and basically ignore me until he wanted something from me.

Other people would ask, "Where's Jake?" and I would come up with the dumbest excuses. Eventually, people stopped bringing it up, except my nosy and loving besties. The shame that would heat my cheeks every time I stumbled through an answer was usually met with empathetic eyes and a caring hug. I always knew they wanted to press me more, but they never did. Sometimes I wish they would, and other times I wanted to run away crying. They were waiting for me to admit it to myself out loud, but the words always got caught in my throat.

"Hold on, guys. Give me a minute." He paused whatever he was doing and looked at me, both corners of his mouth curving up.

My face was blank. "Are you ever going to come to this show?"

"Come on, My, I've been to plenty of your shows." He sat back and huffed out a breath, looking like a petulant child. Food wrappers and takeout containers were littered around him, and I wondered why he decided to stop trying in this relationship. Was it a conscious choice, or one he made passively? Either way, it wasn't fair to me.

"And I will continue to do new shows, and I want to share that with the person I'm dating. If I were a football player, your butt would be at every game," I said, trying to keep my voice even and calm despite the storm brewing in my body.

Scowling, he shrugged. "That would be different. I love football."

I refrained from shouting in his face. "And you don't love supporting me? Do you not love me?"

"Myla, not this again," he groaned, like this argument was

silly and not absolutely life-altering. You did things for the people you loved, even if they weren't your favorite, right? That was the normal thing to do. Did he think I liked picking up after him or picking up his slack around the house? No. But I did it because we were supposed to be a team.

"Fine. Don't come. You know what you can do instead? Clean the house and pay me back all the money I lent you," I bit out. I didn't have time for this fight. I needed to get going. I needed to get ready for tonight. But my emotions threatened to burst out of me anytime I looked at him lately. I wanted this fight with him, but I sure as heck didn't have time for it now.

"You know I'm short on money right now. I'm not getting put on as many shifts. Business has been slow."

I was the artist. If anyone was short on money, it should have been me. But, instead, I was the responsible adult who actually saved, budgeted, and worked my butt off to have my shit together. There was a time in my life when I was working at eight different places; the least he could do was cover his half and get another part-time job.

And where the hell was his money going? He never left the house, and he barely offered to cover anything between the two of us. What happened to the savings he used to boast about?

"It's been slow for several months, Jake. I already pay for all the utilities and the food you eat. If you can't pay your half, then you need to find another job." Was I shrieking right now? It felt like I was slowly unraveling at the seams, and Jake was content with watching me fall apart.

"Babe, I'm working on it," he groused, his bright-blue eyes pleading and his bottom lip sticking out in a pout.

"Are you, though? Because it feels like you just do this all day, every day." I waved at his game. He had no boundaries with it, and it absolutely consumed his life. I was all for escapism, but Jake desperately needed a reality check. Lots of people could play video games and have a job. Why exactly was that difficult for him?

"Just give me another month or two, and I promise things will be good." He went to grab his headphones and put them back on. Suddenly a mental image of me shoving them in the garbage disposal consumed me, and it brought me just the smallest kernel of joy.

"I guess we're just done with this conversation?" I wanted to throw something at him. My whole body hurt from how aggressively I was clenching.

"Don't you need to go to your show?" He nodded at the bag I was death-gripping in my hands. He was right. This couldn't happen right now. I took my job seriously, and I really hated being late, especially for something like this.

"I do. I'll see you later, then." Stomping out, I slammed the door to the sound of him getting back on to greet his buddies. Throwing my bag in my car, I shot off a quick text to Logan saying I was on my way and apologizing for being late. She would understand. Logan always did.

Angry tears fell down my face, and I swiped at them with my hands. Thank god I hadn't done my makeup yet, or it would have been ruined. I couldn't keep doing this with him. I felt so alone, even with him there.

It wasn't that bad being my partner, was it? Lots of people thought I was fun and interesting. People loved coming to my shows, and other people had partners who were devoted to seeing them every weekend. The urge to call my parents and be comforted by them was strong, but I didn't want to bother them while they were in... I didn't even know where they were. France? Maybe Germany? My head felt cloudy, fogging my memory.

My phone dinged and, as if I had summoned them, there was a good-luck message from my parents with a selfie of them kissing in front of the Louvre, and the tears fell down my face even harder.

I wasn't even asking for much. I just wanted him to come see *one* show. Being a performer was a hard-ass job, and I had worked relentlessly to do this full time. Why couldn't he just do the bare minimum for our life together?

I drove, trying to let muscle memory take over and calm the raging tsunami in my body. I wasn't doing a very good job of it, though. Being this keyed up for my performance wasn't good. My body needed to be centered and calm in order to go on stage, not one second from collapsing and sobbing.

Checking my face in the mirror, I tried to take a few deep breaths before I left my car and walked into the dressing room. My friends would see right through me, but I could pretend it wasn't a big deal as long as it didn't look like I had just been bawling my eyes out. This is what I did—I put on a show, even if it was my life.

Exhaling, I told myself to get it together, because we had a performance to do. This was my job, and I needed to do it. I pushed open the doors to the theater and made my way into our dressing room where Logan, Aven, and Jess were already standing.

As soon as I walked in, they all whipped around to look at me. I gave my best dazzling smile. It was an absolute, catastrophic fail of a happy, smiling face. I winced, cracking the mask I was desperately clinging to.

"Myla..." Logan started, and my smile slid off my lips. Then I burst into tears all over again, and they all rushed around me.

"Shhh, it's okay. We're here for you," Jess cooed, her warm, familiar vanilla scent comforting me.

"Cry it out, babe." Aven stroked my hair gently.

"Men are so stupid!" I cried out to no one in particular.

"They really are," Logan soothed and handed me some tissues as I blew my nose aggressively.

"Jake and I aren't doing too good. I want to destroy his Xbox," I confessed, and they giggled.

"I take it he won't be coming to the show?" Jess asked, handing me some water. I nodded.

"He said he's seen too many of my shows. Why does he have to see this one?" My body shook as I cried even harder.

"Because you're a hottie who is incredibly talented and deserves to be seen again and again and again." Aven held my face in her hands and stared into my soul. I searched her hazel eyes like they could give me the answer to this Jake problem, but all I saw was what I already knew. This *needed* to end, yet I wasn't sure I was ready. I wasn't strong enough to kick him out. Instead, I continued to snuffle.

"Yeah but he doesn't want to support me," I said, gulping down air. I tried to get myself together and was doing a terrible job of not leaking more tears.

"Myla, are there other things going on?" Logan asked, her arms crossed and fire lit her eyes.

"Yeah." What was I supposed to say? That the guy I'd fallen in love with wasn't really there anymore? That I was sick and tired of letting him walk all over me when he gave absolutely nothing in return? My friends were all badasses and said whatever they wanted with confidence. Yet here I was hiding from my emotions and the hard truth that I needed to leave this relationship but somehow couldn't.

"He doesn't deserve you," Logan said quietly, like the words might scare me.

"I don't know what to do," I whispered.

"You don't have to do anything right now. Let's get you cleaned up and ready to go so you can go out on that stage and do what you love. We'll help you figure out Jake after, okay? You're a strong, independent woman who doesn't need a man!" Jess said with conviction. Easy for her to say considering she was a hot lesbian who had women fawning all over her, including her ex.

"I know. I need to do something about him, but I just don't know what. We've been together for years. How do you extract yourself from that?" This was too much right now. I couldn't think about ending things at this exact moment in time, could I?

"You just need to make it through the next few hours. You can do this, Myla. Then we will devour a whole tub of cookie dough and make a plan for how to get you out of this." Aven began styling my hair as Logan sat me down and started on my makeup. I just nodded and let them fuss. They would take care of me no matter what, even if that meant I stayed with a shitty guy like Jake.

The show went off without a hitch, and I got tons of cheers for my aerial silks solo. The people loved the big drops and spins and splits. I moved through the performance like I was floating. My body went on autopilot, and I did what I needed to do.

Afterward, my friends tried to get me to come over and talk it out, but my body and heart were spent, so I drove home in silence. I needed time to think and breathe. When I got back to my house, Jake had fallen asleep on the couch. Normally, I would wake him up and tell him to come to bed, but not tonight. I didn't want him anywhere near me.

I curled up in my bed and thought about how I was going to get through tomorrow, when all I needed was to be left alone.

CHAPTER 2
DANI: SEVERAL MONTHS AGO...

"That was marvelous, Dani!" A woman beamed up at me, and I grinned back politely.

"Thank you," I said, wanting to go anywhere but here and sit in silence with the lights off, but unfortunately I *needed* to network. It was part of my job to be available after shows. Even if what I really wanted was to decompress and put on soft, flowy pants.

"What a fantastic last performance!" another patron said. I nodded, trying to slip away into the crowd. Slowly, the other performers joined me as we looked at our generous donor, Mrs. Williams. It wasn't her fault I was overstimulated. I tried my best to lock down my discomfort and put on a mask.

"You all did marvelous, and I'm incredibly thankful for all your hard work." She dabbed at her eyes with a worn handkerchief. This woman had to be at least seventy years old, and she poured all her old money into the arts community. I was grateful for her investment in us, but that didn't fix my social anxiety. I looked to see what everyone else was doing and tried my best to replicate their elated faces.

"It has been wonderful to work with and for you, ma'am."

Our director, Katie, bowed her head, and we all clapped as Mrs. Williams blushed.

She went through and thanked every individual performer. She was truly a gem, and we were lucky to have someone who loved and cherished us as people, not just performers. Not everyone had donors like that, and it was nice of her to stop by after the show and congratulate us personally.

"Dani, do you have a second?" Katie waved me over, away from the rest of the company.

"What's up?" My social cup was already depleted. I desperately hoped this conversation would be short and to the point.

"I wanted to check in and see how you are doing. And see what your plans are after this. I know you only signed a contract for this show, but we would love for you to stay and be a part of our regular performance schedule, if you want." Katie looked at me with wide, hopeful eyes.

"That's an incredible offer. I don't have plans right now, but I've really enjoyed my time with you and the company. This show has been incredibly rewarding. Do you mind if I think about it?" I tugged on my ear mindlessly, wanting to take off this costume and this makeup immediately.

"Of course, no pressure. I'll send you an email with all the details of what we can offer you and a timeline that works for us. We've really enjoyed your talent and character, Dani. We would be honored to have you!" She gave me a quick, hard squeeze, then went off to greet the rest of the audience.

The truth was, this company was great. Katie was kind, and the performers were professional and hardworking. But it didn't feel like where I was supposed to be exactly. I had a restlessness in me that didn't seem satisfied to stay here. My plan had never been to settle in this place, but to be here for as long as I was needed and then go on my way.

I lingered for as little as was appropriate, trying to stay on the outskirts of the crowd. But a few people snagged me to take a few photos with some of the audience members of our show. We were lucky to have such a dedicated community around us who loved the arts and contributed to our sold-out shows. God, I wished I was better at this part, but small talk made me want to squirm, and I was close to running away from the noise in here. Truthfully, in the short term, I needed to get out of here and get comfortable. Long term, I felt like I needed something else entirely.

I was ready for a new adventure. Maybe I would go back to Spain, where my grandparents lived, and look for something there. The idea flooded my body with warmth, but I wasn't sure if that was the answer. Or maybe I would go somewhere where I had no ties, like Thailand or Brazil.

An upsetting thought pierced my brain. Was I running away or toward something? It was hard for me to say. There wasn't any urgency from anyone but me. It was my own monster chasing me to something new.

This show had given me grace to explore and create, really perfecting my flute and straps acts, as well as some of my clowning. A new challenge sounded fun and exciting. This could be exactly what I needed. I just didn't know if now was the time or what exactly those next steps looked like. I needed to see what Katie would offer, then broaden my horizons to see what else was available.

Kind words were exchanged between the other performers, and a lot of them were going out to celebrate the final run. It wasn't my thing, though, therefore I politely declined. Instead, I took the drive back to my brother's house slowly, trying to think of what to do next. Lately, it seemed like every day I was being existential. Sometimes, I had to remind myself I had nothing but time. The sense of immediacy that shoved at my back didn't need to be there. It was often just society's expectations and my personal rigidity that kept my mind racing. Both of which were difficult for me to shake off.

"I'm home!" I hollered as I walked in, and Macy, my brother's adorable little wiener dog, greeted me. "Hi, Macy. Where's everyone else?" I cooed at her and gave her some belly rubs. She looked up at me adoringly with dark-brown eyes, and a little bit of the tension in my shoulders released.

"We're in the living room!" my brother yelled. I snatched a snack from the fridge and made my way toward them, where my brother was sitting on the floor in front of the couch while my niece put butterfly clips in his hair.

"Daddy is my beauty queen tonight," Lily said proudly as she clipped and unclipped chunks of my brother's dirty-blonde hair. He looked absolutely wild.

"And he is very pretty." I tried to stifle my giggle at how ridiculous my brother looked with makeup smeared all across his face like a watercolor painting. Lily had really done a number on him, and I had to admire her craft.

"Dani, you already look pretty," Lily said, pausing and looking at me. Her hair was in two dark pigtail braids that looked just like her mom's, and she had blue eyes that looked just like my brother's.

"Thank you. It was the last day of my show, so I had to dress up." I did a little twirl as she oohed and ahhed at me. I hadn't bothered to take off my makeup or mess with my hair after the show. Instead, I had put on different clothes and sprinted out of there to listen to my music in my car with no one else around me.

"Daddy said we couldn't go for some reason." She pouted, abandoning the clips and patting the couch for me to sit on.

"I know. It was sort of an adult-only thing. But one of these days, you'll get to come and see me at other shows." I gave her a little squeeze, and she giggled. My brother had made it to the show opening weekend, but it was definitely not child friendly. It was already bad enough my brother was there while I was wearing nipple tassels and other performers were throwing dildos around. Most of my shows were not like this, but even if they were, Soaren would be supportive.

"Do you fly like you do in your videos?" she asked, bright-eyed. Lily loved seeing my training videos and said one day she would learn how to soar, too.

"Yeah, just like my videos." I tickled her side, and she laughed wildly.

"Okay, Lily, it's way past your bedtime. I said we could wait for Dani, and we did." My brother's tone was stern, but I knew he would cave if she whined enough. He had a hard time saying no to her, and I really couldn't blame him.

"Okay, Daddy." She gave me one last squeeze as they headed to bed.

"I love you, Lily. Sweet dreams!" I called out as my brother carried her out.

"I love you, Dani!" she proclaimed.

While they went through her bedtime routine, I grabbed some more food and caught up on Instagram and my emails. The show had run for several months, and it was truly the end of a beautiful performance. The final show was always a little bittersweet; a sense of melancholy that stuck to my skin and made my eyes prickle.

Maybe I would stay. My brother could always use the help, and I loved being here even though it wasn't exactly what I wanted. The communities here were just not exactly my people. I was still looking for that place that felt just right. They were all nice enough, but I felt like the odd one out most of the time despite their kindness.

Scrolling on Instagram, I saw Cirque Callisto calling for guest artists. I had worked with Logan before. She was a badass, so that could be interesting. I knew they were very queer, and that made my heart do a little happy dance.

Logan was known for not taking any shit and welcoming everyone from all walks of life with open arms. There were whispers, especially among the male circus artists, that she would chew you up and spit you out if you threatened, harassed, or harmed any of her performers. She wasn't someone you wanted to cross. However, if you were part of her family, Logan would go to the ends of the earth to protect you. It sounded like somewhere that I could really settle in, too.

My current company was wonderful, but there weren't a ton of queer people here, which was a bit tough. Everyone was respectful of my pronouns and my identities, but it wasn't that same sense of community queer spaces provided for other queer folks.

"How was the last show?" My brother came in, wiping his face with a baby wipe.

"God, Lily did a number on you." I laughed fully now that she had gone to bed. He was a great sport about it. I was proud of the dad he was; Lily was in great hands with him.

"Tell me about it." The corners of his mouth tipped up as he continued to rub off the red lipstick.

"It was good. They asked if I wanted to stay longer for the next show. Not sure for how long, but they pay well and seemed enthusiastic about me doing another round of shows with them." My voice fell a little flat. Job security was obviously ideal, but I couldn't get myself to be excited about it. The money was tempting, but I knew in my soul this wasn't the opportunity for me. I knew my enthusiasm sounded forced and fake. Soaren could sniff it from a mile away. He knew me better than anyone else, sometimes even better than I knew myself.

"And what did you say?" He sat down across from where I was eating at the kitchen table.

"I asked for time to think about it." I picked at my food in front of me.

"Do you want to stay, Dani?" Soaren asked gently. Even though he probably already knew the answer.

"I don't know. I have a lot of confusing emotions about it. I've loved being here with you and Lily, but I don't think this is it for me." I pulled at my ear and looked into Soaren's understanding eyes.

"I know. I never expected you to be here long. I appreciated you coming when I called all those months ago. Since Millie's passing, it's been tough being a single dad. You've always been my best friend, Dani, but we can manage on our own now. You helped a lot this past year, and I know it's been a lot. We would love it if you stayed, and we will love you if you go. You will always have a home here, and if you leave, it will give us an excuse to go visit someplace else." Soaren's eyes were watery as he spoke.

Tears welled in my eyes. "Are you sure you and Lily will be okay?"

"Yes. We're in a much better place now. Therapy, medication, and a whole slew of other things have helped me find myself again to be a better dad and brother. Our foundations are strong, and we can survive without you being here." He nodded, swiping at his eyes.

God, he was such a good dad and brother. I was really proud of how far he had come this past year. Grief was a bitch, and I couldn't imagine what it was like to lose the love of your life. It was already tough losing our parents at such a young age. Our grandparents in the States had rushed over to where we'd lived to raise us in our childhood home, and then in the summers we'd go visit our other grandparents in Spain. It was a wonderful childhood in many ways but incredibly hard in others.

Now, it was just the two of us here with Lily. Life was an

absolute bitch sometimes, and it seemed to hand out grief in large handfuls to Soaren and me. We had both done a lot of work to be able to live with what that meant. Every day was a little different.

There was a part of me that felt like if I left, I would be abandoning him. But he had made roots here with friends and his own career and community. I knew he would be okay. I just wanted to really make sure he could handle it before I uprooted myself for my selfish desires.

"I love you both very much, but I think I just need a new start somewhere. But if you need anything, you can always call, and I'll come running back, okay? You're my family, and I wouldn't abandon you." I walked over and gave him a big hug.

"Where do you think you will go?" he asked, holding me tight.

"I'm not sure yet. There's another circus company I've been interested in for a while I want to check out. They just posted a listing for guest artists for a new show, and I know the creative director—we trained together before. I'm wondering if they're looking for any more full-time or part-time residents." I could always see how it went, then try out somewhere else if I didn't like it.

That was the beauty of this work—I could move and be free without the confines of a regular nine-to-five. Plus, I had a decent amount of money saved up from living with my brother for free and babysitting Lily, as well as consuming all their food.

"I think you should try it out. You can always ask for financial help, too. Your big brother is more than happy to share." Soaren grinned at me, and I rolled my eyes.

"Yes, the capitalist hellscape of this earth does tend to pay corporate lawyers very well," I teased. He was incredibly generous with his money and privilege since we were our own little family unit. Anything I needed, he had provided since I'd moved in with them to help with Lily after Millie's passing.

She had been a wonderful woman full of life and love. I had loved her like my sister. The world was a cruel place to take someone like that away.

"It's the least I can do. But, Dani, wherever you go, we will stand by you. You have saved me numerous times over. I'm happy to return the favor again and again."

Tears slipped down my cheeks at his confession.

"Okay, I'll reach out to this other company and see what they say."

"They would be lucky to have you."

I hoped he was right. Otherwise, I didn't know where else I would end up. I was confident whatever happened would be meant to be.